Good Friday

Tony Wolk

OOLIGAN PRESS
PORTLAND STATE UNIVERSITY
PORTLAND, OREGON

Illustrations © 2007 by Jessica Wolk-Stanley

Ooligan Press
Center for Excellence in Writing
Department of English
Portland State University
P.O. Box 751
Portland, OR 97207-0751

Cataloging-in-Publication Data

Wolk, Tony, 1935-
Good Friday / Tony Wolk
p. cm.
Includes bibliographic references.
ISBN 978-1-932010-19-0
1.   Lincoln, Abraham, 1809-1865--Fiction. 2.   Presidents--Un-
tied States--Fiction. 3.   Evanston (Ill.)--Fiction. 4.   Time travel--
Fiction. I.   Title

Printed in the United States of America

For
Samuel V. Sanger
(1899–1992)

and Lindy Delf

Contents

Foreword

You have in your hands a copy of *Good Friday*, Tony Wolk's second novel about Abraham Lincoln, a book which follows on the heels of *Abraham Lincoln, a Novel Life*. The first novel ends on April 4, 1865. Lincoln is in Richmond, Virginia, Robert E. Lee's erstwhile capital. Less than a week away is the surrender at Appomattox. The story also ends in June of 1955 at the home of Joan Matcham in Evanston, Illinois, where Joan is reading a letter from Abraham Lincoln that has just come through the mail slot. How can a book end in two different eras? An ending is an ending. Well, what if they overlap?

Were I to do justice to that last question, I would end up writing my own novel. Or I could settle for this one, since it wrestles with that very question. And wrestling is a good thing. Perhaps I should say, hoping for your goodwill, that tales of time travel inevitably involve paradox. This I know from experience.

Now, being its victim, I will speak of Wolk's writing practice, which sounds like an altogether different issue. As near as I can make out, his books begin as a kind of experiment to see what will happen if he mixes his imagination with a few score words and then lets his pen test that out on paper. If he has got luck on his side, those initial words will grow to a few thousand, or tens of thousands. The story carries him along; he carries the story along. I know for a fact that Wolk's *Abraham Lincoln, a Novel Life* ended to Wolk's satisfaction, until two years later, when like lightning he realized he didn't know who had mailed the letter to Joan Matcham. For two years he had taken it for granted that this anonymous person was well-intentioned. What if that were not the case?

Only one way to find out: write.

A few more words and I'm done.

In Wolk's first novel, Abraham Lincoln suddenly finds himself in the year 1955, on the north side of Chicago. He spends a night at the Orrington Hotel, a restless night, mind you. The next morning, Easter Sunday, he is on the campus of Northwestern University, where first he meets Rusty, Joan Matcham's Labrador retriever, and then Joan herself. One thing leads to another, you know how stories go. You are the living one. Then comes the pivotal Chapter VII, where the novel divides into his story and hers, Lincoln's and Matcham's, hence the two endings. But now I'm doing Tony Wolk a disservice. The novel doesn't divide; it intertwines, like good thick yarn. It is a good story, and true. So now the time is ripe to turn the page, except for one more sentence. If it is not already clear, I am Abraham Lincoln, speaking of myself in the third person.

A. Lincoln
Springfield, Illinois

Good Friday

THE NXT DAY

—Friday, June 10, 1955—

Joan Matcham sat at the broad desk in her living room, her arms folded across her chest. It was June, 1955, an ordinary enough day for Evanston, Illinois, with sunshine, a picket fence, trees, a street.

It was the next day. Next days were piling up, it seemed. There was the day after he disappeared, the day after the examination with Dr. Riggs, and then today.

On the desk was an envelope with a Portland, Oregon, postmark dated June 6, 1955. A Monday. In it was a handwritten letter signed *A. Lincoln*, dated February 10, 1865. A Friday. The name and address on the envelope were in the same hand as the letter. She had a ticket stub from the Granada movie theater, two ticket stubs. They took no pictures. She had her memories. One day and one night together. She had a baby on the way.

Joan had been through this litany, how many times? Not that she had any doubts. Not that it mattered. She could become a true Lincoln scholar and search for hidden signals, buried references in his correspondence, chance remarks, the odd quote in one of the daily newspapers. Or Mr. Stanton, Lincoln's Secretary of War, might have jotted in his diary:

> *Tonight Mr. Lincoln let slip an odd remark at the War Department while we were going over telegrams from the front. I had remarked on his looking more relaxed since the Peace Conference at Hampton Roads, and the President said it was not just the meeting with the Peace Commissioners, it was the vacation that went along with it. You mean the boat ride, I said. And he said, No, another*

vacation. Different. Then he would not say more. I have learned to read his face more than a little, and I know he is hiding something. Well, either it will out or no. Time is the ultimate story-teller.

But Joan was in no mood to subject the library to more than her usual hauntings. Maybe later. Her journal was still another piece of *intangibilia*. It had been so hard, so hard, to write down what had happened, to tell the story plainly. She had met Abraham Lincoln on Easter Sunday, the tenth of April, on the east side of Deering Library. The moment was such that he had blurted out his name and his predicament, suddenly so far beyond his own time and everything unfamiliar, and soon enough she had believed his story beyond a doubt. She had invited him home for lunch. Morning turned to afternoon and then evening. He shared her bed and slept in her arms. She made no apologies, no attempt to defend her sanity.

An array of books about Lincoln stretched across the back of the desk: the last couple of volumes from Roy Basler's edition of the *Works of Lincoln*, various biographies (Ida Tarbell, Lord Charnwood, Benjamin Thomas—there was no end to them), Allen Rice's thick collection of *Reminiscences*, the diary of John Hay (Lincoln's young secretary), not to mention the several diaries from members of his Cabinet. All that and more she brought home, whatever caught her eye on the shelves of Deering Library or the various bookstores she happened to visit. She had grown fond of browsing through her shelf of Lincoln miscellany. The day would come when her habit of reading would become more deliberate, and she would wax eloquent to her daughter or son about that son or daughter's father. Or would it be nothing like that? Sooner or later, round-bellied Joan must confront her brother-in-law who fancied himself responsible for the welfare of the family widow. Well, nothing to do in that domain but improvise when the time came.

Moments of her day with Lincoln flashed before her eyes: the omelette they shared, his fascination with her refrigerator, the drive into Chicago, his presenting a five-dollar bill at the ticket booth of the Grenada and commenting on the handsome figure of the person adorning the bill, the ride home. For the umpteenth time Joan got out a five-dollar bill and looked at the big-eared, sallow-faced, bow-tied sixteenth president of the United States. Did the father of her child-to-be look like that little green man in the oval engraving? No, the icon was nothing like the jaunty man who tugged at Rusty's leash to get her going, nothing like the man who guffawed helplessly at the sight of poor Mr. Magoo bumbling about on the screen, and he was nothing like her lover. Joan smiled at the term "lover." It sounded so Bohemian, so sinful. George Sand and Chopin, Gauguin in Tahiti with his native woman. Joan put the bill back in her wallet. Funny how she wasn't comfortable with his first name, Abraham or Abe. Mostly she thought of him as Lincoln, plain and simple.

She looked at her watch, half past five. Time to think about dinner. Resolutely, she got to her feet. Why, she wondered, was she such a solitary person? And why should her habitual solitude trouble her after so many years? The freezer section of the refrigerator was stacked to the gills with little boxes of turbot pot pies, from Mudd's of Grimsby. Mudd pies, on sale at Field's—she'd bought every single one. Her usual Friday night dinner. Why must it take a thunderclap to free her from routine? Any time she pleased, she could go to dinner, see a movie. Even on a Friday.

* * *

Joan parked right in front of the Little French Café. No wonder, not quite six o'clock—what civilized person goes out to dinner at six o'clock and no theater or movie afterward? She thought to have the restaurant to herself, but she didn't. Inside the café were eight or nine tables, and only two were empty. She chose the table away from the window, said no thank you to a glass of Chablis, and ordered the evening special. At work it was hard to keep everything bottled up inside. The genie wanted its freedom, wanted to shout from the housetops that Abraham Lincoln, her lover, had been thinking of her. He had remembered and cared. She smiled. Probably no one noticed a tall, gawky woman in her mid-forties sitting alone in an inexpensive French restaurant amusing herself.

Joan glanced around the restaurant. Everyone was minding their business. Red-and-white-checked tablecloths, posters of Brittany and the Dordogne. One clock, one calendar. Time. You think it's straight-forward, that it tells every story in the same direction, clockwise, and the months know their order. But yesterday, a Thursday in June, she had received Lincoln's letter telling a ciphered story of how he had come home to his own time, taking not just a shiny penny from the future bearing his image in profile, but the memory, and the consideration, of her. His letter, all on one page, spoke volumes. It said that he had thought back over the day and evening, and then the night; it said he had remembered.

She could recite the letter. *Dear Joan*, it began, and once again her eyes could do nothing but fly to the end, *Please give Rusty my love. Yours forever* with no comma, followed by his signature, *A. Lincoln*, not a scribble, but the same calm hand as the rest of the letter. Her chest heaving, she had willed herself to return to the message, a leap of faith. *So, my little device worked.* It was as though he were reading over her shoulder, no less amazed than she that the letter was in her hands, that his secretary, John Hay, whom he trusted absolutely, had agreed to be responsible for the letter, then to find others along the line to pass it on, like a baton, and the finish line in another lifetime.

A couple with a child, a daughter, had taken the last table—the daughter as tall as the mother, but slender and youthful, angular, gawky like Joan—like Joan's own daughter Emily could have been but never was. Joan had dreamed of the plane crash any number of times the first year after, as though she had been there: Robert and Emily sitting together, and herself across the aisle, her eyes on her daughter and husband—the husband a shadowy figure, the daughter her all. Her sweet all. Then the faltering of the engines and the plane sliding across the skies, Emily's gaze on hers, and nothing the mother can do. Joan would wake in a cold sweat with Emily's eyes still upon her, and she would weep for her dear daughter. Seven, soon to be eight, an eternity ago.

Joan closed her eyes. Again the letter. His presence. It had been all but impossible to keep her eyes focused on the crisp sheet of creamy paper, to see the words on the page one by one, to understand that he had been back in his own time for five days when he sat down to write. Which meant that he had spent February the fifth with her. Except that she had never been to February of 1865; February, 1865, had come to her. The letter was filled with coded secrets: *The trip downriver was swift but uneventful*, where *downriver* equaled traveling back in time. *I have been busy*, he wrote, but he had been thinking of her, the words so cool, so formal, a bread-and-butter note. *Thank you for your kindness and your hospitality.* Then his thought that he might have left something behind, that his visit might have borne fruit. She smiled again. Hospitality indeed, and the power of metaphor.

A young man had come in, a familiar face, a student. He caught her eye and smiled, a quick smile, unsure of itself. She smiled in return. She had seen him in the History office at the university, by the mailboxes. She signaled to the waiter, and in a minute the youth was sitting opposite her.

"Are you sure?" he asked. "I don't mind waiting. I mean I'm glad not to wait."

"It's all right," she said. "It's a French café after all," as though she knew anything about table-sharing in France. "My name is Joan Matcham. I work in the History Department. I think I've seen you there once or twice."

He nodded. You could see the cogs and wheels searching for her and finding nothing. "I'm David Levine," he said finally. "I must've been dropping a paper off for a friend. I'm in Journalism actually."

"So you like to write?"

He shook his head and smiled wryly. "Not that kind of writing. It's what I'm worst at. 'There was a robbery Tuesday night at the Constable Tavern. Two patrons were shot.' And I'm the only one who didn't see the point of the story—it took just one bullet to hit two people. A ricochet. Rack up a C-minus for Levine." Not the first time he'd told the story.

"And yet you're in the School of Journalism?"

He was looking for where to begin. Dark hair, dark eyes, sweet looking. Girls would go aflutter at the sight of him, and he wouldn't know what to do next. Most likely he'd be oblivious altogether.

"Actually," he said, "I'm majoring in nothing. I wish there was a Department of Nothing that just let you go your own way. Besides, it's too late to change. I'll be a senior. I usually order the special; it's almost always fish."

"You come here often?"

"Often enough," he said. "I hate fraternity food. Here and the Huddle and Cooley's Cupboard. I guess I should put the menu down, or I won't be eating here either."

He didn't miss a trick, but didn't know what to say next. "You eat out alone?" she asked.

"Mostly." He shrugged, helpless. "Sometimes I go with my old roommate's girlfriend. He's away at graduate school. We're like friends—we are friends." The waiter was at his elbow, and David ordered the special without prompting.

Those dark eyes, Joan thought, and Abraham Lincoln's eyes, deep-set, gray, inviting confidences. *Guess what?* she could imagine herself saying. She knew better; hers was no story to bandy about. But oh, the temptation. Was it just Monday that she went to see Lorraine Riggs, her doctor and friend ever since the conception of Emily? They had gone out for Italian food afterward, but Lorraine hadn't pressed Joan about the father of her child, and a good thing too. *The father, yes. He was born in 1809, and last I saw of him he was in good health, but—* Joan had been resisting that part of the story, its ending, without much success. She had tried to think of him chewing an apple, or standing by her side at the art museum. Anything but what happened last: Good Friday, Ford's Theater, *Our American Cousin,* a gunshot.

"I can read your mind," David said.

"You can?" Joan said, shocked out of her reverie.

He laughed at her confusion. "No, not like that," and in a trance-like voice he intoned, "You are thinking of a tall, dark-haired stranger and a journey to a distant land." Then in his own voice, "I guess it was my own mind I was reading. The life I lead. Kind of solitary, mostly books."

"It's all right," she said. "It's a free country. Besides, you couldn't pay me to be twenty-one again, wondering if anyone's going to ask me out on a weekend."

"It's kind of like that. I don't have the will or the courage to pick up the phone during the week and start dialing just to look like I belong—belong where, I don't know."

"It's all right," she said again. "I'm in the same boat. Except I'm here as a reward to myself. A week well lived. It's not as though the Little French Café is one of the stops in Hell."

"I know. The food's wonderful. And cheap too. Inexpensive, I mean. And here it comes."

Silence reigned at the table as they ate with few intermissions. He was from Pittsburgh and she was a widow living on Hinman Street. Which added to the silence. They ordered dessert and coffee.

"I was just thinking," Joan said, "just curious. If your heart isn't into journalism and you go your own way, which way is that? I sound like Dr. Freud speaking."

"I'd love to meet Freud," David said. "If he were alive. I've read lots of Freud, *The Interpretation of Dreams*, the book on humor and the unconscious; and *Moses and Monotheism*, and the Ernest Jones biography. Read, read, read, like the Gingerbread Man—try and stop me. One leads to the next. I follow a trail. Cohn in *The Sun Also Rises* mentions W. H. Hudson's *The Purple Land*, and that leads to more Hudson, and Hudson to Conrad." His brown eyes caught hers. "Students don't ask each other questions like yours. Too dangerous, I suppose. I'm lucky. There's no pressure from home to make up my mind, to get a move on, as Martha would say."

"Martha?"

"She's our cook, at home. Kind of our everything. Martha's a malaprop. Says things like 'Guy Lumbago' and 'Open the window, I'm sophisticated.' "

" 'Sophisticated'? Oh, 'suffocated.' I get it. Brilliant."

"She is, in her own way, brilliant. She doesn't stand for any nonsense. Unless you get in the way of her soap operas, *Ma Perkins* and *Our Gal Sunday*. If I were Martha's son, there'd be questions aplenty. Luckily, my folks accept what I'm doing."

"Reading, like the Gingerbread Man?"

He smiled, a conspirator's smile. "They think I'm studying advertising. I'm in the Advertising sequence, so I've done all those courses, and I guess I could get a job in an agency if I wanted."

The waiter arrived with coffee and dessert.

"A job in advertising, if you wanted," Joan continued, priming the pump. "And your parents don't know the true story."

"I wouldn't go so far as to say they don't know what I'm up to, or not up to. Then there's the little matter of the army. At least that's a year off. For some reason I'm not too worried. And I have a part-time job."

"You do?" It was hard to picture. He was so many steps away from practicality, from responsibility—a youth in khaki slacks, a blue oxford-cloth shirt, and a seersucker jacket, no calluses, an eager mind, no history of suffering or loss.

"I do. I work Saturdays at The Bookshop, by Hoos Drug Store. It's mostly used books. I spend so much time there that Mr. Hohenstein offered me a job."

"I've been there," Joan said. "He knows his business. It's as though he's been on a first-name basis with the writers. And I love just roaming around. You never know what you'll find next."

David nodded. "I know, I love it."

"You did say Levine, didn't you?"

"Right," he said. "David Levine."

"For some reason I was thinking Rosenthal."

"Rosenthal. Funny. That was my grandmother's maiden name. Rachel Rosenthal."

"Your great-grandfather was named Rosenthal?"

"Yes," David said, obedient to her cue. "Morris Rosenthal. He was the first Jewish policeman in the city of Pittsburgh. That must've been right after the Civil War. He lived with my grandparents when my father was growing up, and Dad tells stories about him. One goes that he lied about his age to enlist in the war—there's no reason to doubt it."

"No," she said, "no reason at all." Joan was back at Mandell's, the Jewish delicatessen, and she and Abraham Lincoln were having dinner. Lincoln had told the story of the young Jewish boy named Rosenthal who wandered into the White House wanting to ask the President for a furlough. Lincoln had drawn the story from the boy, that he had lied about his age to enlist. He was sick, and Lincoln wrote him a short note to give to Stanton, his Secretary of War, something like *Please see this Pittsburgh boy. He is very young. I shall be satisfied with whatever you do with him.* Afterwards, she and Lincoln drove to the Grenada to see *East of Eden*, the evening unfolding, then him in her bed. And now, was that Pittsburgh boy's great-grandson sitting across from her? She could say, *I think I knew a man who knew your great-grandfather,* but wouldn't. This young Pittsburgh boy would think her odd, or mad, or both.

The waiter happened by. Did they want more coffee? No thanks. Time to go. But Joan had seen a link to Lincoln and didn't want to let it go.

David spoke first. "I was just wondering. There's an Alec Guinness film playing, *To Paris with Love*. I was thinking of seeing it—"

"Now there's an idea," she said, before he could get his foot in his mouth. "Guinness is always worth the price of a ticket. And," she added, "what's a Friday night for if not a movie?" No foot in her mouth—oh, the benefits of world-wearying experience.

* * *

Driving alone at night, especially along this quiet stretch of Sheridan between Chicago and Evanston, the mind adrift, like the ebb and flow of sea wrack. Associations. Dinner and a movie with David Levine, dinner and a movie with Abraham Lincoln. But this time she is alone in the car, going home without him. It takes so little to bring Lincoln to the fore; he is never at many removes from the mind's eye. And Time, with a capital *T*—his finding his way from one century to another. What if Emily—and Joan shuddered at the very thought. No. Certain doors were closed, forever closed.

Imagine the two years, 1955 and 1865, each as flat as a calendar page, time in two dimensions. As though there were a mill where ingots of time, dark as night, were rolled into sheets. And as they cool, Joan takes 1955 in her right hand and 1865 in her left and sets one against the other—it doesn't matter which. Like a child in prayer. Perfect. The two times are one. According to the green dial of the clock on the dashboard, it was a quarter of eleven, her time. Which made it just before midnight for him, the last minutes of April 7, 1865. Lincoln is aboard the *River Queen* on the James River just below Richmond, having spent the evening with the infamous James G. Blaine and Elihu Washburne. It could be he's still chatting with them.

Dates. Joan had worked them out, with help from the library. Lincoln had said that he'd returned the day before from the Peace Conference at Hampton Roads. He was sitting in his office alone, drafting a proposal for Congress to empower him to pay the slaveholding states four hundred million dollars, the value of their slave populations, half to be paid when they ceased all resistance, the second half after the passage of the recent amendment to the Constitution, for emancipation. This sum was equivalent to the cost of war for two hundred days.

The next thing he knew, he was here, in Chicago, on Howard Street, 1955, the tenth of April. He had crossed the River of Time. That made the time of his arrival the afternoon of February the fifth. Then she had counted the days. If days are days, she reasoned, no matter what century, one week of her life equaled one week of his. From February fifth to April fifteenth was ten weeks, less one day. Time, brutal time. Lincoln was shot on Good Friday and died the morning after. Her knowledge of his death was the one thing she couldn't talk about when he was here. But now it was the tenth of June in 1955, sixty-one of her days gone, sixty-one of his. On the evening of the sixty-eighth day, while he and Mary were at Ford's Theater watching *Our American Cousin*, the gun would fire, and the next morning he would die. There was nothing Joan could do. She couldn't work the bullet back down the barrel or turn John Wilkes Booth out of the theater. She couldn't stop time. She could hold her breath at the precise moment, but what difference would it make? This they would not have talked about even if she had known the bullet's precise schedule.

Home, and Joan Matcham was standing by the door, her hand on the doorknob, keys in hand, Rusty's tail wagging hopefully. "Sorry, Rusty. Too late for a walk. Nearly eleven." The tail stilled, the head drooped, and Rusty settled for a routine pee on the lawn.

An odd movie, *To Paris with Love*, Joan thought, dropping the keys into her purse. The generations askew: the father infatuated with the young woman, the older woman with the son. When it's finally straightened out, father and son are once again the happy couple. Alex Guinness, like anyone else, must sometimes have to settle for whatever role comes along. But Joan wasn't willing to crawl into bed with any old Jack of a husband. She had willingly accepted solitude. In a moment Rusty would be back at the door, and Joan waited in the entryway. Routines.

She had parked the car in front of the house after driving home alone from the north side, after saying goodnight to David Levine, who had driven her back to her car parked in front of the Little French Café, after they had sat through the quiet little movie. The story of an evening in reverse. Not really such a bad movie, piquant maybe. "Piquant," not a word one has much occasion for. "A piquant sauce." As though she cooked with sauces, hollandaise, béarnaise. Once upon a time she had experimented in cookery, in marriage. In motherhood. Time, blessed time, was coming round again.

The telephone was ringing. At this hour, past eleven? She picked up the receiver. "Hello."

Silence, and a sense of distance, not a local call.

"Hello," she called into the void, and twice again.

At the other end of the wire only the sound of listening, and the house so dark, just the one small light in the kitchen. Joan shuddered and hung up. Then waited for another ring. But the phone sat there, black and lifeless, empty. She went to the door. "Come on in, Rusty." Rusty gave up sniffing at the gate and trotted in. "Good girl."

Joan switched off the kitchen light and headed upstairs to the bath. She filled the old clawfoot tub, immersing herself. She flipped her hair over the rim and closed her eyes, taking in the warmth. How she hated those calls from the void, especially at night. What were they thinking? If you get a wrong number you say *Sorry* and hang up. You don't go on listening. Listening to the woman say *Hello* over and over. What story does that idiotic voice tell? The story of a woman alone. "Damn," she muttered. "Damn them, damn them all."

THE FACE OF SILENCE

Past midnight. Already the next day. Harry Stein had been thinking about this call all week, even before he mailed the letter. Of course, he'd been thinking about the letter for years. Who was she, this Joan Matcham of Evanston, Illinois? And how would Abraham Lincoln know her address? Assuming it really was Abraham Lincoln writing the letter, signing it. Which it had to be.

His copy of the letter was on the desk. He read it through one more time.

Executive Mansion

Washington, Feb 10, 1865

To Mrs Matcham, Evanston, Ill.

    Dear Joan.

    So, my little device worked. My secretary John Hay who I trust absolutely agreed to be responsible for this letter and to find others along the line. That the letter is in your hands is testimony to their integrity.

    I have been back for 5 days. The trip downriver was swift but uneventful. As usual I have been busy, but that does not mean that I do not find time to think of you and say Thank you for your kindness and your hospitality. I hope that the manner of my departure neither inconvenienced nor alarmed you.

    Since my return to Washington it has occurred to me that I may have left something behind, a little something. The chances are that my imagination has got the better of me. But one never knows. Once is all it takes. I am writing lightly of a subject that is quite serious and I do not wish to offend you. If by chance my visit did bear fruit, or does bear fruit, I am somewhat at a loss for words. I will not say that I was careless. I may have been thoughtless but I would not alter the moment, even if I could. There is so much more that I could say but you will have to understand more from less. From small acorns great oaks grow.

Please give Rusty my love. Yours forever

A. Lincoln

Rusty! The name infuriated him. A dog, a goldfish? One of the new-fangled names, Tiffany, Corky, Sparky? Whatever happened to Ann and Mary, Margaret and Elizabeth? Gone, shot to the four winds. His eye caught a spider, the size of a nickel, by his left foot. "No spiders," he said. "Done."

Alongside the Lincoln letter was the next, with "Adelbert Hay" written on the envelope, Hay's letter to his son. Then the other letters, all the fruit of Harry's tenth reunion at Yale thirty years ago, damn near thirty years to the day. Alton Sweeney telling his story, his link in the chain that included Abraham Lincoln, John Hay, Del Hay, himself, and last of all Harry Stein.

For thirty years Harry had been thinking ahead to a moment like this. He had one word for it: contact. No sense in going over Lincoln's letter again. He had plumbed its depths and been repulsed. *Back for 5 days* from his trip to the Hampton Roads Peace Conference, a fruitless conference, no effect whatsoever. Lincoln and the North held all the cards, and why throw in a winning hand? *Downriver*, down the James then up the Potomac and back to the White House. Thereafter the letter was nothing but a cute parcel of words from a man far from cute. As far as Harry could tell, John Hay did turn out to be trustworthy. No sign that he'd ever steamed open the envelope to see what the letter had to say. Being himself, Harry had done precisely that. To what end? Hay's brief letter to Alton Sweeney, the letter next in line on his desk, said more in half the time.

Granted, Harry had established contact, a single phone call in the night. Still, no more than mere electricity, hollow pulses across twenty-five hundred miles of high-strung cable. More was called for. More what? It was like seeing a river disappear around a bank of trees. And there the knowing ceases. Ahead, you say, lies the sea; that much is known. Rivers can't run dry, can they? Though he knew of one in the Atacama Desert that did exactly that.

He set the letter aside and got to his feet. He had heard her voice, one word's worth. In her place, he would've guessed at the caller, he was sure. He poured himself a Scotch on the rocks and sat in the leather armchair, sipping. How odd to spend half one's life waiting for a specific moment, then to have it go flat as a pancake. Like climbing Mount Everest, but the peak turns out to be a plateau, and there you are in proper attire, and that's it. Journey's end, stasis. "No thank you," he said aloud.

Harry recollected a variety of college reunions, locker-room stories with old classmates, sly glances at the occasional wives, whiskey in paper cups, Alton Sweeney living, Alton Sweeney dead, a withering of enthusiasm as success takes its toll. Inadvertently, Sweeney had inherited the letters. Obliged by necessity and driven to miscalculation, he had passed them on late in life to Harry Stein, star pupil, yours truly, eldest son of an eldest son, inheritor of a dying business, presently in exile in the northwest quadrant of the re-Unionized States of America. That was one version of the story.

Harry set his glass aside, the ice melted, the liquor pale as old brass. It was rather late in the game to question Sweeney's judgment. The pupil had already fulfilled the professor's request.

Were lightning to strike right now, one could say *Perfecto*. Mission fulfilled. But lightning hadn't struck, and Harry, a prime example of a poor, bare, forked animal, imbued with the power of reasoning, had more breaths to breathe, dreams to dream, and questions to answer.

Foremost. Having crossed this threshold, having mailed the letter, could he let go? Could he forget the late-night call, think of it as an aberration, something best forgotten?

Outside, a distant siren. Pity there were no more wolves in Forest Park.

III
TWO TIMES ONE

—Saturday, June 11, 1955—

Joan Matcham stood across from The Bookshop. It was a bit past eleven on a Saturday, and she was at loose ends, her mind caught in a vise. It was nothing after all, she reasoned. It had nothing to do with anything. Just an errant call, a single gray pigeon soaring off from one rooftop and disappearing behind the next. Less than ships passing in the night.

But instead of shedding worry, she was giving it a foothold and clothing it in solid flesh. The telephone call was not simply an anonymous dialer taking satisfaction in the darkness of a woman's fright. It was intentional and malicious, knowing its whole course, a course without a single wisp of fog.

Joan gripped the handle of her purse, crossed the street, and walked into The Bookshop. At a rolltop desk to her left sat David's boss, Mr. Hohenstein. He glanced her way, smiled, and returned to his work. Joan saw that his right arm was in a sling. She surveyed the shelves. Fiction, she knew, was downstairs. History was against the far wall, and she headed for it. "Civil War" declared a label on the shelf. Lord Charnwood, *Herndon's Life of Lincoln*, an old edition of *The Collected Works*, eight or ten volumes. Lincoln's contemporaries and their lives—four or five shelves all told. She had explored the university library but hadn't thought of The Bookshop.

The Boys' Life of Abraham Lincoln, by Helen Nicolay. The name "Nicolay" rang a bell—probably the daughter of John Nicolay, one of Lincoln's secretaries. Joan thumbed through it. Dozens of illustrations, moments no camera ever catches: young Lincoln, a borrower of books; Lincoln riding the circuit in rain and mud; Lincoln in the courtroom *addressing the jury in his defense of Jack Armstrong's son*; Lincoln meeting Grant; a facsimile of the Gettysburg Address. The book was a dollar, a bargain.

"Mrs. Matcham, hello."

It was David Levine.

"Hello there," she said. "I should've known I'd find you here." As if she were just remembering. And heavens, *Mrs. Matcham*. Respect for the elderly.

"Yep," he said. "It's Saturday. Been here two hours, two and a half, doing odds and ends, shelving, making sure things are where they belong. That was fun last night." A pause, the sentence hanging in thin air.

"I know," she said, choosing the words one by one. "We should do that again sometime. Dinner and a movie. I know you're busy with school, but with school out—well, mine's a quiet life, and any time you want company . . ." She let the sentence die, couldn't spur it on. She did want this link to carry on, herself and him, no expectations. She wanted a friend, was tired of being a hermit. She wasn't sure what she wanted. "Any thoughts on plans for the summer?"

"I don't know," he said. "Can't make up my mind. I told my parents I'd call tomorrow. The Sunday night ritual, you know. Looking for anything special?"

"Sort of," she said. "Lately I've gotten kind of interested in the life of Abraham Lincoln. This looks intriguing." She showed him the cover of *The Boys' Life* with its drawings of the log cabin and the White House and the two dates, 1809 and 1865.

David nodded, took the book from her, glanced at it, handed it back. "It seems like such a long time ago, 1809, but it's just ninety years back to 1865. My grandfather's still alive, and he was born in 1860. I guess he could've seen Lincoln—except my grandfather hadn't come to this country yet. It's my great-grandfather, Grandpa's father-in-law, who was here and could've, I guess, seen Lincoln." The sentence ground to a halt, and a sheepish grin at such a convoluted train of thought blossomed on the sweet face of David Levine. "Oh-oh, here's Mr. Hohenstein. I'd better get back to work."

Just like that he was gone, like cotton candy in July, and in his place stood the old bookseller. "I see David has been helping you. Are you looking for anything in particular?"

"No," said Joan. "As I told David, I've been reading about Abraham Lincoln lately." She didn't explain how she knew David Levine—why should she? Then, hearing her own vagueness, she introduced herself.

"I know," he said. "I remember when you first came in—you had your little girl with you. She sat at the table in the children's section, and we talked about rabbit holes."

"You remember that, seven or eight years ago?" She was struggling to stay on an even keel.

"Yes," he said, "like yesterday. I've no control over what I remember. She must be twelve or thirteen by now, a young lady."

"No," said Joan. "She and her father were killed in a plane crash in 1947." Her harsh words froze the air.

"I'm sorry," he said. "I had no idea."

"No," she said. "I'm the one who should apologize. I'm sorry. Sometimes it's so fresh. They say time heals all wounds, but whoever said that didn't have a daughter killed two thousand miles away. For a moment there, with your vision of Emily so clear—" She couldn't go on. Tears were about to flow.

"David," the bookseller called downstairs, "do you mind holding down the store for ten minutes or so?"

"Sure," young David called back. "I'll be right up."

But the tears didn't flow. "You mustn't," Joan said. But she was already being hustled out the door, to Hoos for a coffee or a soda.

* * *

It was hard to judge his age, late sixties, maybe seventy, but his hair was gray only at the temples and he moved as easily as the next person. Still, he was a good twenty-five years older than she was. She hadn't sat at the counter in Hoos for God knows how long, though she very well knew when she would've been here last: with Emily having a chocolate milk shake. Mr. Hohenstein, Emmanuel, had ordered two coffees and was explaining how he'd been in Evanston since before the war.

Joan didn't want to go into how most of the time Emily had receded from consciousness, how what had happened a few minutes ago was rare nowadays, though the threshold of remembrance was never more than a blink away. The void, now more like a gulf, was narrowing. Time's work. She could talk about it now. But she couldn't sit at a drugstore counter planning out an entire conversation, like a solitary chess master marooned on a desert island. "Actually," she said, diving blindly into the conversation, "days, even weeks, go by when I don't think about Emily, or no more than a passing thought. And lately—" Lately what?

His eyes were on hers. When she didn't go on, he said, "I know what you mean. And we feel like traitors. That we have an obligation not to forget. Like Queen Victoria and Prince Albert, or at least that's the common picture. I think it was Leslie Stephen whose first wife died on his birthday, and thereafter there were no birthday cakes. And Mary Todd Lincoln wore black all the days of her life after the murder of her husband, but before that—"

"I know," Joan said. "After her son Willie's death on a Thursday, every Thursday was, I guess we'd say hell for her—though that didn't stop her from paying a fortune for fancy black clothing. But I can't help thinking it was the other deaths piling up, her husband's, then her son Tad's, that destroyed her balance. Though it's impossible to set a marker down and say, *Here the balance shifted*, as though a life is like a book and all the words fixed."

"Yes," he said. "When we think that our lives are set out for us, with no choice, nothing but necessity, then we need help. Without it, we descend into exhaustion of the spirit, or worse, we strike out in anger, like the Titan in Hell who thumbs his nose at God. He might as well, for all the difference it makes. And my oh my," his left hand striking his forehead, "here I am trying to ease your burden, and I can't imagine a more morbid turn to a conversation."

"It's all right," she said. "I think I'm the exception—knock on wood. Don't want to tempt the fates," and here she tapped the underside of the counter. "Mine is a life where the balance has shifted for the good." She stopped herself from elaborating, sipped her coffee. Decent coffee for a drugstore. She could have given Mr. Hohenstein a date, Easter Sunday, April tenth, unless it was past midnight, which it was, and that made it the eleventh when Abraham Lincoln was in her bed. But it was by Deering Library, Easter morning, thanks to Rusty, that they struck up a conversation. Then the dam had burst, not always a bad thing— nature reasserting herself against all our rigid efforts to superimpose our patterns on hers. "You'll have to take my word for it," she added with a smile.

He returned her smile. "Why should I do otherwise? I'm like the stranger you sit next to on the train. You can tell me anything, our ways will part, and no one will be the wiser."

"Not quite," she said, all but laughing aloud at the thought of their busy words heating up the rails of the Illinois Central somewhere down in Sangamon County. "I don't mean to be enigmatic, and one of these days it'll be clear enough, like the day after a storm." She sounded so blithe. "Not that it's all peaches and cream. Just last night, near midnight, the phone rang. Not a wrong number. Someone there, listening. It felt like they were there, in the room, in a dark corner, watching, malevolent. I know it happens all the time and doesn't add up to a hill of beans, and I know I'm dramatizing it, and you can't tell the hand from a single card—"

He broke in. "Nothing? You heard nothing on the line?"

"Nothing, and I guess that's what was so scary: that he stayed on the line and didn't hang up. He could still be there—but that's paranoia, isn't it?"

"Maybe. Sometimes. You haven't used the line since?"

She shook her head No.

"We could dial your number from the store and see if the line is busy. You do live alone, don't you?"

"Yes. And now that you've suggested it, I would like to. I know no one will be there. But the call did frighten me, and if I don't, I'll be thinking about it all day. I'm not ordinarily obsessive, or just normally so. Listen to me go on. It does help to talk with someone."

His eyes were on her, thoughtful, concerned. "Good," he said finally. "Let's go."

Two minutes and they were back in The Bookshop. David nodded as they came in, then went back to his shelving. The phone sat there, menacing, eager. This was crazy, she knew, but she could get it over with, then go on about her business. It was strange dialing her own number. Worse than talking to herself—though she did that all the time.

Busy. The line was busy. She set the receiver back in the cradle and looked up at the old bookseller. Good thing she was sitting. Standing, her legs would have gone to water.

"Busy," he said flatly. She was at his rolltop desk, and he was standing alongside, nonchalant, going through mail, until he saw her reaction. "It could be someone else calling just ahead of you. Unlikely, I know, but possible. Let me try." She handed him the receiver, then dialed the number again. "It's ringing," he said, relief evident in his voice.

"Good," she said, letting out a breath. She glanced at her watch. "I've taken enough of your time already," she said. He held up his hand to deflect her apology. "Besides," she went on, "if I don't get going, I'll never get anything done. I do need to pay for this book."

"How's fifty cents?" he said. She fished two quarters out of her purse, then book in hand, she was on her way. Not that she really had anything that needed doing. She headed toward campus, toward the lake, past the quadrangle of sorority houses, the row of parked cars like so many busy toys gathering up the remnants of the school year for a summer at home. Commencement was this Monday, a matter of interest for seniors, no one else. Then the moving onward, America's proud youth on the royal road to the future. *Oh my*, she thought, recoiling at the burst of cynicism. Had that truly been her frame of mind all these years, maybe even before Emily's death? Had her marriage been that desolate? *I wish you well, fair hearts*, she silently intoned to all the departed and departing.

Truly she was a different Joan, different even from last Saturday's Joan. She would ring up Lorraine Riggs when she got home—damned be the damned obscene caller. A telephone has more uses than one. Her pace had picked up. If she didn't watch out, in a minute she'd be galloping across campus, past Harris Hall and the History Department and over to the lake path. Even in the worst of weather, the immense waters of Lake Michigan let her catch her breath.

The path was deserted, and she found herself remembering her way through the week. Monday, Lorraine Riggs confirming that Joan was pregnant. Then two ordinary days of sleeping and working. Next, Thursday and the unbelievable: finding the well-weathered 1955 Lincoln penny in the box filled with her mother's old pen points. And moments later, the delivery of the letter from Abraham Lincoln, and no one to tell the story to, though she did tell it in her journal. Just two days ago.

She paused and stared at the waves lapping in toward the rocky shore. All in one week, though the real change, the true alteration, had come two months ago, had transformed her from a zombie who had been walking in a fog these last seven years, ever since the news of the plane going down in Bryce Canyon, bearing Emily and Robert. She shuddered, the moment so fresh. *I'm sorry, Emily. I love you, and I always will, but we have another chance, another chance.*

Up ahead was the very bench where she and Rusty had first met Abraham Lincoln. Easter Sunday, sixty-two days ago, which meant he had but six days before Ford's Theater. *I love you too, Abraham, and always will.* "Yours forever" he had signed his letter, and if Abraham Lincoln didn't understand the depth of words, who would?

This week she had been set free. The slate of her destiny had been washed clean, and no one had stepped forth to write a new one. Was that why the midnight call was so upsetting? "To hell with it!" she muttered to herself. She had a secret burden deep in her belly. She would do her best.

She sat down on the bench and took her notebook and pen from her purse. She listened, eyes closed. She caught the sound of lapping waves, birds chattering, her breathing. Footsteps approaching. She wouldn't open her eyes; let them pass. But they stopped, took root. She heard the panting of a dog and opened her eyes. It was Tom Matcham, her brother-in-law, with Prince.

"Joan. I half expected I might find you here."

"Oh, Tom, how are you? Yes, catching a breath of fresh air."

Tom Matcham stood there, right arm outstretched, heels dug in against the pull of Prince. As ever, Tom Matcham went out of his way to speak enigmatically—at least he did with her. *Half* expected to find her sitting on a bench by the lake, as though another half of him pictured her elsewhere, somewhere proper. As though he went out of his way to give her the benefit of the doubt. But no, here she was, indolent Joan being judged by the self-proclaimed boss. A Judge Solomon without the good judgment. Joan closed her notebook and slipped it and her pen into her purse.

"Jotting down the sequence of the waves?" he asked facetiously.

"Might as well be," she said. And damned if she'd give him the satisfaction of saying precisely what she was recording. Just what would Banker Tom, an exacting man when it came to numbers, make of this latest version of her numeric diagram?

Joan glanced toward the quiet waters of the lake. What she had been sorting through once more was her notion that the last seventy days of Abraham Lincoln's life, from the fifth of February, 1865, the Sunday when he departed from her life, corresponded to the subsequent seventy days in her time, from the tenth of March to the eighteenth of June, 1955.

Her limit, the ultimate stone wall and no getting around it, was April fourteenth, Good Friday. She had six days until the Friday evening before Easter when the Lincolns would settle into their box at Ford's Theater. A crazy idea, she knew. That his time and hers were equivalent. Like a mad astrologer, she had constructed version after version of her chart. In the latest she imagined its two elements writ onto transparent plastic, then overlaid one upon the other, a synchrony, a bridge, a revolving door in time that enabled the magical Sunday, the fifth of February, the day when he slipped out of his century, to be identical to her Sunday, the tenth of April.

It had taken half a dozen tries to work it out. In the first few she kept forgetting that he had actually arrived the day before her Easter Sunday, had spent a night at the Orrington Hotel. Not till the next morning had she and Rusty found him on the bench overlooking the lake. Eventually she got it right. She titled it, "Calendar," and it came in two sections:

CALENDAR

A. Lincoln: 1865

Sunday	Monday	Tuesday	Wednesday	Thursday	Friday	Saturday
January 22	23	24	25	26	27	28
29	30	31	February 1	2	3	4
5	6	7	8	9	10	11
12	13	14	15	16	17	18
19	20	21	22	23	24	25
26	27	28	March 1	2	3	4
5	6	7	8	9	10	11
12	13	14	15	16	17	18
19	20	21	22	23	24	25
26	27	28	29	30	31	April 1
2	3	4	5	6	7	8
9	10	11	12	13	*14*	15

CALENDAR

J. Matcham: 1955

Sunday	Monday	Tuesday	Wednesday	Thursday	Friday	Saturday
March 27	28	29	30	31	April 1	2
3	4	5	6	7	8	9
10	11	12	13	14	15	16
17	18	19	20	21	22	23
24	25	26	27	28	29	30
May 1	2	3	4	5	6	7
8	9	10	11	12	13	14
15	16	17	18	19	20	21
22	23	24	25	26	27	28
29	30	31	June 1	2	3	4
5	6--Riggs	7	8	9--Letter	10--Café	11--Bkshp
12	13	14	15	16	*17*	18

She couldn't shake it. She knew the notion had no rational basis. Nor did its corollary, that in his time Abraham Lincoln was still alive, was breathing, eating, thinking about the war, about Bobby Lee and General Grant, and about a woman not yet born, herself. And maybe about another person doubly unborn, his child in the next century, who at that moment was sitting (courtesy of her mother) upon a bench overlooking Lake Michigan.

"What are you smiling at?" Tom asked.

"A complicated joke," she said. "Nothing much. The sort of thing that happens when you take time out from responsibility."

"Oh," he said distantly, not all that interested in the chaos of a woman's mind, especially when it might rub him, her self-appointed guardian, the wrong way. "Actually, I'm glad I ran into you." She loved the phrasing, saying that usually he would rather not run into her. It was a pattern she was used to. She caught it over and over again while he sailed on, unaware of what lay beneath his words.

Finally he got to what was irking him: "I have the sense that you've been avoiding me. I've left messages for you at the university."

"Sorry," Joan said without sorrow. "Things at the department get chaotic at times."

"I'm not surprised. It's not how I'd run a business."

"I don't think a university is quite the same thing as a business." When would she learn not to rise to the bait? God only knew why she let herself get drawn into these pointless conversations.

"Well, that's not the portrait the alumni association tries to paint when fund-raising time comes up. That the university is essential to the community, that a thriving university translates into a thriving economy."

"I forget that you went to Northwestern." Saying that, Joan heard the tense of her verb, the flat present, as though right now, this very moment, she was in the act of extinguishing from thought the fact that Tom Matcham attended this worthy university.

"Well, I certainly did, the class of '29."

"So," she said, "what's troubling you?" Prince, as if intrigued with Joan's question, took this moment to sit attentively, his alert eyes going from one face to the other.

"Did I say something was troubling me? I don't believe I did."

Not for the first time, Joan imagined what it was like to be married to this man, to bear this yoke. Easy to imagine, thanks to Janet Matcham, her sister-in-law, a brow-beaten woman who once upon a time lived a life, but not any more. Joan's reply proceeded from that sad image: "It's not as though you would telephone your brother's widow to add zest to her life. Hence my question. What's troubling you?"

His eyes narrowed. She was an uppity woman, without doubt. "As a matter of fact," he began—and Joan knew that no factual reckoning would be forthcoming—"I'm concerned about the condition of your house, the yard, that dog. But more so, it's your job. It brings in so little. A secretary, a *part-time* secretary, Robert's wife."

Joan let slide the implications about her house, yard, and dog. "Do I not live within my means? Do I not pay my bills? Am I overdrawn at the bank? Is it not then my business how I choose to make a living?" (She could hear herself underscore the word "business," so important to Thomas Matcham.) Prince nodded his assent. It's a wise old dog that knows a sound argument when he hears one.

Two to one, and Tom Matcham wilted. "Do what you will," he said. "I was only thinking—" but precisely what the man was thinking she could only guess, thanks to a more welcome passerby.

"Joan," he said, "what a day for sitting by the lake and nothing to do but stare out to sea." He paused to allow for the introduction.

"Professor Studebaker, my brother-in-law, Tom Matcham; Tom, William Studebaker." They exchanged hands so obediently that Joan added, "And Prince, Canine of Evanston."

"Canine of Evanston," Will Studebaker said with a smile. "Imagine that. A dog putting on the dog. Nevertheless, Prince, I'm pleased to make your acquaintance," and he and Prince also exchanged forelimbs.

"Well, I can't dilly-dally all day. Pleased to meet you, Professor," and giving Prince's collar a tug and Will Studebaker the evil eye, Tom Matcham continued on his merry way.

Will Studebaker was the first to speak. "Is he always that way, or am I over-reading the moment?"

"Probably not," said Joan. "It doesn't take a lot to put him on his high horse, and I'm afraid I just did that, not taking seriously my role as the still-bereaved widow of his dear departed brother. He thinks working in the History Department is inappropriate for a woman of my station, my station being dependent on his." Joan shrugged. "I view him as a strange man, a difficult man. His life depended on his brother's; now his image hangs on mine. And being a banker, his money is a product of everybody else's. It's as though he were invisible, taking color only in the presence of his opposites. Beware the biased portrait."

"We all know people like that, so unsure of themselves that they take their identity from anywhere but within. Do you mind if I sit?"

Joan gestured him to her side. "Besides, Tom was probably suspicious of your height." At nearly seven feet, Will Studebaker had to be the tallest historian on either side of the Mississippi.

"Not much I can do about that. My grandfather on my mother's side was even taller. He made appearances before the royal houses of Europe until the First World War. He was relieved when his life took an ordinary turn, as ordinary as it could." He was thoughtful for a moment, then said, "You just passing the time of day here?"

"I guess," she said. "Until whatshisname came along. I shouldn't be so snide. But I know that his height, or lack thereof, bothers him. I don't think he likes being in a room with me when I'm standing. It's true though. I took the job without thinking about other opportunities. It was there when time was heavy on my hands, and I fell into it—kerplunk. I think there's a line from Shakespeare, 'It wearies me; you say it wearies you,' and where it goes from there I don't know. But he does wear on me, and he brings out a side of me I don't much admire. So, where were you heading?"

"The library, I guess. I've finished most of my papers. Reading exams is the hardest, especially at the end of spring term. Hardly anyone ever comes by to pick them up, so any comments I make go for naught. Like holding a conversation with a statue. Anyhow, I thought I'd take a break and catch up on what's new with the Civil War."

"That's right," she said. "Your specialty." Of course she knew that Professor Studebaker taught the American history survey and the occasional seminar on the Civil War or Reconstruction. But in her almost half-dozen years at the department, she had rarely gone beyond commonplace chitchat with the professors. ("Badinage," a word she'd never said aloud—she'd try to remember to look it up; and another, "costive," for the sake of Tom Matcham.) "You'd expect that, after sitting at that desk all these years, I wouldn't need prompting."

"Well, sometimes I forget it myself. I mean it. It's like outgrowing the clothes you wore in college. I still teach the courses I first taught, but I've moved on. At least a little. Mind if I take a look at that book?"

"Oh," she said. "I forgot all about it. Sure."

"By Helen Nicolay," he said, flipping through it. "Interesting. From 1908, though it looks like it might have been serialized in the *Century Magazine* a few years before. The daughter of John Nicolay, Lincoln's secretary. In fact, that's the very name of a book that she published a few years ago, forty years later—a worthwhile book. I hope I'm still writing forty years from now! Listen to me go on."

"No," Joan said, "I'm interested. I just picked it up for fifty cents. I liked the illustrations. Sometimes a children's historian can take certain liberties—not that a real historian has to be dry as dust." She stopped. She couldn't say that she wanted a more intimate portrait of Abraham Lincoln than any professional historian could provide.

"It's all right," he said. "What's the famous analogy? Like a blind woman at the Acropolis trying to piece together the ancient Greeks. I'm always forgetting half the puzzle, like you and the Shakespeare quote. It drives my students crazy. But it's true: we're so cautious—we're trained to be—that it's next to impossible to paint a picture that comes to life. Sometimes it happens. I ran into a little book called *The Lost Years*, by Oscar Lewis, that has such a convincing portrait of Lincoln it's hard to believe it isn't real."

"Maybe it is," said Joan.

"I wish it were, but it can't be. It's the story of Lincoln if he had only been wounded by John Wilkes Booth. He recovers and serves out his term, not very happily. Then he all but goes into exile. The story hinges on an event in 1869, with Grant in office, when Citizen Lincoln intercedes for a little girl out in California—she delivers the coal, which is how he meets her. Folks there won't let her participate in the Fourth of July celebration because her father had served under Jubal Early, a Confederate. Anyhow,

Lincoln springs back to life, to public awareness, and you get the impression that he'll be reelected come 1872."

"Wonderful. From small acorns. But a sad tale."

"Yes," he said, weighing her response, and then finding the balance. "In the sense that it can't be true. But I was swept up in its simplicity. Lincoln recoiling at bigotry, and his wit, his love of irony. What was the point of shedding all that blood for the sake of union if you're going to bear a grudge? Anyway, it looks like you've made a find. I'd love to see it when you're done."

Joan nodded. "Sure." Will Studebaker was rising, the interlude completed, and she couldn't think of a way to extend it.

A VOICE FROM THE PAST

IV

The Hoyt Hotel on a Saturday evening, and not much of a crowd. It wouldn't be long before this landmark faded and went the way of the dodo. An apt image. The dodo on the isle of Mauritius with no natural enemies and a leisurely life at ground level; the Hoyt, a Portland landmark, a block or two from Union Station, built in the heyday of the railroads with an endless stream of traveling salesmen filling her boxy rooms.

Little comfort in his having forgone the life of a salesman. As though time marched for others only.

> *Golden lads and girls all must,*
> *As chimney-sweepers, come to dust.*

Almost Harry's favorite lines from Shakespeare. No matter what, the story had but one ending, and that a grim one. Still, life had its commendable moments. Such as an occasional late dinner at the Hoyt with its overwrought Roaring Nineties plush velvet decor and the lobby's pièce de résistance, a massive, throne-like chair that was Theodore Dreiser's very own—according to the brass plaque alongside. Truly a gross object. To fit it, Dreiser would have had to be nine feet tall. And upstairs would be a bed appropriate to the sleeping giant with its own plaque. Theater of the absurd and no one but himself as witness.

A rainy Saturday night in Portland. Not the first and certainly not the last. He stared idly out the window. A couple, not young, not old, passed by and in a single glance swept up the scene: the cup of coffee, the half-eaten wedge of berry pie, the diary, the pen crossways on top, and the solitary man—handsome, yes, but past his prime—sitting primly at his table. He returned the favor: raincoats, but no umbrella and no hats, the woman's dark hair glistening with shards of light like moonlit whitecaps. In Portland you learn to ignore the rain.

Joan Matcham. It took little these last few days to bring her to mind. Knowing no more of her than the sound of her voice, and no more than one word spoken, he had settled on the image of a woman in her middle years, still shy of her forties, dark-haired and slender. No way to give features to her face; there his imagination fell short.

If this were Evanston and not Portland, by now he would have driven down her street, seen her car in the driveway. He'd have a sense of what kind of life she leads, her family and friends. He'd have seen Rusty, surely a dog or cat.

The letter had him in its spell. What could have possessed Abraham Lincoln to write such a letter and send it forward ninety years? Only Joan Matcham could provide an answer. Too many mysteries for Harry to ignore, too much trust to burden a soul with. And worth a king's ransom. So now what? It's mailed, it's no longer his, it's received, a heartbeat's skipped, and a new character is waiting in the wings. Named Harry. Does he know his lines? Not yet, but give him time.

Harry ate the last of his pie, a good crumbly crust, drained his coffee cup for the third or fourth time. He gathered his raincoat, paid the bill, and stepped outside. He enjoyed the walk as much as any other element in his excursions to the Hoyt. Right on Glisan, left on Broadway, over to Davis, and up the gradual slope to his apartment ten blocks to the west. The streets were quiet. Was it the rain, or the hour, or some other factor he hadn't considered? Television. Everyone's eyes glued to their sets? Ahead was a young woman and her Scottie, both small, the dog sniffing at the giant bole of a maple. Both clad in plaid raincoats.

"Evening," he said. "Evening" she said back, a little pipe of a voice. Meaningless chatter.

He was in no hurry to get home. The drizzle had softened to a mist, and a half moon had broken through the thinning clouds. On impulse he looked over his shoulder, but the sidewalk was all his—no plaid dog on a leash. Just as well. Those days of striking up a conversation on a moment's notice were long gone.

Uninvited, another literary allusion presented itself: *Long promise and short keeping.* Wasn't he a walking dictionary of familiar quotations? Three cheers for Harry Stein. Dante, *Inferno*, Guido's despicable advice to Boniface VIII. Though its present application was altogether different from Master Dante's. "The Subconscious knows," Harry said aloud, drawing it out, syllable by syllable— as though Harry Stein, Yale University, class of 1915, spent his evenings listening to the likes of *The Shadow*. And subconscious, hell! Who's kidding who? It was his all-knowing father consigning him to the infernal depths. *Harry*, says Papa, his index finger stabbing the dense air separating father and son, *you're the greatest disappointment of my life. Last summer, running around with that shiksa. Now you're panting after Rose, worse than a dog in heat. By God, she's your first cousin! Either give her up and settle down. Or leave, get out of the business. Is this what I sent you to college for? To fritter away a life?* His words like bullets aimed at the heart and no way to dodge them.

What was Harry supposed to do. Change his stripes? Turn into J. P. Morgan? Besides, that wasn't what he went to college for. He didn't go to Yale to become a lawyer or a doctor, and certainly not to become a businessman. All he knew was that he wanted to go on learning. He wanted his life to go on, the only life he knew, a life of the mind. Then, just as he was about to graduate—and who knows what door might have opened—Papa was diagnosed with ALS—amyotrophic lateral sclerosis. At the age of forty-one. Finito. Kaput! Pittsburgh could wave goodbye to Nat Stein, the retail genius, and welcome his brilliant son, Harry, fresh from college. Perfect timing.

No. No use going over that sorry ground again. Clocks don't turn back. But God, how he hated the daily grind. Downtown, taking his turn on the floor, anything to make a sale: *Sir, now that's what I call a distinguished suit of clothes. Have you ever seen the like? Why, it fits you to a T. Pay attention to my clichés and hand over your money. You won't get out of here unscathed, you know. I'm none other than Harry Stein, son of the famed master salesman, Nat Stein the generous, Nat Stein, philanthropist. No, I didn't say "philanderer," though that's an intriguing term.*

It was enough to turn your stomach, the same lines day after day. Not once had he seen his father pick up a book. Year after year in a wheelchair, and all he did was issue orders. Until his voice went. Then came Mama's sweet revenge. Pampering her dear husband, treating him like an infant, knowing full well that if he had two good legs, he'd have two good legs and then some. The errant Jew who wooed and married a Gentile, telling his son to forego his turn at running after the shiksas!

Jesus! He was almost to Westover. He'd walked clean past his apartment.

"That you, Harry Stein?"

He looked in the direction of the voice. A woman on a porch, her arms folded across her chest.

"Yes, it is," he said. "Nobody but. And who might you be, if I may inquire?"

"Come on up, Harry. I won't bite, I promise."

As if the creature on the porch were feral and the promise not to bite meant the very opposite, Harry edged his way forward. Houses in northwest Portland were like sardines in a can, and hers was like any other: tiny yard with a picket fence, front porch, then a middling four-square, three-story house. When he was at arm's length and face to face, the woman grinning like a fox, he willed himself to speak. "Looks like you're holding the ace. I'm afraid I can't quite place you."

"I can see that clear as daylight. Though I always figured nights were your specialty, the darker the better."

He studied her closely—she was giving him world enough and time to answer the riddle. To no end. She looked to be older than she looked, if that made sense. Mid-fifties was his bet, despite the Dutch Boy haircut like a kid in grade school. In this light it was the color of wet sand. What struck him most of all was how poised she was, like a dancer, absolutely in her element, loving the mystery.

"Harry Stein, meet Becky Hirschberg," she said finally. "I do have the advantage. I knew you were living in Portland when we moved here—that was after the war. I've even seen you once or twice, from a distance. Harry, you don't look all that different from that night at Child's—"

"Becky Meyer," he exclaimed. "Goddamn! What're you doing out here? No one back home ever said a word. Let me tell you, the years have done right by you."

"No thanks to Harry Stein, the two-timing lout."

He shrugged. She had him nailed.

"Well, don't stand there like a sheep. Come inside." She held the screen door open till he obeyed her command.

* * *

It was Armistice Day, 1924, a year or so before Becky and Max Hirschberg tied the knot, and she and Harry were out on the town, first to a show, then to the Nixon and on to Child's. Becky was pretty enough, with an up-turned nose and sky-blue eyes, but with a mind all her own. In those days Harry was used to things going his way, especially with girls. But Becky was a challenge. They'd have a good time, then go home by way of Schenley Park for a little loving, but he knew he was dancing to her tune, not the other way around. He couldn't figure how she did it, and why it should have made a difference.

They had gone to Child's to drink and dance, and he had spied the cutest girl imaginable, no more than five feet tall, a redhead with hair bobbed like no proper Jewish girl, and her voice squeaky as a mouse. Dancing with Becky, he exchanged quick smiles with the mouse, and later, when she was alone at her table, gave her his phone number. Sure enough, the next morning like magic she phoned. It turned out she was from the south of France, pâté de foie gras country. Her story was a far cry from Pittsburgh. As a young girl she was as fat as the geese her father raised and force-fed, all for the sake of plumping up their livers. By the time the Americans entered the war, she was as sleek as a cat, and the next thing you knew she was in love with a soldier and vice versa, more vice than versa. *He was a strange one*, she used to say; then she'd refuse to elaborate. Four years after the first Armistice Day, she found herself crossing the ocean and entering the country of matrimony. It took less than a year for the marriage to go sour, and a year later they were divorced. Enter Harry. Exit Becky Meyer.

* * *

Harry looked around. He had grown up with houses like this. No signs of extravagance, no ostentation, but not much evidence of good taste either. Department store furnishings, wall-to-wall carpeting, a familiar wallpaper design. All very harmonious but devoid of artistry. Not that he held himself up as the standard for others to aspire to. But he did have hardwood floors and Oriental rugs, each with a name, each made up of knots tied one by one. *Crafted*. No craft in evidence here.

"Too late for coffee, Harry, but how about a whiskey? Or now that it's legitimate, maybe you don't partake? You were a persnickety cuss, you know. That Chevy of yours, as though it were the high-water mark of automotive design."

"Scotch if you have it would be fine, a little ice. And you're right, I did take pride in my little Chev, like no other car since. The rest have been mere transportation. You said 'we' out on the porch, moving here after the war. Is that you and Max?"

"It was," she said. "Max died not long after the move. Took a position at Meier and Frank, managing the first three floors. He was a sweet man, Max. I met him just a few days before you and I went out for the last time."

"I guess I didn't know that," Harry said. Harry, still the sheep, and Becky, the shepherd.

She handed him his drink. He had followed her into the kitchen, a room that did rise above the generic, and now she led him back to the living room. "I said Max was a kind man. When we were courting he used to take me straight home. He didn't deliver me back to Mama and Papa by way of Schenley Park like some people I know. But I have no regrets. The proof is in the pudding."

Harry smiled. "I was never one for pudding." He gestured at the photos on the mantel. "Your children?"

"Yes, a son and a daughter. They live back east. Mine's a predictable life. What about you, Harry?"

"There's not much to tell. The family business going to hell— you knew I was no businessman. We moved to Florida after Sis got married, real-estate boom and all that. Got out before things went completely flat. Then Papa died in '31. My brother was married by then, his ticket out."

"Howard?"

"Yes, Howard. He's still at Kaufmann's. With Papa gone, we had to pare down. Mama and I took an apartment."

"I remember your mother. I used to worry about her if you and I got more serious. She had a heart attack, didn't she?"

Harry nodded. It was odd to find someone here in Portland, just a few blocks from where he lived, who knew so many pieces of his story. "She died in 1940. It was pranksters, knocking on the door, jangling the bell, and she jumped up to answer, tripped over the carpet, and fell like a stone. The kids ran away, and by the time the super got his keys, it was too late."

"All those years you lived with your mother. It hardly adds up, Harry. I never could figure that out."

"Some days I can't account for it either. One thing leads to the next. I guess I'm not the adventuresome type. I'd been as far west as Indianapolis. It seemed like Mama needed someone to stand by her."

"Seemed? Come on, Harry. Tell the truth."

"All right. With Mama it was all or nothing. I'd probably be there at this minute if she were alive, shopping at Pearl and Richbaum on Murray Avenue. I don't want to think about it."

"So you picked up stakes and moved out west? Here, let me freshen that drink for you."

He stood by the refrigerator as she added Scotch and a couple of cubes of ice from the bucket. "Thanks," he said. "I don't mind telling this story. It's a strange thing though, you knowing so much of it."

"It does seem odd. I want to hear what brought you to Portland. Just give me a minute," and she headed for the bathroom.

Harry wandered back to the living room. True, he was enjoying telling the story of his life. But he wasn't telling the whole story, was he? No, he'd left out 1925, the year of his tenth reunion. Like forgetting to mention Rumplestiltskin as you tell the story of the miller's daughter. Imagine Hugo or Dostoevsky deciding to get along without Quasimodo or Alyosha. Or Shakespeare concluding Prince Hamlet was more trouble than he was worth, and besides, a truer story would let King Claudius live to a ripe old age. What would be the true version of Harry Stein's tale? For some years Harry thought he knew the answer. Years when he used to wonder how Sweeney couldn't wonder at the contents of the Lincoln letter. Imagine having such a treasure dropped in your lap. One in a million.

There was no question: that evening in Alton Sweeney's office was like a hinge in Harry's life; thereafter his days opened onto another landscape. A good simile, the hinge, though it left to the imagination what that other landscape might be. He was still discovering it. Or was that evening more like the moment when a compass loses its bearing, and from then on the arrow veers? Or when a board, once true—or true enough—warps beyond recall? No—he wouldn't miss this for the world, the expression on her face, Matcham's. The realization that her secret lay in the palm of his hand. A secret he would find the key to—he could all but taste the damn thing. So sweet. And right around the next bend.

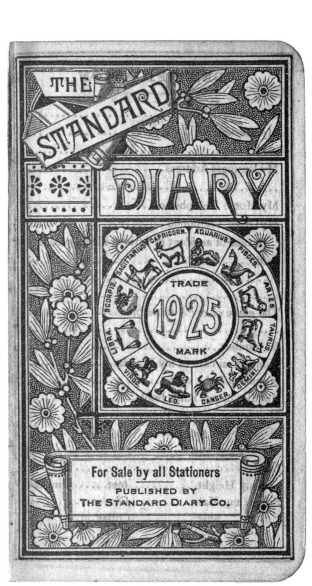

THE STANDARD

DIARY

TRADE
1925
MARK

CAPRICORN. AQUARIUS
SAGITTARIUS PISCES
SCORPIO ARIES
LIBRA TAURUS
VIRGO GEMINI.
LEO. CANCER.

For Sale by all Stationers

PUBLISHED BY
THE STANDARD DIARY Co.

THE PAST

Harry Stein followed Alton Sweeney up the dimly lit staircase to his office. It was Harry's tenth reunion. He had been there often enough in years past, when he was a student and Sweeney his professor. There was never a line outside Sweeney's office. Always it was just Harry and Sweeney, Harry following Sweeney after class or Harry meeting Sweeney at an appointed hour. Harry the heir-apparent, Harry the crown prince. Sweeney the lord and master, Sweeney keeping alive the spirit of the past: Homer and his heroes, Trojan and Greek, and centuries later Virgil, translating the story to Rome; after more centuries Dante and Chaucer, then Shakespeare, pen in hand, keeping the story alive. Troilus, Cressida, Pandarus, Hector, Ulysses. "Someday," Sweeney would say, "the story-teller will pick up his pen and tell Lincoln's story, the story of union and secession and assassination, my father's story, your grandfather's story."

Sitting behind his desk, Sweeney leaned toward Harry. "I have a story to tell."

Harry sat across from him, listening.

Sweeney, gazing nowhere, searched for the beginning. "I'm not a young man, Harry, not even in my middle years." He waved Harry's silent protest aside. "I'm sixty-two years old, Harry. In two, three years, I'll step aside. I was younger than you when I came to Yale—there are times when I can't believe I was born in 1863. Dalton will carry on, no problem there—he knows Virgil backwards and forwards. But that's not the story I want to tell."

Sweeney half-swiveled his chair, withdrew a packet from his briefcase and set it on his desk. "It's not easy to begin," he said. "I've waited for this moment for a long, long time."

Harry nodded, doing his best to narrow the gap.

"Close on thirty years ago I had a student, nothing like you, Harry. Del Hay, Del short for Adelbert. Del was not devoted to the straight and narrow. Smart enough, to be sure, but he was not at all serious. Until it came to women and gaming and carousing. Not that he was the only one. But he was the only one whose father was the Secretary of State."

"John Hay, father to the Panama Canal?"

"Yes," Sweeney said. "I made it a project to redeem Del Hay. I wasn't that much older than Del. We sat in this office and talked, man to man, heart to heart. I tried to tell him how he was throwing away a life, that it wasn't too late to turn himself around. I told the story of Priam and his fifty sons, as though it were yesterday. As though Del Hay were one of those sons, but which son would he turn out to be? Paris, the root of the fall of the kingdom of Troy? Or would he resemble Aeneas and carry forward his father's work? I reminded him that he was born in the year of our nation's centenary. I pulled out all the stops. Tears would gather in his eyes when he spoke of the pain he'd put his father through, his father's headaches, his nerves, one wretched malady after another. Yet Del would go off on another spree. He graduated, class of '99. Then, unexpectedly, President McKinley appointed him to the post of General Counsel to South Africa. Del was a success in Pretoria, a surprise to his father. It was not entirely a surprise to me. I came to see a very different person that last year. There were times, Harry, when you put me in mind of Del Hay. Del was never the student you were, but you were both high-spirited lads."

Sweeney's eyes closed. As a student, Harry had seen this moment more than once: Sweeney turning inward, as though he were stepping outside of time, picturing in his mind the next scene and its cast of characters. Then he returned to the present.

"I received a telegram from Del—it was 1900. He was back in this country and wished to have an evening with me. Could he meet me for dinner? I wired back Yes. I was already at the table when Del came in, a few minutes late, the fault of the train from Washington. It was mid-March. I remember the night was mild, though there was still snow on the ground. I asked if anything was wrong, suspecting the worst. 'Nothing,' he said. He was doing quite well, wonderfully well in fact. But he had a matter of considerable import to discuss, and could it wait till after dinner?"

"Suspense," said Harry.

"Yes, you're right. I suggested we adjourn to my home, which we did. And there he told his story, which I will do my best to retell. It's not that long a tale."

Sweeney paused. Harry couldn't read his mind. Again some inward process was at work. Almost as though Sweeney needed a rewinding. Then he resumed.

"It begins with Abraham Lincoln."

"Lincoln?"

"Yes," said Sweeney, holding up his hand that he might continue. "In February of 1865, two months before he was shot by John Wilkes Booth, Abraham Lincoln made a strange request of John Hay—'Panama' Hay—in those days a young man and personal secretary to the President. It is expressed in this letter." Here Sweeney took an envelope from the packet on his desk. "That mild night in 1900, at my home, Del Hay showed me this very letter, written by his father, then Secretary of State to President McKinley."

Gingerly, Harry accepted the proffered envelope, withdrew the letter, and proceeded to read it.

Department of State
Washington, New Year's Day, 1900

Dear Del,

As I said on Christmas day, I have been in a running fight with ill health. Folk think I exaggerate, especially since the death this year of Vice President Hobart which has placed me next in line for the presidency. At times I think I shall have to die to silence their skepticism. I hinted then that I would choose you to inherit a delicate mission. Hence this letter.

In February of 1865, when I was a secretary to President Lincoln, he entrusted me with a letter. The president's instructions were simple enough yet mysterious. He wanted me to arrange it so that a letter, his own, should be mailed long after his death, early in June of 1955, a date which is still more than half a century away. He had already addressed the envelope and sealed the letter within. He asked me to entrust the letter to another, with like instructions, at some time in the future.

It has been close to two years since your graduation from Yale. Speaking frankly, I have often had misgivings about entrusting the letter to you. I'm sure this comes as no surprise to you. But those days are behind us. Now I ask you to take the necessary steps to ensure the delivery of the letter. For me the process has been twofold. First, I composed a cover letter in the event of my untimely death and left it and the letter with other vital documents. Second, as the keeper of the letter, in time I would yield to the next in line. As such, I have had my eye on a moment such as this. Though you may well be alive come 1955, and God knows I wish for your continued good health, we never know from this day to the next what will transpire.

With these few words I hand you the letter which was given to me by Abraham Lincoln.

Your loving father,
John Hay

"Like you," said Sweeney, "I read the letter through and was rendered speechless. Finally I spoke. I asked what it had to do with me. Del was still a young man. He explained that he had no choice but to accept his father's estimation of himself, the prodigal son. But his life was not entirely stable. He wouldn't be returning to Pretoria, though another tour of duty was imminent. Then he said—I remember the exact words—he had a premonition of something untoward, like a dark hand reaching for him. I didn't tell him he was being foolish. I'm no Horatio, subjecting all to the test of reason. Del said he wasn't passing the letters on to me as next in line, but he asked if I would care for them until such time as he should reclaim them. With that he handed me the second letter, an older envelope, sealed and fully addressed. The handwriting seemed familiar to me. Now I should say it is the most familiar hand I know. With that Del rose, looked at his watch, and said that with a little luck he would catch the night train to Boston. Like a whirlwind he was gone."

Harry looked about the darkened room. He could begin to make guesses.

"Del Hay was right," Sweeney said, "in more ways than one. In June, while at his second college reunion, Del fell from a window and was killed. One moment he was sitting propped in the window frame in sun and breeze, chatting with friends, and the next he was gone. His father was in New Hampshire at the time, doing his best to recover his health. That night a local reporter burst into his bedroom with the awful news. I too was stunned, though I was no father to Del. Then in September came the assassination of President McKinley at Buffalo. Had it been a year earlier, before the election, Mr. Secretary John Hay would have been President John Hay."

Harry stared at his mentor. He had read Sweeney's recent biographies of Charles Sumner and Edwin Stanton, both published in the years since the war, stories of two complex men living in complex times. "Did you ever meet John Hay?"

"Yes," said Sweeney. "Del introduced me to his father at his graduation. I had already seen him once before when he spoke at his own reunion, at Brown. Did you know I went to Brown? That I'm not all Yale?"

"At least it wasn't Harvard."

"Thank the Crimson Lord," said Sweeney. "You're wondering, aren't you, Harry, whether I ever said anything to John Hay after the death of his son?"

"Yes. Did you?"

Sweeney stared straight ahead, then nodded thoughtfully. "I knew he must be thinking about Lincoln's letter. I also guessed that Del had never told his father that he had passed the letter on to me. My plan was to speak to John Hay when the shock of his son's death had subsided."

"Then?"

"In September came the assassination of President McKinley. I saw the letter John Hay wrote to President Roosevelt just days afterward. It was never printed, but it circulated." Sweeney took a folded sheet of paper from the packet and passed it to Harry. "Read it at your leisure. It's quite a letter. Mind you, Hay was not enamored of Roosevelt, so the letter is a delicate one. At one reading, it sounds like a letter of resignation. At the next, it's just the opposite, as if Hay, though his natural life was drawing to an end, should be the one to carry on unfinished business, including the canal treaty. In all, I read the letter as though it were written by the hand of a wise Abraham Lincoln. Roosevelt read the letter rightly and reappointed Hay."

"Lincoln casts a long shadow," said Harry.

"Yes," said Sweeney. "Seeing the letter, I wrote a note to John Hay, congratulating him on the appointment, with a postscript to the effect that Del had passed the letter on to me and that I would safeguard it."

"Did Hay reply?"

"Yes," said Sweeney. "That letter's here as well."

"It seems there's no end of letters, each begetting the next."

"Yes," said Sweeney. "You will find it interesting. It renews the obligation to sustain the bridge from the hand of Abraham Lincoln to the eye of Joan Matcham ninety years on. I want you to read that letter aloud, in my presence."

Harry took the letter.

"Aloud, Harry."

"Sorry, it's hard not to leap ahead." And Harry began:

Department of State
Washington, Oct. 21, 1901

Dear Professor Sweeney,

I read your letter with great relief. I knew neither Lincoln's let-ter nor my letter of explanation was among my son's effects. Your offer to safeguard the letter is an answer to the question that hith-erto I could address only to the four winds. It also allows me to sustain Del's own choice.

If memory serves, President Lincoln gave the letter into my care in February of 1865. The President had recently returned from the peace mission at Hampton Roads. He told me nothing of the circumstances under which he had written the letter, and I did not question his motives.

I am now older than Abraham Lincoln was when he was killed. My life has taken surprising turns. I came within a hair's breadth of becoming the twenty-fifth president of the United States, a long road to have traveled from Warsaw and the amphibian days of my boyhood along the banks of the Mississippi. Writing this letter, I am mindful that you and I and my son, all are links in a chain that sustains the private wish of a man I admire beyond all others.

Once more I express my gratitude and great relief that the letter is safe in your hands.

Your obedient servant,

John Hay

"Quite a letter," said Harry. He set it back on Sweeney's desk. "And quite a burden."

"Yes," said Sweeney, "a great burden. Mine for nearly a quarter of a century. It's a burden I should like to transfer to your hands."

"I would be honored," Harry began. "But—"

"Harry, I understand your reluctance," said Sweeney.

"Professor Sweeney, you're choosing me because of what you know of me, or think you know. But that Harry Stein is a phantom. I can see right through him. He's like the mist in a valley. He only looks solid."

"Harry, we're all like that. That's every one of us. Lord knows, we're put together with invisible thread and—"

"No," said Harry, knowing what Sweeney was about to say. "Sure, I read. I read every night. And I write too. Every day. And I earn an honest living. But the books I pick up could be anything. There's no pattern. I'm like a scavenger—whatever dies, I'm there to gobble it up." Sweeney's mouth was open, as though he were about to speak, but it was his turn for silence. "This is what I write," and Harry reached into his shirt pocket and held out his diary, the size of a pack of cards but half as thick. "Hamlet says we're bound in a nutshell. Well, I write in a nutshell."

Sweeney took the small book, opened it, held it close to the light. "I can't read this, Harry. How can anyone write so small? Is it all like this? What does it say?" He handed the diary back.

"What does it say?" Harry echoed. "Listen," and he opened the book at random.

> *Germaine met me at the Pitt at 8:15 and we saw a good mystery play,* In the Next Room. *Holding hands. I do like G. Later drove around town—then down to the Nixon Café. We drank Benedictine wine there and danced.*

"Then there's a list of all the people I knew, the old crowd.

> *After 12 up to Dormont—*

"That's up high, some view—

> *and out in the car we sat and petted. G is charming. She loves and kisses adorably. I can go only so far with her—*

"It's all I can do to read it—

> *but she promises more. I like the way she talks, her accent. It was so late when I got home.*

"That's my life, Professor Sweeney. That and selling suits and overcoats. I sleep in, go to work late, hide from customers, talk to girls on the phone, avoid my family, and hope for a little loving. I can't think of marriage. The money's frittering itself away on my dad's medical bills. He tells me I'm the biggest disappointment of his life. For this he sent me to college! Then I write my squirrelly notes about my eventful day."

"Are you finished?"

"I didn't say that Germaine is French, a divorcée, was married to a soldier. Not Jewish. Jewish girls are all I can marry, but without money—this sounds so pitiful! I'd sooner swallow hot coals than marry for money. I try not to think about this. I'm like a sleepwalker."

"If it weren't for the war—"

"I know. You wanted me to study at Heidelberg, like my grandfather. Then Dad was diagnosed with ALS. Two strikes. Being Jewish is the third."

"Harry. You're telling me not to trust you with the letter. But what you describe is on the outside. What's inside is what matters. Everything went wrong for Hamlet, but he found hope. You've got a good mind, a fine mind. Your health—"

"Now you sound like a Jewish mother."

"Harry, I have an idea. Are you calm enough to listen?"

Harry shrugged.

"Thank you," said Sweeney. "My brother Philip lives out west, in Oregon. After my mother died, he took his share of the inheritance and started afresh—that was back before the war." Sweeney paused. "Harry, I can't promise you a red carpet, but financial security can go a long way toward keeping the wolf from the door."

Harry stood and circled behind his chair. He couldn't believe it. A chance to get away from Mama and Papa, to escape from the narrow circle where being Jewish governed every chapter of the story. Was that what Sweeney was about to propose?

"Harry," Sweeney said, "I don't doubt your ability to survive, but you're no more a businessman than I am. Unlike yours, my family held on to its pot of gold. My father, seeing the cross on the door, took steps to protect my mother and her sons. He died when I was little older than you are now. Philip and his young wife Margot went west. Before the century was out, his wife was dead. Tuberculosis. I never said that it was I who first met Margot, at Saranac. The two of us loving one woman." Sweeney sighed.

"Saranac," said Harry. "I was there myself, after the war. My folks worried that I was losing weight, was listless. But it was just my psyche being out of sorts. Before long, the good doctors sent me home, well-fed and rested."

"Life is no bed of roses," said Sweeney. "The short story is that Philip never remarried. He lives alone. He has a degree in law, but he's never practiced in the common sense. He lives simply, he's managed his affairs well, he's respected in the community. He's like my father in so many ways. Thanks to Philip, I live a life free of financial care. But I worry about my brother's solitary life."

"I follow you, and yet I don't."

"Be patient, Harry. It's clear to me now that there's more to this than handing you the letter. What I haven't said is that my own days are numbered. A tumor, slow growing, but persistent. I get headaches, and I've had a few episodes where the lights have gone out. Let me continue. I know what you want to say. I understand. But it's getting late. You can see that I don't live an extravagant life. And thanks to Philip, it's been some years now since I have touched my salary, meager as it is. With a small supplement, you could live on what my estate provides. If you marry, that will change. But you're no fool. The Harry I know wouldn't lay all his dollars on a single roll of the dice."

"No, not very likely. Nor will my handwriting suddenly grow fat."

"So, with your permission, I will do two things. I'll write to my brother about my trust and faith in you. I'll ask him to treat you as my own son. And I'll set up a fund in your name. You'll still have to find your own way out of the maze. But at least I will have given you a thread to follow."

Harry's grip on the back of the chair was firm. "I came up here this weekend thinking only of escape, a moment's respite. It's as though you've sat a starving man at a table, handed him a menu, and taken his order. You're right. I don't want to abandon my

THE RIVER OF TIME
VI

—Saturday, June 11, 1955—

The clock was just chiming eleven when Harry got home. Becky Hirschberg was precisely what he remembered: a woman whose deficiencies canceled her virtues. Would the mysterious Joan Matcham be cut from that same cloth? He'd seen it again and again. Frances, Germaine, Molly: a whole host of lookers, who start out bright and beautiful, even interesting. But they end up drab and insistent, calling at all hours of the day and night, tiresome, Harry this and Harry that, and Harry woncha please, Harry, Harry could we huh, Harry? It was such a relief to get home to a good book. Granted, it might take a week or two for the infatuation to die down, for the novelty to wear off.

And why had he done that, natter on about the good old days as though that's what they were? Old times, old friends, hallelujah! If he wanted that, he could have lived his life out in Pittsburgh where he knew the streets like the back of his hand and half the people in half the houses. He knew what he seemed like to Becky: a rediscovery, like coming across an old jewel, or the novelty of a long-forgotten book.

His eye had caught the glint of a spine, *The Son of Tarzan*. Harry tilted it off the shelf. A first edition, 1917, probably worth a pretty penny. Harry turned to page 100. Some folk read the first few paragraphs to test the mettle of a book, but he knew better and picked up the story in mid-paragraph:

> *"And now white men, men of my own kind, have fired upon me and driven me away. Are all the creatures of the world my enemies? Has the son of Tarzan no friend other than Akut?"*
>
> *The old ape drew closer to the boy.*
>
> *"There are the great apes," he said. "They only will be the friends of Akut's friend. Only the great apes will welcome the son of Tarzan. You have seen that men want nothing of you. Let us go now and continue our search for the great apes—our people."*

It was like using a Bible for prophecy. Pick a passage at random. Was the whole world Harry's enemy? Had it come to that grim pass? The next paragraph explained how the boy spoke ape, meanwhile the boy *was immersed in deep thought—bitter thoughts in which hatred and revenge predominated.* Hard words. The chapter ended with Akut catching an unwary rodent, tearing it in half, and delivering the *lion's share to the lad.*

Hatred and revenge. Becky Hirschberg was nobody. He could see her again—if that's what she wanted, and she certainly did. Why not? In small doses a woman can be good company, and the Scotch didn't hurt. He could be at her house right now, the two of them on the couch like the old days, his hand inside her blouse. She was still a looker.

Time to wrap up the evening. He tidied the kitchen, added *milk* to the grocery list, showered, wrote the balance of the day's worth in his diary, double-checked the locks, and got in bed. The nightly ritual. *Son of Tarzan* had piqued his interest, and he began at the beginning. He was not at all tired—plenty of time to get well into the book before turning out the light. Harry propped the pillows behind his shoulders and turned to the opening chapter.

> *The long boat of the* Marjorie W. *was floating down the broad Ugambi with ebb tide and current. Her crew were lazily enjoy-*

ing this respite from the arduous labor of rowing up stream. Three miles below them lay the Marjorie W. *herself, quite ready to sail as soon as they should have clambered aboard and swung the long boat to its davits.*

Harry paused, something in the back of his mind trying to catch his attention. He looked closely at the page, the illuminated capital *T*, a small line drawing serving as a frame for half a dozen men in the long boat, four at the oars, one man in front, and another braced in the stern with the steering oar. Didn't ring a bell. the *Marjorie W.*? He shrugged. Then, like a flash, it struck him— the pieces of the puzzle slipping into place seamlessly: *with ebb tide and current . . .down the broad Ugambi.*

"That's it!" he said aloud. "Damned if that isn't it!" The words from Lincoln's letter were flashing like neon, in plain view: *I have been back for 5 days. The trip downriver was swift but uneventful.* Harry had taken it as a given that Lincoln was talking about his voyage on the *River Queen*, down the James and up the Potomac. But let your eye slow down, and that doesn't make sense. Lincoln wasn't talking about his return trip from Hampton Roads. Look on any map: Hampton Roads is at the *mouth* of the James; the subsequent voyage on the Potomac to Washington, D.C., is entirely upriver. There simply was no "downriver" unless Abraham Lincoln meant the River of Time. Harry was sitting up now. It fit. The envelope with the correct address. He'd bet his bottom dollar the house at 1607 Hinman Street wasn't there in Lincoln's day, just as no Joan Matcham was alive and well in 1865. And why pick early June, 1955, for the delivery? Unless you'd been there! Been there two ways: in space and time. Which is exactly what the letter was about.

Harry got out of bed, went to his desk, unfolded his copy of the letter. He read it through for the umpteenth time—he all but

VII AWAKE

In 1927, the summer she turned fifteen, they drove west—mother, father, daughter. Her father exactly four times her age. At sixty he was an old dad, older than any of the other dads. Yet he seemed just right, always. Give him a younger face and darker, thicker hair, and he wouldn't have been her dad.

For a moment there, he was almost alive again.

Joan lay her palm upon her stomach. "Patience, my friend."

Next to the alarm clock was the green and white tin of soda crackers. She set it on her stomach, worked the lid up, and withdrew a single cracker. She nibbled at the corners one by one till the square became an octagon. She held it up to the light—already a sunny day. An octagon was as good as she could manage—crackers were much too brittle for an early morning experiment at squaring the circle. "Edible geometry," she termed it. She wondered, did Isaac Newton perform edible geometry? It would be nice to claim kinship with old Isaac. Kinship for herself, kinship for her womb child. As though having Abraham Lincoln as a parent wouldn't be sufficient.

Lately, at odd moments, solitary moments, while walking Rusty or reading late at night, even while waiting for the kettle to come to a boil, she'd been thinking: just how would she tell the child *the story*? It would depend on the child, wouldn't it? And what if she waited too long, what if she were struck down by lightning, and hadn't said to Lincoln's daughter or son, *Today I have a story to tell, a story that you will not believe, not at first. But it's true, and you will treasure this story. You will love this story, as I hope you love me. This is the true story of your father.* Joan could carry the story no further, knowing that *young Master*, or *Mistress Lincoln* would look at her skeptically, and from there on the story would be in the hands of Improvisation, perhaps the best of all story-tellers.

All this from nibbling on a soda cracker.

In her dream—the snag-end still in her grip—her father was hiking in the Rockies, youthful, with a bounding spring to his step, as though he weighed no more than a feather. Lying here now, with Rusty on the oval rug beside the bed, Joan saw herself, sitting sideways in the back seat, Father driving, Mother with map in hand, the car and its trailer like toys on the undulating road across the endless miles of cornfields. They had hitched their small two-wheeled, turtle-backed trailer, white with green stripes, onto their little Chevy. The Turtle performed well, carrying their tent, sleeping bags, cookstove, everything for camping. After Iowa came Nebraska, more miles and miles of farmland before turning to range country. At Grand Island they'd turned north late in the afternoon, and driven through the Sand Hills, a succession of sparsely grassed hillocks that extended in every direction. Come twilight they had parked by the side of the road, Dad turning off the engine. Theirs the only car for miles.

They had stood on the shoulder, the engine cooling, tick-tick-tick, slower than a clock. And slower. Almost cool. Dark, and overhead a billion stars. Then came the gentle rising of the moon, as though it had been lying in wait for them from its berth down down down among the unearthly hills. When the three earthlings were back in their car and heading north, Mother began to speak of the Cheyenne who not so many years ago had camped in these Sand Hills, one entire winter, hiding from the U.S. Army, and how a huge herd of elk migrating south had saved the Indians from starvation. That night, in O'Neill, near the South Dakota border, the Colfields spent the night in a tourist home, and a much younger Joan had drifted into sleep, thinking of the Cheyenne, secret campfires and the feast of venison, and later, the women flensing elk hides.

They got as far west as Estes Park in eastern Colorado, feasting night after night on breaded rainbow trout—nothing had ever tasted so good. She remembered one day when it was just her father and herself hiking, Mother shooing them off. Not a lot of talk, one or the other leading the way, telling each other little stories, accidental memories, then silence again. If she could relive that day, she would find the moment, ripe like a sweet pear, and it would be her story she told to her father. She'd begin with Emily, sweet Emily. She would tell him how the granddaughter he had never met had died in Utah, farther west, in the plane crash. Now they would be in each other's arms, the father and his daughter, both weeping for the lost child.

They would find a fallen log to sit on. *Father, there's more. Another child, waiting to be born. Listen.* And she would tell it as simply as possible, like perfect music, unfolding its melody, telling its bittersweet tune. Her father, born just three years before Abraham Lincoln was shot—or would be shot, as she reckoned time— would listen closely. *Father, what can we do?*

"Oh my," she said aloud.

She replaced the tin of saltines on the nightstand. Not even eight o'clock. Time passing, time frozen. What was she straining for? Things so far away. Things beyond boundaries. The impossible. Something no clock could ever discover. *There is no time but the present*, she thought. No, there will be no telling her father the story of this child's father. The clock, with its two uneven hands, is telling lies. A clock, an honest clock, could say no more than *Now*, again and again. *Now*, the story of an endless present. Yet

"So do you always go home for the summer?"

He nodded. "I can't tell you what a relief it is not to be going back to a summer of the same old thing. The land that time forgot. I'll spell you on the leash if you like."

"Sure," Joan said, transferring the loop to David. Rusty sensed the new hand and picked up her pace. *Summer in Pittsburgh*, Joan thought, *what if that's all it took to go back in time, a detour through the Smoky City? Would I do it?* Today being Sunday of Lincoln's last week, she wouldn't have much time to think about it. She grimaced. The image of the two calendars again, so vivid, his and hers, 1865 and 1955, April and June, his date the ninth, hers the twelfth. Come Friday he would be going to Ford's Theater to see *Our American Cousin* with Laura Keene, and the last word he would ever hear would be such an odd one, *sockdolager*. Booth had timed it to the second—knowing the burst of laughter that strange word would beget, his cue to pull the trigger of his tiny Derringer, the barrel inches from Abraham Lincoln's head.

Joan shuddered, her elbows hugging her sides, her neck and shoulders bracing for the shot. She'd read about Japanese soldiers killing captured Chinese soldiers with a baseball bat, swinging at their heads. The mind is such an assembly of horrors, all the nightmares we have stored away. All it took was the memory of that one word, and Booth listening for it, poised to strike. Outlaw the word and stop the killing. And what if Pittsburgh really could take her back a century, would she try to prevent him from going to the theater? Of course she would; she'd find a way.

Rusty and David were galloping along. "Don't worry," she called ahead. "I'll catch up." She was picturing herself at the White House doors, standing off to the side like the Soothsayer in *Julius Caesar*, as Lincoln emerged. *Beware the Ides of April.* The day of his death. Then she saw herself standing in front of Lincoln's carriage, blocking its progress, crisscrossing her arms, *Stop! Stay home! It's me!* She couldn't bring herself to say, *It's Joan.* And Mary would ask, *Who is that woman? And what is that strange attire?*

Oh, what a fool she was—frantic to stop the President from going to his death, yet chock-full of concern over how to dress for the occasion. Occasion? Assassination! *Red, wear red.* Mary, Joan remembered, was spattered with blood. His blood. Even if Joan were to gain access to Abraham Lincoln, how would he respond to her warning? When he was with her, she had avoided the subject. Joking, he had asked whether the history books spoke of the president just disappearing, as though the trip to the future was one way only. *No*, she had said, *he hadn't just disappeared.*

Mostly they had kept his presence in the present, as though neither dared risk breaking the spell by coming within reach of his own inevitable history. But what if she were actually to prevent him from going to the theater on Good Friday? Or what if John Wilkes Booth were intercepted, he and his cohorts arrested? What would that reweaving of history provide for the years to come? Lincoln's life would not be cut short; he would serve out his second term of office; the South would be nursed back to health under his wise hand, *with malice toward none.* Then what? Back to the present, back to Joan alone.

David and Rusty had stopped at the corner. "I have a notion," she said when she caught up. She didn't know whether it would qualify as a decisive act, or was it just one more instance of her instinct to *re*act? "Feel free to say no. It's no more than a thought."

"Okay," David said brightly, at which magical word Rusty's paws dug in. Her favorite word. Tail wagging, she surveyed first David, then Joan.

"O-K-A-Y is a big word in Rusty's world," Joan explained. "It means she can lick up spilled food or go for a walk. It means the world is her oyster."

David reached down and patted Rusty's flank. "How's A-L-L R-I-G-H-T? And is there any particular reason why a black Lab is named Rusty?"

"I can tell you that story later. Here's my idea. I live in a good-sized house. Off and on over the years I've had students live with me. It can work to everyone's advantage. There's company for Rusty and me, the rent is low, and if the student needs a place—"

"You live just off campus, don't you?"

"On Hinman, a block and a half from where Sheridan bends around."

"Jesus!" he said. "That close! It sounds too good to be true. You're sure? You're not just saying it to be kind?"

"Kind would be all right, but no, I've been a little uneasy of late. No real reason. A weird phone call a couple of nights ago. It was probably just a crank call. But I don't mean to put any pressure on you."

"No, not at all," he said. "It would work out great. I lead a pretty sedate life—I'm not a party boy. I do have a lot of books though."

"Space is no problem, and you could move in whenever you like."

Rusty was on the way again. "That would be perfect," David said. "You're sure now?"

Joan nodded. "Sure as sure can be."

"Looks like we have a deal," David said. "Though we haven't talked about money yet. I don't think this is how my father sells fur coats."

Joan shrugged. "Well, I wouldn't be doing it just for the money, which explains why I'm not in the fur business. Your dad's a furrier?"

"Yep, and I have a raccoon coat. That's about the extent of my link to the family business. Luckily, my brother's there."

Joan did her best to wash away the sudden image of youthful David in a fur salon, standing with hands clasped and smiling blandly. "Listen, how does twenty dollars a month sound, about enough to cover utilities?"

"Make it twenty-one and you've got a bargain. Do I have to stay penned up in my room at that rate? Just a joke. I'm still a little heady over a summer's freedom. And that last hit. Dick Strauss takes his sports seriously—he was an All Big Ten linebacker—and I guess it's infectious. He's the same way about bridge, but there I'm the all-star. I mind-read the cards." And he mimed a blind seer, eyebrows twitching.

"I'm more than a little gifted in that realm myself," Joan said. "Not that I relish the gift."

Satisfied, they walked in silence, turning south toward Joan's house. She showed David around the house from top to bottom. He could have his choice, the bedroom on the second floor or the attic rooms, if he didn't mind the cramped ceilings. For hot nights, there was a fan.

He settled on the attic. She said he was welcome to switch furniture around—he had little of his own aside from a couple of bookcases. If it was all right with her, he'd move this very day, since it was Sunday and still early. He could manage with just a few loads. She offered to help; he said it was easy enough to pack up a load, drive it over, unpack, drive back. It was only ten or twelve blocks, and his car being a convertible—a '48 Buick, his mother's old car from after the war—made the move even easier. Joan gave him a spare key and invited him to dinner, which he accepted gracefully. He turned down a ride back to his place, and she waved goodbye, thinking of romance.

She couldn't help it, and she didn't turn it aside. David was a tall and handsome youth with dark hair and eyes, bright and funny and well-read. It was a fantasy that could go nowhere, hence safe. It was as though Abraham Lincoln had awakened the girl within, hidden for so many years. And once awake, she stayed awake.

With one last glance at David, just crossing Sheridan, Joan caught an echo of her cousin Richard, her father's nephew from Denver. He had gone to Northwestern and lived with her family his first term. It would have been 1927, that year again, a couple of years before the stock market crash, and herself sweet fifteen. She and Richard used to walk her dog, a fox terrier named Sparky, up along the lake. Richard was like a brother, whatever a brother was like, maybe too attentive to be a brother. Then one evening, as they were walking Sparky, he took her hand. Innocent enough, yet not so innocent. Just once they had kissed, her first kiss. In December he took the train home to Colorado.

When he returned he moved into a dorm. She remembered standing at her bedroom window while Richard and a friend gathered up his belongings, loaded them into the trunk of a car, and drove off. From then on she saw him rarely, until she too was enrolled at Northwestern. It was her freshman year, his senior. They took no courses together, he didn't come for Sunday dinners, and they had no mutual friends. The last time she saw him was in the cafeteria just before graduation.

"Cousin," he said, "tomorrow I leave for home and then a job." His major was geology. "I've been hired to prospect for gold and diamonds in the Congo. I'll be gone at least three years, and three years is a long while, especially in Africa."

He'd been wary of talking with her, he said, had even avoided her. At fifteen she was so young, and being first cousins…She remembered how his sentence had faltered. If they hadn't run into each other, nothing would ever have been said. But here they were, and pardon his boldness (which she did), but if he didn't say it now, he never would, and he didn't want love to go unspoken. She could hardly fathom his words, hadn't dreamed that he had taken her so to heart. And now he was going away—first to Denver, then to unmapped regions in the heart of Africa.

"I won't write directly," he said, "but you should hear of me through the annual Colville family letter." Knowing that wasn't enough, he held her cheeks in the palms of his hands and gently kissed her forehead. A kiss? A brush of the lips. Then he was gone.

He was tall and slender, like herself, like all the Colvilles. And it was true, the Colville annual letter did speak of him. Then Joan had married Robert Matcham. Strange, she hadn't thought of Richard in ages.

Joan glanced at her watch—twelve o'clock on the button. At Appomattox Court House it would be 1 p.m., and General Robert E. Lee would soon surrender the Army of Northern Virginia. Abraham Lincoln had hoped to be there to witness the surrender. But Secretary of State Seward was thrown from his carriage on April fifth, the very day that Richmond fell, and the President could not continue at the front. Until early evening he would be on the *River Queen*, steaming up the Potomac. Come sundown, the streets of Washington would be alive with people, bonfires everywhere, the end in sight. This evening. And five days from Appomattox. . .

VARIATIONS ON A THEME
OF ROBERT BURTON

Harry got dressed, put the kettle on, poured milk into his Grape-Nuts, and sat down with the *Oregonian* beside his bowl. Last night, before he fell asleep, it struck him that he could chart the Lincoln letter, sentence by sentence, writing out what each phrase revealed. That way he would catch every nuance. All his skills as a lifelong reader would come into play. If Sherlock Holmes could see it, he'd pat Harry on the back for a job well done. It was hard not to start charting right away. But first things first.

He loved that it was a Monday, and yet he had the leisure to savor every crunchy bite. Thank God he no longer had to work for a living. After breakfast, the Lincoln grid. Then he'd see about planning the Evanston trip. He'd have to fly, no two ways about it.

He remembered other Mondays, so many Mondays that it seemed they would stretch on to doomsday. Monday through Saturday at Truman Levine, Just Furs. Truman thought the pun on "just" took the sting out of flattering little old ladies into parting with their husbands' hard-earned dollars. Harry damn near felt his blood pressure rise at the thought of his brother-in-law, darling Miriam's poor excuse for a husband, a stupid marriage to begin with and a worse marriage thereafter.

Son of a gun! What brought on this fit of pique? he wondered. Like poisoning a well of sweet water. Truman Levine was a thing of the past. Here in Oregon the proverb proved true, "Out of sight, out of mind." Why dwell on those last ten years in Pittsburgh? He should thank Miriam for that blasted decade. She had meant well, intending simply to provide for her brother, poor Harry, hopeless Harry, Harry who sacrificed his all for the sake of dear Papa and then again for dear Mama. And so Miriam had persuaded Truman, who couldn't say *no* to his beautiful and distant wife, to give Harry a job in his thriving fur business. At first, to both of them, it seemed like a good idea. He and Truman seemed to get along. Not so many years before, hadn't Truman been instrumental in quashing the rumor that the fire at Conneaut Lake had been deliberate, for the sake of the insurance money? But it didn't take long before Harry saw himself being taken advantage of: *Harry this*, *Harry that*, long hours, lousy pay, never a *Thank you*.

Harry got up from the breakfast table. His Grape-Nuts were long gone. Truman Levine wasn't the only one. There was Alton Sweeney—if you listened to Sweeney, you'd think Death was knocking at his door. Fifteen years! Fifteen years of waiting for Sweeney to die. Instead it was Mama who died first, on the thirtieth of March, 1940. Then came Truman's ulcer attack. Could brother Harry desert his kid sister?

With his 1940 diary in hand, Harry returned to the table and his second cup of coffee. He wanted to relive the moment when good fortune struck. He glanced at the clock. Nine fifteen—the library wasn't going to lock its doors. Plenty of time. Nor did he want to rush ahead with the grid. If all went well, he could call a travel agent, see about a hotel. He flipped pages till he came to June, and Truman in Montefiore Hospital. *June 15. Occasional showers and hot*, Harry giving blood. The sixteenth, a Sunday, *fair and warm*. By half past five he's at the hospital: *Truman awake and feeling pretty good. Sis had me step into the room and say hello*. The diary didn't record what was said—something saccharine no doubt. The seventeenth, *mostly fair*, overhearing on the neighbor's radio that France had asked Germany for peace terms. *Britain alone against the uncivilized Nazi hordes. Truman showing a lot of improvement.*

Close, thought Harry. In less than two weeks, the telegram from Chauncey White, Sweeney's attorney, announcing the Master's demise, *letter to follow*. It was Harry's Declaration of Independence. And not least of all, his escape from the Amsterdam Apartments. Harry surveyed his present surroundings—nobody's taste to pander to but his own. Not so in the old days, with Papa lingering on till 1931 with ALS, not a red cent left from the estate. He and Mama had moved to a single-bedroom apartment on Wightman Street, all they could afford. It was Miriam who found the ad in the *Post-Gazette*, then talked Harry into taking it, *till you find something better*. For nine years Harry had shared a dingy, peach-colored bedroom with his mother.

That's what he loved about his diaries, watching the days sift along, one by one, like grains of sand—days by the thousand. Time for his morning cigarette.

June 20. Fair and much cooler, Harry at the hospital with his nephew Gene (it had been an age since he'd heard from Miriam's eldest son, or for that matter from David, her youngest). *We listened to the broadcast on the portable radio of the Louis-Godoy fight, a technical K.O. in the 8th round.* What you'll do for the sake of family.

He cringed at the next entry. He'd clean forgotten Ruby Wiggins, a young widow, needy as all get-out.

June 21. At 1 Mrs. Ruby Wiggins was in the store to see me. Sitting downstairs, she told me of her hard luck: how yesterday she had to move from E. End over to the N. Side, that she can't find work, depends upon her mother's pension of 40.00 a month to sup-port herself & her 2 boys of 11 and 14, that she has to have 5.00 for her room rent. She asked me for a loan of 5.00. I told her I didn't have it. She said she'd phone me tomorrow at the store. After she left I thought how I would be making her spend 5¢ for a useless phone call, when she had told me she spent her last 12¢ for this a.m.'s breakfast! I decided then and there that after the store closed, I'd ride over to the lower N. Side, to her rooming house, and give her a dollar instead. I wouldn't miss 1.00—and besides I was cu-rious about the woman. At 6 I rode over to Ridge Ave. There, in an old graystone rooming house, I saw Mrs. R. W. and met her 2 boys in a squalid, crowded third-floor room. I asked the woman if I could see her alone. The boys went out. I told her I couldn't loan her money, then gave her the dollar (which she said she wanted to consider a loan). We talked and I put my arm around her and kissed her—once and I didn't want to any more. When I got home, I scrubbed my teeth, my hands & face.

Damned if he couldn't just about taste her, worse than a week-old armpit. He remembered thinking, while the kiss was turning sour, that he deserved his dollar back, and then some. But it was worth the dollar to get the hell out. Granted, she was a customer for his moth crystals, a sideline Truman had suggested years before. If truth be told, the damned stuff was as likely to attract moths as to repel them.

The next day, Saturday the twenty-second. Never mind the rain and a hard day's work, all he wanted to do was listen to *In-formation Please* on the radio—the diary tells all. Miriam phoned and said *Truman's home*, as if Harry hadn't guessed. In her fool's paradise of a world she thought Truman and he were fast friends, like Damon and Pythias. But brother Howard was already there, talking business with Truman, and good brother Harry has called on a fool's errand.

Then listen to this, just listen—the whining cry of an animal in a cage, hungry and bewildered, not knowing that, come Monday, freedom would be on the threshold.

> *I just cannot like Truman. I feel that he constantly ignores me. He never talks with me and then I feel hurt and I make no effort to talk to him. I suppose Truman doesn't realize what all I do for the business, the many details I look after, the way I keep the wheels going around, running things smoothly. Or maybe Truman feels that he has a good "shnuckle" working for him, watching his interests. What I do, I do for Miriam and the kids.*

"Shnuckle," he said aloud. "If that doesn't sum it up—a damn fool, living off table scraps." With a grunt, Harry skipped ahead to Friday. Still bemoaning his lot: *For I'm not happy in my work.* "Tell me about it," he muttered. Now, a few sentences along, driving home, in East Liberty, on Penn Avenue, *a carnival and I went in & just walked around & listened to the barkers.* Harry closed his eyes. No memory of the moment, no barricades closing off the street, no flashing lights, no frizzy-haired dancers in short skirts, no pepped-up voices crying *Come one, come all.*

Harry snubbed out his cigarette. *Just walking around, Harry the shnuckle—lucky they didn't fleece your hide. Send you home in a barrel with suspenders.*

He heard the call of a story—perhaps one by Isaac Bashevis Singer, with its cast of old-world characters, and Harry a desolate peddler. But it wasn't so much Singer he heard calling as Bagdad, with the story of stories, "The Fisherman and the Jinni." Harry got to his feet. A quarter to ten, no rush. Just across the room was Richard F. Burton's 1885 translation of *The Book of the Thousand Nights and a Night,* in no less than seventeen volumes. Volume One was already in his hands. *By the Burton Club for private subscribers only,* so said the ornate title page. The next page, supremely elegant:

Bagdad Edition
Limited to one thousand numbered sets,
of which this is

Number 919

No date, no place of publication. He pictured a bespectacled clerk for the Burton Club dipping the extra-fine nib of his pen into his bottle of red ink, then filling in the blank after "Number." One thousand sets, each set seventeen volumes. How long did it take the clerk to write the number of the edition seventeen thousand times?

And what were the qualifications for becoming a member of the Burton Club? Being an un-Victorian Victorian? Which the members must have been. The hundreds of exquisite, lurid engravings testified to that. Harry had found the set in a used bookshop on Ankeny Street the very first week he was in Portland, seventeen volumes, seventeen dollars, a clear sign the move to Portland had been the right choice.

Harry turned to the table of contents, and there it was, the second of all the midnight tales of Shahrazad told to amuse King Shahryar: "The Fisherman and the Jinni," a story of frustration and liberation, a variation on the tale of "The Classics Professor and the Seller of Moth Blocks." As Harry remembered it, the story opened with the impoverished Fisherman long in years and living with his wife and four children. Harry turned the pages, catching familiar phrases, the Fisherman's narrow habit of casting his net each day four times and no more. Then comes the day when the fourth cast reveals the jar of yellow copper, its mouth made fast with a cap of lead bearing the seal of our Lord Sulayman, son of David.

Were the Fisherman without curiosity, there the story would end. Imagine characters so uninquisitive that they would leave the jar unexamined! Like Hay and Sweeney with the letter. If anything, King Solomon's seal was more binding than the word of Abraham Lincoln. And where did it say, *This letter is for the eyes of no one but Joan Matcham?* Harry turned a page, skimming along.

The Fisherman's curiosity having the better of him, with his knife he works at the lead till it is free. At first, nothing. But soon enough a heavy smoke spirals heavenward, finally condensing into the form of an Ifrit, huge of bulk and menacing of visage. Indeed, his head is like a vast dome, his hands like pitchforks, his legs like the trunks of cedars, his mouth like a cavern, his eyes like glowing coals. The Ifrit intones, "There is no god but *the* God, and Sulayman is the Prophet of God. Never will I speak against thee or sin in deed against thy covenant, O Apostle of Allah."

The Fisherman speaks: "O Chief of the Ifrits, Sulayman the Apostle of Allah has been dead nigh unto two thousand years. We are late in the days of the world, and the age of miracles is past. Yours is among the last, and would that I might hear your story."

The Ifrit's ironic reply: "Be of good cheer, good Fisherman. My story you shall hear, then you may choose the manner of your death."

"My death?" cries the Fisherman. "But I am your liberator! Is it not I who drew you from the depths of the seas? Is it not I who broke the seal of Lord Sulayman, son of David, and freed you from the bottle? Were it not for me, more centuries—"

And, O the bitter words of the Ifrit, who knows full well the good done unto him by the Fisherman. But too much time has passed, and the Ifrit has sworn revenge upon the first living being that should present itself unto his eyes. "I swore I would grant but one request: the manner of my rescuer's death. Now that I am free, I am ready to grant you your choice."

Harry glanced at the etching of the terrified Fisherman and the angry Jinni issuing from the copper pot. Journeyman's work. Not so the next, just one page ahead: in the style of Aubrey Beardsley, a portrayal of the contemplative Prince sitting upon his throne surrounded by watchful lions, a moment much further along in the story.

But Harry wouldn't rush the story; he would savor the satisfaction of the analogue, himself taking the part of the horrid Jinni whose naïve expectation is that good tidings will soon be on their way. But the years pass, and Harry languishes in the boundless depths of Pittsburgh, by day confined to the fur storage department, checking coats and jackets and scarves for missing hooks and eyes and broken buttons, cataloging the multitudes of furs, arranging pickups in June and deliveries in October. And by night, behind the wheel of his car, a salesman of moth crystals. *By the block, or would you prefer the perfumed canister?* He might as well have been in a strait-jacket, or confined to a wheelchair and locked in deadly silence like his father. Or buried in a copper jar at the muddy bottom of the Monongahela River.

"Yes," Harry said aloud, "I am the Jinni." And Alton Sweeney must be King Solomon. Who then was the Fisherman? Joan Matcham, who opens the envelope and thereby frees Harry? No, he was getting things muddled. Granted, Joan and the envelope were a match for the Fisherman and the copper jar. But Harry's freedom had nothing to do with Joan Matcham and her damn envelope. No, it was Sweeney's death and the fulfillment of his last will and testament that broke the spell that had Harry tied up in brasen knots. That day had already come and was long gone by the time Harry unsealed the letter. *Unless,* Harry mused, *within the envelope was a voice, not of a Jinni, but of Abraham Lincoln, silent lo these many years. Then, the wily Fisherman—none other than myself.*

Yes and no. He was every one of them. Like the poor Fisherman, he opened the envelope; like Sweeney, he sent it on its way to the ultimate Fisherman, Joan Matcham; and God knows, he'd put in his years as the Jinni.

AN OCCASION SO PLEASURABLE

David poked his nose into the breakfast nook. All morning long, the sudden appearance of his cheerful face had taken Joan by surprise. One moment he wasn't there; the next he was. It had been a white lie when she said she often had students living with her.

"Mind if I try out that men's bicycle in the garage? Doesn't look like it's been used for a while."

"Robert's old bicycle. It's British."

"I know," he said. "A Raleigh."

"Sure, why not? There's oil for it somewhere, with the tools, in the basement."

"Thanks. I have a three-speed like it at home, a Schwinn. I've often thought Evanston would be perfect for bicycling, not like Pittsburgh, nothing but hills."

"Prairie country," she said, taking a deep breath, knowing there was no way to keep the story of Robert and Emily at bay. Better now than later. "Robert and I used to take long rides up north, and when Emily got old enough we planned to start riding again." Then, before he could ask his question: "I realize I haven't explained, haven't said anything about my husband and my daughter Emily. They were both killed in a plane crash in Utah, in 1947. Which is why this house is like a coat three sizes too big."

It was as if she had kicked him in the stomach and he'd gone flat. No matter how she phrased it, inevitably it came out as if it were fresh news.

"I'm sorry," David said. "I didn't know."

Joan nodded. "She was a bright child, a bright star. Time helps, dulls the edges. I take nothing for granted. I don't often talk about it. It's there in the background. And life has a way of moving forward. I'll be glad to see Robert's bicycle in use again. I might even join you sometime."

David was back to breathing normally. "Sure, I'll fix them both up." Then, sensing his way clear of the maze, "Listen, I told Mr. Hohenstein I'd be in by noon, and I wouldn't want him to get all wrung up. I'll let you get back to your work."

She waved a gentle goodbye. Her work. Her calendaring. Her notebook was open to the page with the overlapping timelines, and alongside was Roy P. Basler's new edition of the collected works of Lincoln, the last volume, quoting what Lincoln said on April 10, 1865, as reported in the Washington *Daily National Intelligencer*. Today. A Monday in both centuries. The day after Appomattox—not quite the end of the war, but nevertheless "an occasion so pleasurable that the people cannot restrain themselves." His words.

He is addressing a spontaneous gathering that has slogged through rain and mud from the Navy Yard, along Pennsylvania Avenue, up Fifteenth Street, over to the War Department, where they call for Secretary Stanton—who doesn't appear. There they are joined by two bands for what Basler terms a "Response to a Serenade." All are in front of the White House—one, two, three thousand, thanks in part to a holiday for government employees.

Joan pictured herself on tiptoe, clutching her cloak tightly about her neck, cheering, calling for the President.

"There's Master Tad," and an outstretched hand points to a young figure at the window, clutching a small Confederate flag. Finally the President himself appears on the balcony. Next to Joan is the reporter from the *Intelligencer*, his pencil poised. "Fellow citizens," Lincoln begins. The pencil flies. Joan can't make heads or tails of the reporter's shorthand. Then the President's joke:

> *I propose closing up this interview by the band performing a particular tune which I will name. Before this is done, however, I wish to mention one or two little circumstances connected with it. I have always thought "Dixie" one of the best tunes I have ever heard. Our adversaries over the way attempted to appropriate it, but I insisted yesterday that we fairly captured it.*

He smiles benignly as the crowd bursts into applause. When they're done clapping, he continues.

> *I presented the question to the Attorney General, and he gave it as his legal opinion that it is our lawful prize. I now request the band to favor me with its performance.*

Joan settles back on her heels, the bands begin to play, the reporter relaxes. Lincoln is standing pensively. She wonders, *Is he thinking about us?*

Joan's hand was holding back the stiff pages of the book. If she had been reading this "Response to a Serenade" ten weeks ago, the question would have made no sense. Back on the fourth of April she had no inkling that within a week she would spend a day with Abraham Lincoln. But today, the thirteenth of June in the twentieth century, she wasn't sure. His tenth of April had surely changed. Now, as he listens to the bands play and the crowd cheer, he knows more, as though a second Lincoln were standing by his side, prodding him with his elbow to get his attention. *Imagine Joan Matcham by your side now.* "Not now," Lincoln whispers. "Let us celebrate the present occasion. I'll deal with you later."

wasn't like tallying numbers, any of it. She was who she was. She always had been, and she could rely on that.

Then there was Lorraine Riggs, Joan thought, the one person who knew at least part of the story: that Joan was pregnant. And her clinic, right by Lincoln Park, was the Lincoln Clinic. Fitting. Joan's appointment had been the last of the day, and afterward, at Lorraine's suggestion, they had gone to Zarantanello's for dinner. Joan had given her a ride home to Winnetka. Standing by the car door, Lorraine had said, "We don't have to wait for an appointment to do this again." It was just a week ago today.

Joan climbed the stairs to the History office. Liz eyed her as she walked in. "One on the button," she said, duly noting the break from routine.

Joan shrugged. "I figured things would be quiet the day after Commencement, and I was in the middle of a project."

"Well, you're right. It's as dead as a doornail, just a couple of students in to pick up papers. Dr. Boyce phoned to remind us to get the dean's signature on the hiring form—Sharon will sign it for him. Professor Harmon phoned to ask Will Studebaker, if he comes in, to drop his mail off on the way home."

"I can do that," Joan said. It seemed that half the History Department lived within a few blocks of her home.

"I'm sure Harmon's aware of that. See you. Tell me about your project when I get back from lunch."

Joan had the office to herself. She checked her inbox, typed up a syllabus, ran off a ditto, put the afternoon mail in the boxes, and left a message at the Lincoln Clinic for Lorraine Riggs to call. Finally she opened Basler, Volume VIII, at random, turned a page, then another.

> *Story Written for Noah Brooks*
> *The President's last, shortest, and best speech.*

On thursday of last week two ladies from Tennessee came before the President asking the release of their husbands held as prisoners of war at Johnson's Island. They were put off till friday, when they came again; and were put off to saturday. At each of the interviews one of the ladies urged that her husband was a religious man. On saturday the President ordered the release of the prisoners, and then said to this lady "You say your husband is a religious man; tell him when you meet him, that I say I am not much of a judge of religion, but that, in my opinion, the religion that sets men to rebel and fight against their government, because, as they think, that government does not sufficiently help some men to eat their bread on the sweat of other men's faces, is not the sort of religion upon which people can get to heaven!"

    A. Lincoln

Written December 6, 1864. Joan looked to the small print, which explained that Lincoln sent for Noah Brooks (writing for the Washington *Daily Chronicle*), who found him in the parlor writing with a pencil on a piece of boxboard. When Lincoln finished, he said to Brooks: "Here is one speech of mine which has never been printed, and I think it worth printing. Just see what you think." Then Lincoln added the title by way of a joke, and it was printed the next day. A curious moment, Lincoln writing a story as though he were reporting on himself. *How*, she wondered, *would he report the story of Joan?*

Joan skipped ahead—December eighth, a telegram to General Rosecrans: *Let execution in case of John Berry & James Berry be suspended until further order.* Small print: the two brothers, deserters from Company D, Fourteenth Kansas Cavalry, had been sentenced to be *shot to death with musketry.* The sentence was *mitigated to hard labor and imprisonment.* Almost any page Joan turned to had such an order. One she had come across included branding with the letter *D* three inches high on the left hip. The horrors of war, and the enemy your own countryman.

December twenty-seventh, to Haidie M. Jones: *I have received your pretty present by the hand of Hon. Mr Ashley, and for which please accept my thanks. Yours truly, A. Lincoln.* The note stated that no one knew anything about Miss Jones or her present. James Ashley, however, was a congressman from Toledo. The volume was filled with so many invisible stories, names without histories. Someday her own name would be in a book like this unless she destroyed the letter or kept it secret, and everyone else kept it secret as well.

Joan looked up. It could be that she was already here, in *The Collected Works*, if he had written her name in the last two months of his life, maybe on a scrap of paper found in his wallet, or in the small notebook he carried in his pocket. She hadn't run across a reference to Lincoln's personal notebook, though he'd shown it to her. Things get lost; she knew that. He did know her address—it was his writing on the envelope. He could easily have remembered it, or he might have written it down:

Mrs Joan Matcham
1607 Hinman
Evanston, Ill.

They had talked about paradoxes of time and place. If his notebook had survived, her name couldn't have appeared in these pages two months ago, but now was another matter. A book of changes. A changing book. She turned to his April, her June, and began to read closely.

* * *

"*The Collected Works of Abraham Lincoln*, the last volume, if I'm not mistaken. You're like a hound on a fresh trail. First *A Boys' Life*, and now you've got the man, full-blown."

"I guess," Joan said, looking up. It was Will Studebaker. How such a big man could be so stealthy was a mystery.

He was looking at her askance. "If one of my students were in pursuit of Abraham Lincoln, I'd pull up a chair and join in the hunt. It's what none of my colleagues can afford to do—too much pressure to pursue their own fields."

A pause, a cue.

"Well," she said, "pull up a chair. I'm looking at the last part of Lincoln's life, since the peace negotiations at Hampton Roads in February." She felt like a bull in a china shop, all instinct and no plan.

He scooted over a chair. "Peace conference," he said. "That's putting it a bit strong. Lincoln knew nothing would come of it, but he had to silence the peacemongers—Greeley and the lot. And now you're up to, let's see, April tenth, the day after Appomattox, if I'm not mistaken."

"Yes," said Joan. "Lincoln had hopes of being there himself—"

"Except for Seward's accident. Which, in some ways, saved Seward's life come Friday night."

"It did?"

"It did," said Studebaker. "While Booth was at the theater, Lewis Powell was supposed to kill Seward, who lay at home in bed recovering, his neck in a heavy brace. That brace made the difference between death and a less-than-mortal wound."

"I didn't know."

"How would you? It wouldn't be in Basler. The attack was timed to coincide with the assassination. It *was* a plot, though not a Confederate plot—at least that's my opinion. They were to have killed Andrew Johnson too, but George Atzerodt got cold feet and fled on horseback—not that it saved him from execution."

"I guess I don't know much about the assassination. When I get to that part of the story, I want to stop reading."

It was true. She had never warned Lincoln to stay away from Ford's Theater. Nor did Lincoln want to draw on what she knew; he could have asked. It was a taboo that had been with them from the moment he forgot where and when he was and introduced himself as Abraham Lincoln.

Will Studebaker was nodding thoughtfully. "I know the feeling. I must've read a hundred books about Lincoln, and it never fails but I get so caught up in the living man that come the winter of 1865 and I know what's next—well, if I could just shut the book, I could stop the clock. But I read on, I always do."

Joan nodded. The impossible, and it had been in the palm of her hand.

"So," said Studebaker, "you haven't said what got you interested in the life of Lincoln. I had it figured that *The Boys' Life* was a spur-of-the-moment purchase. Jumping to conclusions, that's me."

"I'm a rank amateur," Joan said, "and it's only been for the last couple of months. I found an old edition of his complete works on a shelf at home, a broken set, every single page with a beautiful watermark, *A. Lincoln*, his signature. The volumes had to be my mother's—she was the reader, not my dad. She had hundreds of books, and she left them all to me. I found myself reading, turning page after page, all the odd things he wrote. Thank you for the salmon, the trial of a new kind of battlefield sock, the widow whose son was serving without pay, and one thing led to another." Part of which was true. "What about you?"

"No one's asked me that in a long time."

Their eyes met briefly—his were gray.

"I'll do my best," he said. "Mind you, mostly I'm asked, 'What's next?' Hardly ever about what launched this unlikely ship. Let's see." A short pause while he did his invisible seeing. "Well, I had this teacher in college who made Lincoln come alive when he said the character of Lincoln was rife with contradiction. Was Lincoln an abolitionist, a conservative, a liberal? Was he an instrument; was he a leader? Was the Civil War inevitable, or was it the product of rank stupidity, on both sides? Then he gave us the freedom to read and think for ourselves. Oddly, he was a Canadian. I went back and forth on every issue. I'd be swayed by whatever I was reading. The course ended but I couldn't stop reading. The professor's name was Lowell W. Abercrombie. I stayed on for a Master's degree, did more work with him. He'd never say not to bother with so-and-so, or tell me that Gurowski was unreliable. He let me come to my own conclusions. We'd talk, and I'd find myself taking the next step."

"Sounds like a wonderful teacher."

"He was. He never made a name for himself, though he might've. He wasn't much older than I was. He joined the Canadian army in '39 and was killed before Dunkirk."

"I'm sorry," Joan said.

"Thanks." There were tears on his cheeks. "Just before he was shipped abroad he got married. To a former student of his. My big sister, if you can picture me with a sister who's bigger. She's remarried now and has a son named Lowell Abercrombie Price. So that's one story of how I got interested in Lincoln."

"Lots to that story."

"I guess so," he said, getting to his feet. It was like watching a folding ruler undo itself, one segment after the next—the legs, then the thighs, chest, and head.

"Listen," he said, "I'm working on a paper in my office. I don't know when you get off today, but would you be interested in continuing the conversation over dinner?"

"I would," she said.

"Well, hot dog. I know you live nearby—how does six or six-thirty sound?"

"Fine. Six-thirty would be good. I live at 1607 Hinman."

"Got it. See you then," and he was gone.

What had she just done? Nothing much. Achieved the promise of a conversation at dinner. Fair enough for a woman with child by a phantom.

THE GOOD LIFE

—Monday, June 13, 1955—

Harry took his new clothes directly to the bedroom. The other items from his afternoon's extravaganza he set on the coffee table. When was the last time he had been on a shopping spree? Not since he was living at home and Dad was alive. The tiger *can* change its stripes.

It wasn't even half past four. Every item on his list was checked off: travel agent, hotel, Meier and Frank, Triple A for maps, the Central Library for the Evanston phonebook. It listed two Matchams: besides Joan at 1607 Hinman, a Thomas at 734 Judson—given how uncommon the name was, Harry's guess was that Joan and Thomas must be related: most likely a divorced couple. From the *Yellow Pages* it was obvious there was one choice of hotel: the Orrington, on Orrington Avenue, just a few blocks from Hinman. A hotel, the perfect base for anonymity; and being afoot, he could come and go whenever and wherever, and no one the wiser.

Alongside the maps and the envelope with his plane ticket lay Volume I of Burton, still open to the engraving of the turbaned Prince upon his throne. Harry looked hard at the image of the enthroned Prince surrounded by lions. Say that Harry corresponded to the Fisherman and Sweeney to King Solomon, who might the Prince represent? The answer was obvious now that he thought about it, though he'd never made the connection before. No wonder. The Prince was far too beautiful, while Nat Stein, his philanthropic father, nearly bald and with the full Stein nose, was like a block of ice that refused to melt. But the Fisherman—no, it was the Sultan—has a way to go before he meets the ensorcelled Prince. As Shahrazad is telling the story, the Jinni in his rage at King Solomon, towering high above the poor Fisherman, is about to fulfill his vow to kill the first living being that should appear before his eyes. "The manner of thy death—choose!"

* * *

"But what is my crime?" the Fisherman asked once more. "Was it not I who unsealed you from the jar so that now you are free upon the shore?"

"Enough!" roared the Jinni. "Choose and be done, for I must kill you."

The Fisherman bowed his head as if considering the manner of his death, and said to himself, "This is a Jinni who takes counsel only of his malice, and I am a man faithful to Allah—though poor, I am still possessed of wit." He raised his head and spoke as one who stands upon the verge. "If it is true that you must kill me, O dread Ifrit—"

"More than true!" said the Jinni. "Choose!"

The Fisherman fell to his knees. "I am prepared, O mightiest of the Jann. But if in the Most Great Name, graven on the seal ring of Sulayman, the Son of David, I should ask a single question of you, will you answer truly?"

"Yea," replied the Ifrit, though his wits were troubled by the mention of the Great Name. "Ask, and be done with it."

"Your majesty stands taller than the cedar of Lebanon. How did you come to fit within this bottle which could not contain even your hand, let alone your arm, and never the whole of you?"

The Jinni's eyes glared like twin bolts of lightning. "You doubt that I was contained within the jar! I tell you I was. It was a sight your own eyes beheld."

"Nay," said the Fisherman. "My eyes were turned inward with fear. Before I believe, I must see the impossible with my own eyes."

"Fool," cried the Jinni, whose flesh was already dissolving, until it was naught but a dark cloud which little by little flowed into the jar.

When all was within, the Fisherman took the leaden cap with the seal and stoppered the mouth of the jar. "Now," he said, "what say you to me before I cast you back into the seas? By Allah, I will build a lodge here upon the shore, and I will say that in these waters lives an Ifrit who would slay his deliverer, so beware."

"I did but jest," called the small voice of the Jinni from within the jar.

"And now you lie, O most vile of all Ifrits." Here the Fisherman set off for a high promontory from which to hurl the jar into the deepest of waters.

"Nay, nay," cried the Jinni.

"Aye, aye," said the Fisherman, quickening his pace.

"Where are you going?" the Ifrit asked in a softer voice. "What are you doing?"

"From the cliff tops I will hurl you into the deepest sea, and there you will lie till Judgment Day. Did I not say, 'Spare me, that Allah shall spare thee?' "

"O Fisherman," said the Jinni, "let me do unto you the good turn I should have done for your good deed, had I not been blinded by foul rage."

"You speak to no avail," said the Fisherman. "I know your words to be as hollow as was the vessel when you bade me choose the manner of my death."

"The blessings of Allah be upon you, O wise Fisherman. Is it not said that whoso returns good for evil shall reap a double harvest?"

By now the Fisherman stood on the very edge of the cliff, his arm poised. Once more the Jinni spoke: "I hereby swear that not only shall I do you great good, but I shall never harm you or your kin."

The Fisherman lowered his arm. "I accept both conditions. Repeat your promise and affirm your vow in the name of Allah the most merciful."

This the Jinni did, and the Fisherman removed the stopper from the jar, whereupon the column of smoke issued forth a second time and the gigantic Ifrit stood before the Fisherman. With a great swing of his leg, the Jinni sent the jar flying far out to sea. Seeing how it went with the jar, the Fisherman was sure of his immediate death. Yet he fortified his heart and spoke: "O Ifrit, as Allah hath said, 'Perform your covenant.' "

"Follow me," said the Ifrit, and without glancing back he set off toward the city.

The Fisherman followed at a safe distance. Passing beyond the last of all houses and into uncultivated ground, they reached an untamed wood, in the heart of which lay a mountain tarn, its waters still and dark. "Cast your net," said the Jinni.

The Fisherman did as he was commanded, and when he drew up his net he saw therein four fish: one white, one red, one blue, and the last yellow.

"Present these four fish to the Sultan," said the Jinni, "and he will make you a wealthy man. This is the limit of the good which I may do unto you. My time at the bottom of the sea has been so long that I cannot wait another minute to see once more the face of the world. A warning: do not cast your net in these waters more than once each day. Godspeed, and Allah grant that we may meet again." That said, the Ifrit rose to his full height and with a mighty blow struck the earth, which promptly opened its jaws and swallowed him entire.

The Fisherman marveled at the sudden departure, then proceeded homeward. He dared not approach the Sultan in such mean attire. To keep the fish fresh, he put them into an earthen bowl filled with water, whereupon they began to thrash. With fresh clothing upon his person, he put the bowl upon his head and did as the Jinni had instructed. At the palace he was taken directly to the Sultan as though he had been summoned. The Sultan stared in wonder at such fish as the world had never seen and ordered his Wazir to carry them to the cookmaid immediately. When the Wazir returned, the Sultan commanded him to bestow upon the Fisherman one hundred dinars. The Fisherman clasped the coins to his bosom and ran home, stumbling all the way, fearful that the dream would dissolve before he could reveal the treasure to his wife.

The cookmaid cleansed the fish and put them in the frying pan, basting them with oil till one side was done. Then carefully she turned each fish over, the white, the red, the blue. But the moment the yellow fish touched the oil, the kitchen wall split open with a crash like thunder, and out stepped a young lady, fair of form, her face a perfect oval, her eyelids graced with kohl. Her dress was all of silk, with tassels blue as the sky. A gold ring hung from each ear, and gold bands set with priceless gems encircled her neck and wrists. In her left hand she held a rattan cane, which she thrust into the frying pan, saying, "O fish! O fish! Be ye faithful unto your covenant."

The cookmaid well-nigh swooned at the sight of the wondrous young lady, who repeated her words a second and then a third time. The fish raised their heads and with one voice cried, "Yes!" Whereupon the lady upset the frying pan into the coals and departed as suddenly as she had come.

The cookmaid threw herself upon the ground and sobbed aloud, "All is lost, all is lost." In such a case the Wazir found her.

Becky smiled broadly. "We'll save that story—it's a good one. You said you were retired. Retired from working for Philip Sweeney?"

"Yes and no. Sweeney had retired from his law practice and was getting on in years when I came along. He owned some property here and there, and gradually, once he saw I knew my left hand from my right, he turned the management over to me. I had a small nest egg. Mother had been saving for her old age, but she died sooner than she expected. I saw Phil's system and began to play the real-estate game myself. Soon I was busy enough with my own properties, and Phil and I went our separate ways. Before long, he'd dismantled his little empire and set up a trust fund. When he died, Reed College was the big winner. He did leave me a token for my years of service. So goes the story of my retirement." *And*, thought Harry, *there's even a fair amount of truth to it.*

"Sounds like you've put together a pretty good life for yourself, Harry Stein."

They took their drinks to the living room. Becky talked about her life as a widow, her routines, one day drifting into the next. Her chatter had him remembering those early years in Portland, Alton Sweeney's legacy, and the supposed privilege of working for the younger Sweeney. Though it was clear from the first day that he'd traded one sour apple for another. Indentured servitude all over again. Marking time: D-Day, the Bomb, Dewey and Truman, and finally, goodbye to P. Sweeney, Esq.

Harry looked at his watch. Half past five already? Harry, his own Shahrazad, swept away by the Tale of the Disgruntled Servant. Becky yammered on, her words going in one ear and out the other. If they had sex now, it would spoil dinner. If they waited till after dinner, how would he get rid of her? He did like her looks, the blonde eyebrows, the striped blouse that accentuated the line of her breasts. Maybe dinner, then her place—that way he could be the one to gather up his marbles when it was time.

"I have an idea," he said. "We finish up our drinks, then we have that dinner. How's that sound? What did you have in mind?"

Becky glanced at the time. "I guess. There's the Oyster Bar or Henry Thiele's. There's Chinese. What do you think?"

"What about that Italian place across the river on Sandy, Sylvia's?"

"Sure," she said. "I've been there, with all the Chianti bottles hanging from the rafters. Good food too." She crossed her legs the other way. "There's no rush, is there?"

"Not at all," Harry said. "I skipped lunch today, that's all." His glass was half full. "I remember you used to be a reader."

"Still am," she said. "More than ever these days. I see you are too. If books were water, you could drown in this apartment."

"So I could, though it's more the other way around—books keep me afloat. Who're your favorite writers?"

"Willa Cather, probably. I read her books over and over." He nodded. Yes, he liked Cather. And they both liked Edith Wharton, and Fitzgerald, and the Russians. Subsistence conversation. As though he'd lost the knack of talking to a female. In the old days, he had a clear goal: to keep things alive till they got to Schenley Park. He glanced at the mantel. Six o'clock, dinnertime.

THE NEXT THING SAID

—Monday, June 13, 1955—

Joan and Will settled on Fanny's out on Simpson—a little bit of everything: spaghetti, steak, Southern-fried chicken, including their "World Famous" salad dressing for sale in small mason jars. Walking in, Joan had blanched at the sudden smell of fried oil, but sitting in a booth by an open window calmed things down. Will Studebaker's Studebaker, like an odd stutter, sat in the parking lot, its chrome grill facing them, though Joan still thought of Studebakers as facing forward no matter which way they were going, forward or backward. One hoped the living Studebaker was less two-faced. Joan had avoided all the obvious Studebaker jokes, other than asking if he was related to the car family. "Distantly," was the answer, though he couldn't resist owning one. There had been the odd moment at her house, with David answering the bell and the two of them knowing each other from the tennis court. Small world.

They had ordered, and the waitress brought them their iced tea (iced tea, an ever-present reminder that Evanston was world headquarters for the Women's Christian Temperance Union). By the clock it was a quarter of seven, and Joan had no way of knowing what Abraham Lincoln was doing just then. A couple of hours earlier he had delivered his second "Response to a Serenade," an impromptu speech in which he said that he had nothing to say, but that tomorrow evening he would be better prepared. Yet he had taken enough time to say he had nothing to say so that the crowd was not unfulfilled.

"Cheers," said Will, holding his iced tea up for a toast. "As of five o'clock today, I'm on holiday: the last paper read, grades turned in, no classes till September."

"Here's to an eventful summer," Joan said. "What will you be doing?"

"Oh, the university pays me a little money to keep up with my book on political parties of the '50s, the 1850s, leading up to the election of 1860. If I didn't have my summers, I'd never catch up, and the book would end up being written without my help. By somebody else, that is. Leave it to me to specialize in an area so broad it has no boundaries." He spoke with a straight face. "What about you?"

"Me? I'll work till mid-August, the end of the regular summer session, and then I'm not sure. Things are kind of up in the air for me." *To put it mildly*, she thought. "Though I'm sure I'll go on with Lincoln."

"Glad to hear it. I wouldn't want to hear you'd dropped Lincoln."

Indeed, she thought. Everything they said was doubled-edged—that she couldn't help but go on with Lincoln; the possibility that Lincoln (a very young Lincoln) would drop; that day by day she was less up in the air and more bound to the earth.

Here was their minestrone and a basket of French bread. Studebaker passed her the shaker of Parmesan. "Good soup," he said. "I could live off this stuff."

It *was* good, thick and rich, with kidney beans and tomato and every other vegetable under the sun, and parsley and sage and bits of pasta. A "world soup," it should be called. "Look." She had balanced her spoon upright in the bowl, and there it stayed. "I wonder what *minestrone* means in Italian."

"I don't know," he said. "It has to be an Italian word, maybe something to do with the Latin verb *ministro*, like 'minister,' or

God forbid, 'administrator.' I'll bet it means something like the word 'serve.' Either that or it doesn't."

"Some teacher you must be—when push comes to shove, you're a know-nothing."

"That's one brand I reject," Will said. "With a foreign name like Studebaker, I'm on the other side of the street from the Know-Nothings. How did Lincoln put it? It was in a private letter to Joshua Speed—Lincoln was being careful not to offend a considerable group of people, not when the Republicans stood to inherit their votes. Something like this: 'We began with All men are created equal; then we said Negroes weren't men. And when the Know-Nothings get control, they'll exclude foreigners and Catholics.' Then he added, 'When that day comes, I'll move to Siberia where there's no pretense at liberty.' "

"Good timing," Joan said. "Wait till I have a mouthful of chewy bread, then charge me with a major crime and send me to the gallows. I forgot it was a political term."

"Yes. They called themselves the Native American party, but they really were a secret society, like the Order of the Star-Spangled Banner. If anyone questioned them, the members were instructed to say, 'I know nothing.' Lincoln expected them to die off and was surprised when they didn't. The trouble was, he needed their votes—no getting round their being a popular force."

"Doesn't sound like they're altogether gone."

"No," said Will. "Lincoln recognized the irony of the Order calling itself the Native American party. He answered someone who pressed him for support by saying he thought Native Americans wore breech-clouts and carried tomahawks, and that we had pushed them from their homes, and now we were turning on others not so fortunate to arrive as early as we did on these shores. It'll be a good while before such sentiments disappear. I think Shakespeare has something to say on the subject: " 'when such days come,' meaning Utopian times, 'We'll be able to eat our soup with a fork.' "

"Shakespeare said that?"

"Words to that effect. I'm just a historian—don't ask too much of me. It's a miracle I can come anywhere near what Lincoln said, let alone Shakespeare. If Walter Jones, my high school history teacher—and a good one—knew that I'd grow up to become a history professor at a reputable university—well, God only knows what he'd think. I'd write him words to that effect if I didn't fear what it might do to his faith in his own good judgment."

They had moved on to their pasta. "Were you really that bad a student?"

"Yes and no. I loved reading about the past, but if you asked me to give nine reasons why the Hittites died out, I'd be stumped. Even now I'd have a hard time telling you what precipitated the Civil War. I get at those kinds of questions by mulling around, by looking at old newspapers and diaries and letters, by reading one book and another and then another. And next year I'll read yet another that changes the slant on all the others. Why am I doing all the talking? They ought to prescribe teachers for insomniacs."

"I'm interested," Joan said, "maybe that's why. I'll do my sleeping on my own time. I'm glad to hear how someone else goes about being a historian. I'm brand new at this. Mostly I'm going back to Lincoln's own words to find out what I can about Lincoln himself. Roy Basler's edition of his works astonishes me, though I know how far short of the person it comes. How can you capture a person on the pages of a book?"

Will shrugged. "I don't think we ever do. Certainly Lincoln's biographers didn't, not the whole person. But what little we do in that direction is better than being kicked in the side of the head by an ornery mule."

Joan smiled. A couple of times it felt as if William Studebaker was not unlike Abraham Lincoln himself. It could be the homely expression, the common-sense approach. Plus the gangly physique. And both of them were automobiles. "I was thinking," she said, "that even when we live with someone, we know them only to a limited degree. I honestly believe we're strangers even to ourselves."

" 'Strangers to ourselves,' I like that phrase. It has a ring. Mind if I borrow it sometime? But first tell me what you mean by it. And keep up the talking so I can work through my spaghetti."

"You're a funny man, Professor Studebaker. Feel free to draw on the phrase any time. I don't require credit for it. And what I think I mean by it is that at any given moment we're completely unpredictable. We're the sum of countless habits, but at the same time new ones are shaping themselves and the old ones are shifting. I'll admit I think of myself in familiar terms—my reflection doesn't surprise me, or not very often. But the next thing I say to you could shock me half to death."

"Say it," he said, and the air was suddenly as unblinking as the eye of a hurricane.

"I'm pregnant."

He set down his fork and spoon.

She said not a word.

He said, "You're not married."

Joan nodded.

"And it has nothing to do with David Levine, does it?"

"No, though I've thought about that, and how it might look, and that concerns me. But as I said, it was pure happenstance that led to that arrangement, or nearly so."

She watched him, could see him searching for how to phrase it, whatever *it* was.

"You said that you could be surprised—no, shocked—by the next thing you'd say." He waved aside her nod. "Then you said what you had no intention of saying. Which was very brave. It surprised me too, but not in the sense that I'm a stern prophet from the Old Testament. I mean 'surprise' simply in the sense of 'unexpected.' "

"Yes," she said simply.

"I have one more question." His palms were flat on the table, as though for balance. "It feels so presumptuous to ask it. I think I know the answer, but I want to be sure I'm not mistaken."

"Ask it."

"You're happy to be carrying this child, aren't you?"

"Yes," she said. "I'm just beginning to find that out. It was confirmed just a week ago."

"Then that's all that matters," and he picked up his fork and spoon. "I could ask any number of questions, and the answers matter to me, I assure you. But I'll be more than happy to go on with our dinner. And the next one too."

"I think I'll do a little eating myself. Something to be said for nourishment."

* * *

They finished dinner, then drove back to Joan's house. It was still light, and at Will's suggestion, they headed for the path along the lake with Rusty for company.

"I've been thinking," he said.

"So have I."

"I'd be surprised if you weren't," he said. "I was about to say that I'm at a crossroads in my life. I know next to nothing about you. You know very little about me. I hesitate to presume, but at the same time I'm afraid not to. Ordinarily, time would let questions come to the fore and find answers. But right now nothing seems ordinary."

He was walking at a deliberate pace, his eyes focused on the path.

"I know," she said. "I seem to be at a crossroads myself, a whole slew of them, one after the next." She was trying to remember the first, Easter Sunday, in front of the library, just up ahead, when she'd met Abraham Lincoln, and then the rest of that day—whether any moment along the way was like a crossroads, with a choice. But her memory of that day wasn't like a map where your finger can trace how you get from here to there. She could make a list of what they had done, from lunch to dinner, the movie, and then afterwards. But it was far from a series of decisions, each with a Yes or a No. Will Studebaker was a nice man, more than nice, but she was afraid to push her judgment on such short notice. *On the other hand*—she was almost speaking aloud, and then she was: "Nothing ventured, nothing gained."

Will stopped cold. "Was that said for my benefit? It sounded like the words just leaked out."

"They did," she said. "A slip of the tongue." Then, "How old are you? I'll be forty-three come Wednesday."

"Congratulations. So I'm younger than you by a few years. Does that make a difference?"

"Some. I'm conventional, but I guess I'm in no position to worry about what's unconventional."

"It sounds like you want me to feel sorry for you, but I have no reason for that, unless you give me one. At dinner you said you were glad you were pregnant."

"I am," she said. "I'm trying to be forthright, but it's hard. It's as if I know where I am but not where I'm heading. Maybe if I take one step at a time—" She fell silent, looked at the sky, then out to the water. She wondered why suddenly she felt so small.

She was tall and he was taller, but it wasn't that kind of small. More like the image in the wrong end of a telescope, that kind of small. And so distant.

He was standing up straight, looking her in the eye, listening carefully, just like Rusty. "Step one," said the man, "if you please."

"All right. The father of my child, he isn't in the picture."

"Isn't in the picture," Will echoed.

"No."

"Well, I guessed as much, but I'm wary of guesses with you. You did agree to have dinner with me, and you don't strike me as the two-timing sort."

"I hope not."

"Can I ask a direct question?" Then before she could answer, "You know, this is hard for me too. It's like I'm watching a play and I call out from the audience, 'Hurry up—it's okay to skip the next scene.' Except I want the whole story."

"You can ask, but I can't promise I'll answer."

"Is the father anywhere nearby? Is he anyone I know?"

"That's two questions."

"That's what comes of being tall: part-way up asked one, and the rest asked the other. I read a story once about a man with two heads that didn't cooperate very well, but I always agree with myself."

"Good," she said. "Wish I could say the same. We'd better walk, or Rusty will feel shortchanged, and then I'll answer."

"Fair enough," he said. "Do you ever let her off the leash?"

"Sometimes, especially when the path is free. But you never know when a student will be afraid of dogs. She's overeager sometimes."

He was already undoing the leash. Rusty shot off, then stopped to investigate an elm tree. Satisfied, she squatted to pee.

"The father's nowhere nearby," Joan said. "That's one answer. The other one—" She hesitated.

"You don't have to answer."

"I know," she said. She was looking for how to phrase it. "He's no one you've ever met. There's no way you could ever meet him."

"I hear a 'but' lingering at the end of that sentence. Are you saying I do know him, in some fashion? This feels like some kind of guessing game, like *Twenty Questions*."

The sun was close to the horizon. "What if we turned around?" Joan asked.

"Sure," Will answered. "Listen, I meant what I said. You don't have to answer anything. I know enough for now. I don't want to intrude. And I'm stumbling for the right words. Come on, Rusty," he called, and the three headed toward Hinman Street.

* * *

Joan opened the door, and Rusty dashed inside. Will was holding the screen door open. "I'm not going to ask you in," she said. "It's been a full day." And then they were both talking at once. He was saying how she was certainly free to go in her own house unencumbered, and she was saying how actually there was a sense in which he did know the father of her child. They both paused, and Joan went on: "I don't want you to think I'm crazy."

"We're both crazy," he said. "I'm thirty-six and single. I was engaged once, when I was teaching in Fargo, but neither of us could get serious about the next step. Or maybe I should say neither of us could picture us being a married couple. As though we were miscast. And so here I am half a dozen years later, lingering on your doorstep like a gawky teenager." Whereupon Joan rose on tiptoe, put her arms around his shoulders, and kissed him on the lips.

When her heels were back on the ground and her breathing had slowed, she spoke. "The father of my child is Abraham Lincoln. And now goodnight, Will Studebaker. I'll be in the office tomorrow at one. Thank you for dinner, and everything else." The next thing she knew she was inside, and the door was closed.

ANCIENT SPELLS

Not bad considering, Harry thought. He'd done a lot worse. Becky was the first woman he'd screwed for quite some time without having to ask what her name was. Usually it was like the all-too-frequent moments in the *Arabian Nights* where the Prince spurs off into the waste chasing after the enchanted stag, and the next thing you know he's lost, it's nightfall, and who should appear but a beautiful damsel who tells him that she is the daughter to a King among Kings, but while traveling with her caravan she grew drowsy and fell from her beast, and now she is cut off from her people and sorrowfully lost. In reality she's a hideous Ghulah, a spell-binding Ogress, a monster from the graveyard who has said to her brood, "O my children, on this day will I bring to you a fine fat youth for dinner." "Hurry," said her sweetlings.

That the Prince and the beautiful damsel should find themselves coupling and carousing, her legs wrapped around his as a button-loop clasping a button, signifies for the handsome Prince nothing out of the ordinary. He shouldn't be surprised. Isn't this ease at falling to it the result of an altogether different and most ancient spell, a spell originating in the Garden with the first of all women?

It was ten-thirty by the clock on the dresser. Becky was asleep, one arm tucked under the pillow, the other cradling her chin. He had cast his spell. He dressed by candlelight. The candle added a touch of romance—no harm there. But more, thanks to its gentle illumination, he could see what he was doing. He liked to watch the movement of his hand on a woman's breast, as though it were happening in a movie. But movies, alas, at that very moment, cut to moonlit clouds, and the imagination, like a blind man with a cane, can only wonder how it went.

He tiptoed out of Becky's bedroom, down the stairs, turned out the lights, and closed the door. She'd want more of that when he got back from Illinois. They'd used her car to go to dinner, but a bit of a walk was all right. He liked the physical awareness in his groin, the spent feeling of a fresh orgasm, the sense of accomplishment. A good prelude to tomorrow and the next few days. And just who in the hell did Abraham Lincoln think he was kidding? He might have left a little something behind! Harry may have left a little something behind too, but it was a little late in the game for Becky Hirschberg to do much with it. And what if, as the letter suggested, the spell-binding Ogress of Evanston was with child? Now wouldn't that just be the trick of the century?

At home, Harry once more went over what to take on the trip. A reference book or two—there would be plenty of libraries in the vicinity, especially when it came to Lincoln. His eye caught Benjamin Thomas's *Lincoln*, that and the last volume of Freeman's *Lee*. What about Asia Booth Clarke's book about her brother? And for something different, a volume or two of Burton. He'd pack his bag in the morning to keep things from wrinkling. He couldn't think of anything to add to his list. What about his travel iron?

After a shower he propped himself in bed. He'd left off where the Wazir carried the second batch of fish to the cookmaid, and again

* * *

the wall divided, and now a somber woman in modest raiment stepped forth, of an age past the begetting of children. She thrust her wand into the frying pan and commanded the fish to be faithful unto their covenant. So saying, she upset the frying pan and promptly departed, and the wall gaving no hint of its cleavage.

"This must I see with my own eyes," cried the Sultan.

"So be it," replied his Wazir, and upon the morrow, not a woman in the prime of life, but a crone appeared to stir the fish, upset the pan, and swifter than the hare, was gone.

"Call for the Fisherman," commanded the Sultan. "Surely these fish are under an enchantment."

Soon the Fisherman stood before the Sultan. "Out with it, fellow! Whence come these fish?"

All atremble, the Fisherman replied, "O my most merciful Lord, they come from a tarn lying just behind the ridge which commands a view of your city—a walk of less than an hour."

The Sultan wondered that such a tarn should be so near. He ordered his men to march and his horsemen to mount, and with the Fisherman as guide (privily damning the Ifrit), they fared till they came to the ridge and the familiar path to its summit. Without pause they ascended. Beyond lay a great desert and in its midst the tarn, and in the distance a great wall of mountains. Had the Sultan's men in all their lives ever seen this desert or this water or these mountains before? "O Sultan of the age, never have our eyes beheld such sand, water, or stone, not in all our days."

They camped by the shore of the tarn. Now the Sultan took his Wazir aside. "You must guard the entrance to my tent, and should any ask, you must say that I am unwell and must not be disturbed."

Whereupon the Sultan changed his dress and ornaments, and with his sword slung upon his shoulder, he pursued the path which led toward the nearest of the mountains. All through the night he marched, and the morning too, until the mountain lay at his back. When the sun reached its zenith, he found shade and rest.

Come evening the Sultan resumed his march, and come the second dawn he spied in the far distance a habitation all of black. Haply, he said to himself, someone here will know of the tarn and the fish of four colors. When he drew close, he discovered a castle built of stone as black as night. His spirits rose, for he was weary with travel. He stood before the gate and rapped smartly, and again, and again. Receiving no answer, he tested the latch and the door swung open.

"I am a wayfaring stranger and hungry," he called, firm of voice. "Have you aught of victual?" Hearing no reply, he called again, but his words echoed hollowly from within. Strengthening his heart, he entered the vestibule, then continued to the very middle of the palace and found not a single person. Yet it was furnished with costly stuffs of silk and gold.

The Sultan looked left and right. He was within a spacious courtyard, flanked on either side by an open saloon with a raised dais and a canopy for shade, beneath which a fountain jetted water as clear as crystal. The Sultan stilled his heart. When did rushing ever help resolve a mystery? Were those chimes he heard? He glanced upward. Overhead, birds darted this way and that, their wings brushing a net of silver wire. Surely this palace was complete in every way, save for the presence of a human soul.

The Sultan chose the saloon to his left. He sat upon the edge of the dais and lamented that he had come all this way in hope that someone would reveal to him the secret of the tarn and its fish, the desert, the mountains. But instead of revelation, he had naught but the void of this black palace. Sitting thus, deep in thought, there came unto his ears a mournful voice. "O Fate, O bitter grief and no escape, world without end, O what my eyes have seen and shall never see."

Hearing these words, the Sultan sprang to his feet and followed the voice to a curtained door. Drawing the curtain aside, he saw a young man upon a couch, fair to the sight and well shaped. His forehead was broad, his cheek like the rose, and upon his upper lip a downy mustache. The Sultan rejoiced and saluted the Prince, but the youth in his kaftan of silk and gold did not stir from his couch. Though his crown was studded with gems, his face betrayed only sorrow. "My Lord," said the Prince, "I crave pardon that I do not rise to your greeting."

"No excuse is necessary. It is I who intrude," said the Sultan. "I come from the far side of the mountains, a journey of two days, in hope of unfolding the secret of the tarn and the fish, the desert and the mountain. Now I add to these mysteries your palace of stone that outshadows the shadow, and within it your solitary self, wretched and palely grieving."

"Why should I not grieve?" asked the Prince, who raised the hem of his kaftan. Wonder of wonders, from the waist down to his feet all was stone, while above he was flesh.

"O youth, sorrow upon sorrow, yours is the story I would know. There is no Majesty and there is no Might save in Allah, the Glorious, the Great! Lose not a moment and tell me your tale."

"Attend closely," said the Prince.

* * *

"Like Papa," Harry said softly, "the man turned to stone."

Gently (for what requires more care than a volume so rare and fine?) Harry closed the book. The voice of Shahrazad faded till it was softer than the whisperings of the valleys of the moon. Harry surveyed the story. *We have solved the mystery of the jar with the seal of Solomon; we have survived the Jinni and his wrath; we have seen the four fish and their bitter covenant; we have come to the enchanted palace and the ensorcelled Prince, in whose flesh is buried the darkest secret of all. What story will the Prince tell? Come tomorrow, the unraveling.*

A DAY FOR UNFOLDING XIII

Joan woke with a start and then relief that this was her world and not the other. Her dreams were a muddle: floods, water pouring through the kitchen ceiling, trying to start her car (it was a convertible like David's Buick) when it was half submerged. Now the sky looked clear, though there had been a rainstorm in the night, with thunder and lightning and Rusty whining to go out and immediately wanting right back in.

Then came the other flood, of memory. First her telling Will Studebaker that she was pregnant, then the impossible scene on her doorstep. If she could just have kept her mouth shut. He was probably halfway to Timbuktu by now. But oh, they had hit it off like long-lost souls. It was strange, Joan thought, how she could see a person day after day and not think twice about it. As if there were different drawers to her life, and Will belonged in the work drawer. When she walked out of Harris Hall, that drawer closed. But seeing him by the lake—was it just Saturday?—he took on an added dimension. He wasn't bound up like a mummy in the narrow confines of the History Department anymore, but was out and about, a person and not a fixture. Which made it all right to say she was pregnant. It had just slipped out—it was undeniably a fact—and the longer she would have waited, the harder it would have been to go on. But how could she have said next, just like that, that Abraham Lincoln was the father?

"I'm a nut," she said as she got out of bed and headed for the bathroom. It wasn't even seven o'clock—no need to worry about competing with David.

Downstairs, she put water on to boil for oatmeal and a cup of tea. *Oops*—in plain sight on the kitchen table sat her journal. Too many years of solitary living. Last night was the first time she'd written in it for a week, since her appointment with Dr. Riggs Monday last. A week and a day. Lorraine Riggs telling her, *Yes, you are pregnant*. No surprise there, with the missed period and the queasy stomach, but it had crossed her mind that it might have been a hysterical pregnancy, though she'd only read of the phenomenon. Think enough upon a thing, to paraphrase Hamlet, and no knowing what transpires. Maybe if she'd been a diarist like her mother and her grandmother, keeping diaries all the way back to the 1840s, sheer force of habit would have kept her pen going. Small matter—*Diaries are there to serve us, not the other way round*. At the table she added brown sugar and a bit of butter to her cereal and took a bite—perfect. As always.

She opened her journal. The first entry, a week and a half after his "manifestation"—a cumbrous word for discovering a tall and lanky man sitting on a bench by Deering Library. By the twentieth of April she had purchased a blank book at Kroch's and was ready to tell her story, save that she didn't know where to start, which was where she started. Then, rather than tell the story in its proper order, she introduced the issue of whether she was pregnant or not, as though if she weren't, that would unhinge the story. Next, with assurances that she was of sound mind, the spare announcement that the father of her child, if she was with child, was Abraham Lincoln. Again it was like telling a story backwards, where the person falls dead, is shot, and the trigger pulled. Joan is pregnant, has sex, meets Lincoln. As though the next part of the story would have her in pigtails and playing hopscotch. Well, what was a diary supposed to be? Was it a straight record of daily events, or did it encompass the errant tracings of a mind, like the trembling needle of a seismograph?

Joan turned the page, and there, as if taking fright at the sight of two blank pages, the creature found its voice: *It all began when I saw him sitting on a bench overlooking the lake, and it didn't cross my mind that he resembled the man on the five-dollar bill.* Though even that sentence no sooner flowed than ebbed. Across the next few pages the story unfolded, and when it finally caught its tail it fell silent until Lorraine Riggs happened along. Then last night's entry. No mention of Thursday's letter, no mention of the inexplicable reappearance of the 1955 penny. No time like the present.

Joan set her dish in the sink, lifted the cozy, and poured her second cup of tea. She uncapped her pen and began to write.

Last Thursday afternoon the 9th of June. While reading randomly in the diary of Grandmother Morrow, on the spur of the moment I opened her little prescription box filled with pen points. I'd never looked through them before. I didn't even know if they were hers or my mother's. No two were alike. Some were from banks, others from printing companies, railroads, a few were from England. It was a collection. I'd never done more than lift its lid. Which meant that ever since my 30th birthday when Mother gave me Grandmother's things, it has been mine. Looking at the points one by one, I noticed a dull-looking penny underneath. I looked at it & saw it was a Lincoln penny, not an Indian Head penny as I expected. It couldn't be Grandmother Morrow's since the Lincoln pennies weren't minted until the centenary of his birth, 1909, a common coin for a man of the common people. Grandmother died before the turn of the century. Still it was old and tarnished. Then I looked at the date. 1955! I jumped to the answer. This could be none other than the penny that he had showed me, Abraham Lincoln, when we were together. He had found it & put it in his pocket & when he left, it was in the pocket of his pants.

Joan capped her pen. She had wondered about this miraculous reappearance. But the how of it eluded her. He wouldn't have excused himself and snuck up to her bedroom, examined her chest of drawers, found the box with her grandmother's things, and hidden the penny. *To what end? No, somehow the penny had got from Abraham Lincoln to Grandmother Morrow, though she wasn't a Morrow yet, was still Sarah Prentiss, a widow from the state of Maine. No way to know how she got the penny. It's not as though you can phone up a woman who's been dead close to sixty years.*

"Oh my God!" Joan cried out. She ran for the stairs, took them two at a time, got the box of diaries from the closet, and found the volume with 1865 on its cover. It had to be somewhere between his appearance in Evanston and—she'd come to hate the very word—the assassination. Somewhere between February fifth and April fourteenth.

Joan took the diary back downstairs. The writing was small but readable. By early February Sarah Prentiss had returned from visiting her brother in England and was staying in Boston. Joan skimmed along. March twentieth was headed *Washington*. Sarah was staying with her uncle, William Pitt Fessenden, Chase's replacement as Secretary of the Treasury, and spending every possible hour with her old friend Elizabeth Lee on Lafayette Square. Toward the end of the entry for March twenty-first, Joan's eye caught what she was looking for, the one word, *Lincoln*. Vice President Johnson was recuperating at Lizzie's house, and Sarah and Lizzie Lee had dined at Willard's Hotel before going to the opera. The Lincolns were dining a few tables away and were also going to the theater. Lizzie being a friend to Mrs. Lincoln, there were introductions. The matter-of-fact description of the meeting ended with Sarah Prentiss writing that *the President seems a gracious and friendly man*. Not earth-shattering. Then March twenty-second:

Washington City. This morning I went across to the White House where President Lincoln wrote out a pass allowing me to visit Richmond. He was reluctant at first, though I explained how difficult it was for Emma to keep order in a house & at the same time amuse nine year old Jourdan who must be confined to a darkened room. Still he withheld his approval. He kept insisting that my friend must have her own friends in Richmond who could help. He said that while wars are fought on battlefields, Richmond as the capital of the Confederacy commands the attention of the Federal army & one never knows. He did his best to dissuade me as one friend to another. It was my telling the story, & I dont remember why, other than pulling out all the stops, though its real enough God knows, of how Emma came to my support when my Meg & her father were drowned in the Kennebec flood that led the President to relent. At the end of the interview he asked if he might impose one condition. He then said, should Richmond be evacuated, would Emma & I hold our ground & he would direct our soldiers to watch out for us. I agreed to his condition & told him where Emma lives. I am afraid that when I told Mr Lincoln of my Meg I put him in mind of the death of his son Willie for we both had tears in our eyes. He said I must not trouble myself for doing that, & these are his very words, "I catch myself every day talking with him as if he were with me." He is a very kind man & it is hard impossible to match him up with the blood thirsty monster one reads about in the papers.

Joan brushed tears from her own eyes. She had never known this part of the story. Still, there was no mention of any penny. She looked ahead. From the twenty-fourth of March the pages were headed *Richmond*. Joan turned to April the fourth, after the evacuation of the rebel capital. The entry went on for several pages, with a description of President Lincoln and his small party of marines

Prentiss and recognize, two generations early, the features of her granddaughter.

Joan imagined herself, back before Easter, with her eyes riveted on the diary, then the melting away of one account and the emergence of another: the same handwriting, the same faded ink, different words, different story. How different? And would she note the difference? Would she see time divide and witness its passage down both tracks? And here in mid-June, should she say anything to Will Studebaker? She may already have said more than enough. And Abraham Lincoln's strange words, like a soothsayer's, to Sarah Prentiss: *Another day may come when more can unfold*—such a day was left to the granddaughter. This day.

UNCOMMON STORIES

—Tuesday, June 14, 1955—

Harry gazed out the window—sunshine and mountains, peak after peak, endless. The airline map was spread across his knees. Must be Wyoming. He caught sight of the airplane's shadow trailing effortlessly behind. The stewardess (a pretty girl, Margaret Thompson, who was from Dallas, Texas, but now lived in Chicago) had just taken away his lunch: tuna-fish salad, fresh fruit, blueberry pie, and coffee. A far cry from what his life would have been like if he were still in Pittsburgh, living with Mama, working for Truman, taking in remodeling jobs, parking by the wharf so vandals could put pieces of old rubber in his gas tank, eating the same lunch (coffee and a muffin) at Donahoe's day after day, and in the evenings delivering moth crystals to the likes of Arnie Bondura on Album Street, and the highlight of the day: watching the Lux Theater or maybe Jackie Gleason and the Honeymooners perform their stupid skits. And complaining about being stuck in the same dingy old apartment and doing nothing about it.

"Professor Griffin, mind if I get by?"

"Please call me Rita, Mr. Stein. I'm only a professor when I profess."

"Rita," he said, as she stood in the aisle to let him pass. Harry couldn't imagine calling any professor from his day anything but Professor. Not that it mattered what title you gave Alton Sweeney—he'd have trouble hearing you from six feet under. Certainly

"You got me there. I can't explain it, but the one other time I was up in an airplane it was a two-seater, half an hour for five bucks. We flew loops and figure eights, and I didn't stop to think about how we did it."

"You mean you haven't flown since then?"

"Right," he said. "Thirty years ago on the button. Since then I've stuck to vehicles that cling to the ground."

"The ride was that bad?"

"No, it wasn't bad at all. But then came the *Hindenburg*, and before you knew it airplanes were falling out of the sky left and right. Just this year, by my count, there've been sixteen crashes involving American planes where at least nine people in each flight were killed."

"Sixteen? All in the United States?"

"Oh no," he said, "just seven in the United States; four of those crashes were military flights, and that includes Alaska and Hawaii, one each. A lot of our military planes go down, nine of the sixteen. Of the seven commercial planes, four were foreign flights. I'm not exactly sure what those numbers signify, whether we're less safe. Maybe it's the sheer quantity of U. S. flights. Besides, it's not a large sample. Still. The most killed was sixty-six, everybody aboard. Imagine the day when airplanes are all jets and hold ten times that number."

Rita Griffin was staring at him in shock. Sometimes he forgot that not everyone saw things the way he did.

"I'm sorry," he said. "That recitation doesn't make the air any less buoyant. It's not like I'm predicting the next crash. I didn't say 'Watch out for Midway Airport in the next two months.' It's just that you asked why I hadn't flown in thirty years. I'm sorry. How about we change the subject?"

"How do you know all this?"

He shrugged. "I read the newspapers, and there's nothing they like to report more than an aviation disaster. I'm not sure when

I started. For a long time it was hard to have a real disaster until the planes got big enough. I keep a diary, and sometimes I like to include what's going on in the world. The last crash was in Germany, ten days ago, a U.S. Air Force plane hitting a mountain. I keep track of the people I know who die, but I'm just a speck in a wide, wide ocean. It would be pretty narrow of me to restrict myself to just people I know."

She nodded. "And you claim mathematics isn't your area?"

"I do?"

"I thought you did, something you said."

"No," he said. "I love mathematics. One of my favorite stories is about Srinivasa Ramanujan and the taxi. He was that self-taught Indian genius—it's harder to remember the names than the math. You probably know the story."

"I don't. Go on."

"Well, after he was invited to England—this was back before the First World War. In fact he died not long after the war, being a Hindu and a vegetarian. I'm getting the story all tangled up—maybe it was the flu epidemic. He was brought to England by G. H. Hardy from Cambridge."

"I know of Hardy."

"Well, Ramanujan and Hardy were in a taxi together. Hardy noticed the number of the taxi, 1729, and said, 'Now there's a dull number.' And Ramanujan cried, 'No. It's a most interesting number. Why, it's the lowest number that's the sum of two cubes in two different ways.' "

Rita Griffin was looking at him from the corner of her eye. "Do you know the two ways?"

Harry smiled. "Ten cubed plus nine cubed. That one's pretty easy if you recognize the powers of three: 3, 9, 27, 81, 243, 729. And everyone recognizes a thousand as ten cubed. And the other one's pretty easy too: a gross of a gross of a gross is 1728, and one is always itself no matter the power. So I can see how he did it, but actually doing it, that's another matter. And knowing it's the lowest such number. He was thirty-two when he died. Two to the fifth."

"I have a question for you, Harry. You've been keeping track of the numbers of airplane disasters, and you say you haven't flown since 1925. So what brings you up here now?"

"Well, over the years I haven't had much reason to get anywhere in a hurry. But when time is of the essence, the distance between Portland and Chicago looms large. If I was like you, with a father out west and a responsible job, it would be a different story."

"So where is your family, if you don't mind my asking?"

"Oh," Harry said, "I have a kid sister in Pittsburgh, and she did fly out a few years back. My brother, I don't expect to ever lay eyes on him again." Howard, everybody's friend and then some— Aaron Gold wouldn't be asking him about his sex life. "Sis and I talk on the phone some, and there's an occasional letter. When the time comes, she'll fly out again."

"But you won't go visit her in Pittsburgh?"

"No. Forty-seven years in the Smoky City did the trick. You know how you can get tired of something: spaghetti, grape juice, baseball, chess." He felt like adding, *waiting for a person to die*, namely Alton Sweeney, but why turn a conversation sour when you can't help but sit elbow to elbow for another four hours? "You don't happen to know the story of the Fisherman and the Jinni from the *Arabian Nights*, do you?"

She was thinking. Rita Griffin was what you'd call a "nice-looking woman," which translated into "skin and bones and bordering on homely." But she was no doubt some poor fool's wife, to judge by the gold band on her wedding finger. No accounting for how the human race matches up. Maybe there's some poor village in Wales with enough people like her that such looks are accounted pretty.

"Let me think," she said. "It takes a while to straighten the stories out, the way they intertwine. Is that the one where the fisherman tricks the enormous genie back into the bottle? That's the only part I remember."

"That's the one," said Harry. "It begins with the Fisherman who snags the bottle in his net; then the Jinni says he'll kill the Fisherman; then comes the part where the Fisherman tricks the Jinni. Do you remember why the Jinni wanted to kill his deliverer?"

"You're sure taking me back to when I was a kid. Is it because he's angry at waiting so long to be rescued?"

"Right. Even the best thing in the world, if it's too long in coming, goes sour. Then you're like the Jinni: you swear you'll kill the first thing you lay eyes on."

"Which explains why King Solomon bottled him up in the first place." Rita's face was like a bulldog's. "Because he was warped and twisted. It wasn't being in the bottle that deformed him. He was like Satan, the bent one. You think that if the fisherman had found him earlier, it would have been a picnic on the beach?"

"I thought you couldn't remember the story." Harry sounded to himself like a little boy whining.

"It's coming back in pieces. I'm a slow enough thinker most of the time, but I'm steady. And what does that story have to do with Pittsburgh, unless you're angry about your past?"

He sat stunned. Rita's leap caught him by surprise. She'd read his mind: Aaron Gold and all things Pittsburgh, and Sweeney, both Sweeneys—

"Do me a favor," she said, "and wait a moment before you tell me to mind my own business. I have my own story to tell. We're miles up in the sky, and I don't know you from Adam."

"All right," Harry said. "I'm the perfect stranger. Go ahead." He realized his eyes were checking to see who was listening in on their conversation. But the plane wasn't even half full, and folks were either dozing or reading their books.

Rita cleared her throat. "I think I said I was using the few days between the end of term and summer session to visit my father."

"Yes, that's what you said. In Cannon Beach. I own a bit of property there, out of town a ways."

"Good for you. Cannon Beach didn't do much good for me. My father taught in the high school there. Some of the time he was the principal, and the whole town looked up to him. Wonderful Joshua Stallings. What my sister and I learned from him was to keep our mouths shut. He did things to us no father should do, and our mother was no help. She had her own row to hoe.

"Well, Joshua Stallings is at the end of his row. I doubt if he looks at me and remembers a little girl with pigtails, let alone the foul urge to lay his hands on me and my sister. So why should I spend my hard-earned money—and even more, my time—to say goodbye to the fucking bastard!" Her voice was such a fiery whisper by the end that Harry wasn't sure he'd caught her last words. He'd never heard a woman say the word "fuck" before, if that's what she'd said.

"Lena," he said softly. "It's Lena."

"Who's Lena?"

"It's the same story. Her parents were long-time friends of my family. I don't know how my mother got wind of it—maybe Lena said something to her. But her father was what they call an alcoholic. Not like a drunkard. There was nothing to see; he was all charm." He had said enough.

Rita Griffin nodded. She'd been staring out the window. "It should be an uncommon story, as rare as Solomon's genie." A deep sigh. "Now it's my turn to say I'm sorry. You can keep things penned up just so long. Do you mind if I read for a while?" She had picked up her book. "It isn't just my father. When you're in academe, especially if you're a woman, you put up with a lot, and there are so damn few of us."

Harry said nothing. He'd unleashed a monster, that was for sure. If the conversation had continued without going off like Mount Vesuvius, God only knows how he would have answered her question about why he chose now to take to the air. There was a moment when he was on the verge of bringing up Alton Sweeney's name. He'd better watch it.

He glanced Rita's way. She was deep in a mathematics journal, equations with sigmas and deltas; it was all Greek to him, as the joke went. He dug out his briefcase. Not for the world would he entrust a volume of Burton to any baggage handler. He found where he'd left off, the Prince, stone from the waist down, addressing the anxious Sultan.

* * *

"Right wondrous is my tale and that of the four fishes. My father was the Lord of the Black Islands for threescore years, and when his reign reached its last hour, I became the Sultan. I took as my wife the daughter of my paternal uncle, and she loved me to the utmost. If I was absent, she neither ate nor drank until my return. For five years we lived in harmony. Then by chance, upon that day of the month when by custom she went to the Hammam bath, all changed. As usual I instructed the cook to prepare our supper. I then lay upon the bed and bade two damsels to fan my face, one on the left, the other on the right. My eyes were closed, but sleep did not pay its customary visit. I lay there thinking of my wife and her soft words and sweet breath. Presently I heard the slave girl on my right say to the girl on my left, 'O how miserable is our master, his kindness all for naught. O the shame of our false mistress, the accursed whore.'

" 'My very thought,' said the other. 'Here he lies with all his fair gifts, while each night she ranges abroad. Allah curse women faithless and adulterous.'

"The other sighed. 'I would he would wake and wonder at her absence, but each night she serves him his drink, and in it is a distillation which produces a sound sleep. Immediately she rises, dons sumptuous raiment, and is gone until break of day. Returning, she burns a pastille by his bed, and with a smile he awakens from the utter depth of his sleep.'

"When I heard their words, a black curtain descended upon my life. I dismissed the slave girls, and when the daughter of my uncle returned from the baths, I behaved as though all was as it should be. When she called for my wine, I only pretended to drink, and she knew not the difference, so sure was she of my ritual. When it seemed that I slept, I heard that voice, no longer sweet, curse me. 'Sleep and wake into death. I loathe every pore of your flesh, and daily grows my disgust that I must share a bed with such as you.' She then donned her richest dress, and with my sword slung upon her shoulder she went her false way.

"I rose and followed in her footsteps. We threaded the streets until she came to the city gates, where she spoke strange words, and the gates sprung open. We continued until we came to the worst of all the hovels of my domain. It was less than a sty, and one had to bend half over to enter. I climbed upon the roof and peered through the rough thatch. At first I saw naught but broken straw and filthy rags, and then I saw the tattered heap stir. It was a hideous shape, scarce human, incapable of ambulation, every feature gross. I saw my wife kiss the earth at his feet, whereupon he raised his head and cried, 'Where have you been? Do you not know my need? Others visit. Each has his paramour, and they carouse until the dawn. I can but envy their satisfaction.'

" 'O my Lord, know that I am married unto my cousin whose very breath turns sour my stomach, and I hate each moment when I must suffer his rude touch. Did I not fear for your safety, I would turn his city to such a heap of filth that even the ravens would circle wide to avoid its stench.'

" 'Lies,' he cried. 'Damn you and your lies. I swear, by what I deem most sacred, if ever again you fail me and my friends, I will find me another to straddle my loins and tune my flesh and pluck my strings and sing her merry song.'

"What I then saw and heard made blood run like a red curtain across my eyes. 'O breath of my life,' sobbed my wife, 'desert me not,' and she wept bitterly till he relented.

" 'Enough and be quick,' he said. She stripped off her clothing until she was mother-naked. Following suit, he brushed aside his rags and, taking her hands, he guided her loins onto his.

"Seeing this, I lost my wits, climbed down from the roof, and entered the hut. My sword lay by the entrance. I drew its blade from its sheath and struck at the slave's throat. The stroke no sooner was performed than my shoulders were through the doorway and I was on my way back to my palace."

* * *

Harry looked below at the cloud-studded landscape. Mountain peaks had given way to barren ranges. The engines droned. The Fisherman and the faithful Wazir were camped by the side of the tarn awaiting the return of their Lord. The Jinni was making up for lost time according to his kind. The Sultan sat rapt at the foot of the ensorcelled Prince. The foul slave hovered between life and death. The faithless wife swore vengeance. And Harry Stein plunged dark into sleep.

* * *

Someone was fiercely gripping his left arm. "Harry, Harry, get your seat belt on." A high-pitched siren was screeching overhead. He fumbled at his belt and heard the click as it engaged. The plane was tilting to the left. Rita Griffin, as rigid as steel, her fists clenched, shot him a frozen smile. Nothing to see out his window but the wing pointing to an ominous bank of clouds. Across the plane it was a different story: the ground rushing up, rows of tiny houses, narrow streets, cars, a parking lot. The plane banked hard to the right and then leveled out. Where was his book? Under the seat in front, out of reach.

"Heads down," said a mechanical voice. "Now!" Then the plane hit, bounced up, hit again, slewed left, its belly ripping across the concrete runway with a horrendous scraping sound, a hangar rushing madly at them, sliding by, then sudden silence. The torso of the plane looked like a rag wrung out. Up front, people hung sideways from their seat belts; others lay like rag dolls in the aisle. Sirens wailed from all sides; then the emergency door in the row ahead wedged open. A face crowned with a fireman's hat peered in and stared at him with a horrified expression.

"Harry," said a voice by his side. "Harry, we've landed. You were out like a light. Here's your book."

SISTER JOAN

—Tuesday, June 14, 1955—

Joan's eyes returned to the clock on the mantel—just past seven. Papers and books were spread about the desk—one thing to thank Robert for was this mammoth slant-top desk, rescued from an Iowa courthouse by Matcham Père years ago. Poor Thomas positively slavered over it, but it was hers, dammit, hers.

By her reckoning this evening, Tuesday the fourteenth of June in 1955, corresponded to the eleventh of April, 1865. Before long the crowd would assemble, and then would commence what Roy Basler termed Lincoln's "Last Public Address." The President had alluded to it the day before in the two spontaneous responses to the Serenades, speaking adroitly but saying nothing beyond that he would say nothing until the next evening—tonight. Every biography Joan could lay hands on, every book about the war, devoted a fair amount of space to it. Delivered from the second storey of the White House to the assembled masses on the portico below, by all reports it was a disappointing speech. Following victory at Appomattox, the people wanted a victor's celebration; what they got was a full and considered statement on reconstruction, with detailed analysis of how and when a so-called seceded state such as Louisiana should return to the Union—if it had ever been out of it.

The speech would begin in about an hour. It was odd. Joan had such a vivid sense that when it was time, the thumb and forefinger of her right hand would twist the knob on her radio clockwise, the vacuum tubes would warm up, and moments later his voice would emerge from the speaker. She and little Lincoln would settle back and listen to what for her, and for no one else on the face of the planet, would be a familiar voice.

"Rusty, it's all right, girl." As usual, Joan had heard the bark before the bell. On the doorstep was Will Studebaker. She opened the door. "Come on in." He had an odd grin on his face as he passed through under the doorway. She realized he had never been in her house, had never made it beyond the porch. Nor had he been at school today, at least not in the afternoon. Their last communication had been last night's declaration as to the paternity of her child.

"I worked at home today," Will said. "Less distraction. And you are a number-one distraction."

Joan nodded foolishly.

"Can we talk?"

She nodded again. "Sure. Would you like some tea or something? There's a program I want to tune in to in about an hour."

"Tea's fine," he said, and he followed her into the kitchen. "Nice house. I especially like that desk in the living room. It's amazing."

"I'll add your name to the list." She put water on to boil, then turned to face him. Damned if she wasn't enjoying this moment. "Let me guess."

"Guess, schmess," he said. "What the hell kind of line is that to drop on your sorry excuse of a doorstep?"

"What do you mean by that remark? It's a perfectly fine doorstep."

"Well, it sure didn't let me cross its threshold."

She shrugged. Her eye was on the kettle, which was coming to a boil.

"I'll hold my horses," he said, pointing to the kettle. She added water to the teapot and topped it with the cozy.

"All right," he said. "You said the father of your child is Abraham Lincoln. I honest-to-God looked the name up in the local phone books on the off chance. There were enough Lincolns but no Abrahams. You sounded so literal."

Once more she nodded, slowly, thoughtfully.

"Joan Matcham," he said, looking her in the eye. "To say I am puzzled, mystified, bewildered, and a host of other words, doesn't begin to get at my state of mind." He glanced upward. "David's not here, is he? I didn't see that old Buick of his."

"No, he's out somewhere."

"You are pregnant, aren't you?"

"I am pregnant, quite definitely with child."

"But you don't want to say who the father is. I understand that, for any number of reasons."

"No," she said. "Sit. Do you take sugar or milk?"

"A little of each."

"Okay," she said when they were both at the table. "When I said the father was Abraham Lincoln, it wasn't a joke. I wasn't being evasive. Maybe I was being a bit of a smart-ass, but mainly it just spilled out. Here's your chance to walk out the door. But I'd like you to hear me out."

"I'm listening," he said. "Go on."

"Here goes," she said, "the short version. Easter morning, the tenth of April, I was walking Rusty along the lake. A man was sitting on one of the benches. The next thing you know, Rusty was sniffing at his trousers. He asked how a black dog got the name of Rusty, and then I was talking about Emily, and suddenly I was in tears. Then he asked if we'd mind if he walked with us a bit. I must have said all right—you couldn't help but trust him. He had such a gentle way. I put out my hand and said my name, and he said his, which I don't think he meant to do. Abraham Lincoln. And oh my, it was him. The clothing didn't seem too out of the ordinary, dark trousers, a tweed jacket—no stovepipe hat, none of that. He said he didn't know how it happened, the shift—he had no ready words for it. It was just the night before. He'd spent the night at the Orrington. He even signed in with his own name and address, in Springfield. He said the clerk hardly looked up." She paused. Will's eyes were narrowed, his posture reluctant.

"I said it would be the short version." She breathed deeply. "All right," she said. "We walked back to my house, and I filled him in on current events, you might say: the two world wars, Hitler, the bomb, Roosevelt's four terms, Communism, the Korean War. We had lunch, we went downtown to the art museum, we had dinner, we saw a movie, *East of Eden*—"

"*East of Eden*," he said, his voice a welcome echo.

"Yes," she said, "with Raymond Massey, of all people. The man who'd played Abraham Lincoln. Then we had dessert on Howard Street with another couple, people I used to know, not exactly friends. And they had an argument, or had had an argument, because on the way back Beth, Beth Silverman, went home alone and had an auto accident—her car went off the road. We got back to her house. Then we went home. Somewhere along the way I found out where he was in his own time. He'd just come back the day before from the Peace Conference at Hampton Roads."

"Early February, 1865."

"Yes. Saturday the fifth. He was working on a proposal to present to Congress that would allow peace by compensating the slave states for the emancipation of their slaves, and the next thing he knew he was on Howard Street."

Joan thought a moment. By the kitchen clock it was half past seven. "Before he met me he'd been in Deering Library, looking at the card catalog under 'Lincoln,' and then in the stacks. By some miracle he didn't find out about his assassination—I have such a terrible time with that word."

Will nodded.

"And then—"

"One thing led to another," he said. "You've got your eye on that clock."

"I know. There's more to it. Tomorrow I'm having lunch with Lorraine Riggs—she's the doctor I went to, at the Lincoln Clinic, last week—everything's Lincoln, it seems. I almost told her about Lincoln, but didn't. It's so hard to keep the story locked up. It wants out. And, yes, you're right about the clock."

"You mentioned a program."

"I know. Not exactly a program. But this is the really weird part. Or one of the weird parts. This one's all inside my head. Since he left—since he disappeared, while we were together—it's been sixty-five days. And I think he returned to the very moment when he left, with the proposal for compensation."

"How would you know that?"

"I knew you'd ask that." She realized this was the moment she'd been leading up to all the while. "I know," she said, "because of the letter I got last week."

"The letter last week." Another echo.

"Yes," she said. "I'll be glad to show it to you later. He wrote me a letter five days after he got back."

"Lincoln wrote you a letter?"

"Yes, dated the tenth of February, saying he'd been back five days. Naturally, he didn't put it in a mail slot—if they even had mail slots back then. He gave it to his secretary, John Hay, to see that eventually it would get mailed in 1955. He even put it in an envelope, sealed it, and addressed it. Everything but the stamp. I guess he could have done that too, though ninety-year-old postage stamps would have been a temptation—too valuable."

"You might as well put me to outright torture, saying you have the letter but won't show it to me."

"It's personal." Joan grinned. "But I simply meant I'd show you in a bit, not 'later,' like indefinitely later. What I was trying to explain was my crazy notion that our two times, his in April of '65 and mine now, that they correspond. Are synchronous."

"Go on," said Will.

"You're thinking I'm crazy as a loon."

"Just go on."

"I will," she said. "Let me get my chart."

"Your chart," he called after her. "At this stage, I wouldn't be surprised if you walked back in the room with Christopher Columbus's personal map of New Hispaniola."

"Nothing that dramatic," Joan said. "Here. I've used onionskin so you can see the overlap. Think of each square as one day. But when you hold the two sheets together, like this, the day is in two—I can't say places; I have to say times—two times at once. At least that's how it is in my head. Today," and she pointed to the bottom row, third block from the left, "is Tuesday the fourteenth of June. It's also," and she lifted the bottom of the 1955 page, "Tuesday, April the eleventh." She heard her own voice, racing, frantic. "Here," she said, handing him the two sheets of paper and stepping back while he held them up to the light.

"I see," he said. "And the end of the chart, the last box, Saturday, the fifteenth of April, the day of his death—"

"Yes," she said. "The morning after he goes to Ford's Theater to see *Our American Cousin*. Four days from now."

Will broke the silence. "I didn't drink my tea."

"I know."

"And the program you're planning to tune in to—which is it, his reply to the Serenades, or his last speech, about reconstruction?"

"Reconstruction. They're already gathering. In ten or fifteen minutes he'll be at one window and Mrs. Lincoln at the other, and

Tad's there, and Noah Brooks—he'll hold the candle so the President can read what he's written. As he finishes each page, he'll drop it to the floor, and Tad will fish it up. Later the Marquis de Chambrun will find the President stretched out on the sofa in his office, and Lincoln will talk about his firm resolution for clemency no matter what."

"So how do you turn on your magic radio?" He glanced at his watch. "It's five of, and it's one time zone earlier there."

"I'm not sure. Yesterday morning, with his first Serenade, I had the sensation—no, more than that. For a moment it felt like I was actually there. Seeing things I hadn't read about, details, the stenographic reporter for one of the newspapers. You can chalk it up to an overactive imagination."

"Do you want me to clear out, while…you know?"

"No," she said softly, almost inaudibly. "Stay. Please. I think I'll sit at my desk, with my books and papers, with my charms and spells. You can be there in the room, on the couch, behind me, kind of out of sight. Why not? You already know everything there is to know about me." She'd run out of words. Could say no more.

"I think I love you," said Will Studebaker, his voice barely a whisper.

* * *

Basler was open on the desk. Joan had read the speech through again last night—she couldn't keep herself away from what he wrote and said. That was the charm, his words: *We meet this evening, not in sorrow, but in gladness of heart*; that the evacuations of Petersburg and Richmond, and the surrender at Appomattox give hope of a speedy peace; that we give thanks to those who achieved the honor, and no credit to himself, neither for the plan nor for its execution. Thanks to these long-awaited successes, the mind looks forward to the *re-inauguration of the national authority—reconstruction.*

Joan knew where he was heading: the deep argument to distinguish the Civil War, a fratricidal war, from a war against strangers. *Unlike the case of a war between independent nations, there is no authorized organ for us to treat with. No one man has authority to give up the rebellion for any other man.* Like a pack of squabbling children, where one cannot step back and say the battle's done. He was not enunciating a broad policy that would fit all cases, but one that would fit individual cases, the first, and then the next— *disorganized and discordant,* as though all the instruments of an orchestra were at odds, one with another. You call for silence, and then ask for them one at a time; and you hope and pray for music once more.

That morning the President had received a letter from Salmon P. Chase, his Secretary of the Treasury, a Radical. There was no direct mention of the letter in the speech, but the speech was Lincoln's reply. He termed it a *pernicious abstraction* to ask whether the *seceded States, so called, are in the Union or out of it.* The President considered it a mischievous question, guaranteed to divide friend from friend. The argument calls for close attention. All agree that the seceded States are out of their proper relationship with the Union, and everyone's goal is to return them to that *proper practical relation.* Once the States are *safely at home,* there's no material reason to concern ourselves with *whether they had ever been abroad.* That the States are home again is all that matters. Let us all join unto that end. Why didn't he allude to the Prodigal Son?

There was so much to see that it was hard to pay attention to the words. The crowd, the illuminated city, the President's struggle to read his words, Noah Brooks taking the candle, Tad scampering at their feet. At the other window, Mrs. Lincoln was like a statue. Joan willed her eyes back to the President, to Abraham Lincoln, to Abe—"Abe," she had whispered in the dark of her bedroom. Now, he was so different, speaking to them all, lecturing to his reluctant pupils. How well his voice carried.

Back to the case of Louisiana. He was relentless. Some would question whether the constituency on which the new government rests is sufficient: twelve thousand only. To some it is unsatisfactory *that the elective franchise is not given to the colored man.* Chase had raised this point: the folly of restored rebels being in control of black loyalists.

Now the crowd was dwindling, the argument so technical. Victory wasn't as easy as you thought. What were the next steps? It was more than dancing, careening in circles, hats flying every which way. In front of her and to the left, a small man in a dark suit, handsome, with a broad forehead—hard to judge his age—his hair almost black and a sleek mustache. She didn't care for his looks, preferred Will's gangly and genuine beauty, free of posturing.

Alongside the small man—the pretty man—was another young man, casually dressed, with a loose tie, a hat with a soft brim, and a mustache barely noticeable. The two of them were listening closely, but scowling, and the smaller man jabbed the other with his elbow, again, and again. Behind them stood a big man, also young, with a body like a gladiator, but with a glazed expression. Whenever the other two would exchange jabs, his head would feverishly nod. Washington City had its own share of "secesh."

Then the President's own judgment: *I would myself prefer that it were now conferred on the very intelligent, and on those who serve our cause as soldiers.* The small man erupted, like a Rumplestiltskin. "That means nigger citizenship," he said through gritted teeth. "Now, by God, I'll put him through." She missed what he said next, something about the President's last speech. If he didn't like Abraham Lincoln's speeches, why had he come to the White House, tonight of all nights, when half the crowd was black?

The President's pacing was deliberate, unlike yesterday when he was without a prepared text. And unlike at her house, at lunch, and later, saying whatever suited the moment. It was as though he were saying, *Listen closely. Follow with me, step by step. Louisiana has held elections, organized a State government, adopted a free-state constitution that confers the benefit of public schools equally to black and white, and empowers the elective franchise upon the colored man.* Joan glanced to her left, but the trio who took the speech so bitterly had slipped away.

The President had paused for a moment, was looking for his place on the next page, and it struck her again that this man who was laying out his plan for reconstruction—for reconciliation—was also the Abraham Lincoln who had spent a day with her, and a night, part of a night, enough of a night that at this moment she was carrying his child. *He has been in my bed*, she said to herself, *by my side, not asleep*, and she remembered how they had spoken of the paradox, that in ninety years, according to his calendar, he would find himself sitting on a bench by Deering Library, and she and Rusty would come along, and none of them would remember that they had already met. And the woman in the other window was his wife, the mother of his children, the mother of his other children.

Thanks to Brooks he had found his place, and he carried on, holding each page as close to the candlelight as possible. The new government of Louisiana asked for the nation's recognition. If we rejected them, we would discourage and paralyze both white and black, and what had that to do with bringing Louisiana into a proper and practical relation with the Union? But if we accepted them, all would be inspired. Granted, the black man desired the elective franchise now, but how much better to proceed with the already advanced steps than run backward over them. "Yes, yes," cried a gray-haired black man by her side, his eyes on the President.

Lincoln was down to the last page. What had been said for Louisiana would apply generally to other states. Let no plan be exclusive and inflexible, otherwise it would become a new entanglement. A pause. He was almost done. In the present situation it might be his duty to make some new announcement to the people of the South, and when satisfied that the action was proper, he would not fail to act.

Silence, then applause, but nothing like yesterday, and no military band to play "Dixie," then "Yankee Doodle."

"Sister," said the gray-haired man, "don't you just wonder what that man has up that sleeve of his?" A good question. A question without an answer. "Joan, Joan." Someone calling her name. But no one there knew—

* * *

"Joan, are you all right?"

She looked up at Will, so tall, by her side. "Yes, I'm fine. What time is it?"

"Getting on to nine, about ten minutes till."

"Was I just sitting here, the whole time?"

"Yes," he said in an odd voice, tentative, as though her question were askew.

"Just sitting?"

"Sitting. Turning a page once or twice, and your finger tracing the words on the page."

"I was tracing the words? Which words?"

"The words written on the page."

He had caught the implication of her own question: words on the page or words from his lips? "So it was close to an hour."

He nodded.

"And what did you do the whole time?" she asked.

Will's hands were in his pockets. "I watched you. I couldn't help myself. Though about all I could see was that thick braid of yours and your back. Sometimes you'd nod a bit, or shake your head, a No. Like I said, your hand was keeping pace with your eyes. But—"

"But what?"

"If you were a cat, I'd say your ears would prick up—you know how you can judge a cat's thoughts by its ears. I've never seen anyone sit the way you did. People move, they wiggle, all that involuntary stuff. But you didn't do any of that. Maybe I didn't either. You had me hypnotized. You were there again, weren't you?"

"Yes. I don't understand, can't explain—I'm just there, the way you are in a dream. There's no entering, no beginning. It just happens, the same as when you're awake. But I had the benefit of knowing the speech already, knowing what he would say, though he said things that surprised me, that I didn't remember. Too bad I didn't have a notebook with me. Like when he said it was like children squabbling, and one of them can't call it off for the rest."

"Was that at the beginning, when he says no one can give up rebellion for anyone else?"

"Yes," she said. "Early on."

"That's not in the books, not as I recall. They go by his written text. It could be there in old newspaper accounts. Were those the exact words?"

"I think he said, 'like a pack of squabbling children, where one can't step back and say for all that the battle's over.' "

"Anything else you noticed?"

"Things I know from reading. Mrs. Lincoln at the other window, Tad picking up pages as the President dropped them to the ground after he had read them, and Noah Brooks holding the candle for him. How his voice carried, how every word was clear. The crowd, probably half were black, though a lot of people didn't stay to the end. What else?"

She closed her eyes, to nurse memory along. "Let's see. It was a misty night. He wasn't wearing a hat, but why would you indoors? And there were three men nearby who got more and more upset as the speech went on, a big man and a second who looked, oh, indolent, indifferent, casual. But the third was a meticulous man, short, well dressed, with a cane, or a walking stick, like a dandy. What drove him crazy was the President talking about citizenship and the vote in Louisiana, that it looked like the black people would have it, and that was his own preference, for the more intelligent and the ones who had been soldiers. What was it the short man said? Something like, 'That's it. Citizenship for niggers.' Or maybe 'Votes for niggers.' Then something I didn't understand, like, 'Now I'm through.' He used the word 'through.' I didn't catch all his words. It was more like he was talking to himself, furious. And later when I looked their way, they were gone."

"And then?"

"At the end the President said his famous words about having a new announcement for the South, and the man next to me, an older black man with gray hair, said, 'Don't you just wonder what he has up his sleeve?' And he called me 'Sister.' No one's ever called me 'Sister,' and I don't mean because I'm an only child."

"You don't call him 'Lincoln,' do you? You say 'the President,' or just use the pronoun."

"I guess not. If I were a historian I probably would, but—"

"You know him differently, personally."

"Yes, like I wouldn't call you 'Studebaker.' "

"You know who the three were, don't you?"

She shook her head. "No."

"It was John Wilkes Booth, with Herold, David Edgar Herold, and Lewis Powell, the big man. He's the one who attacked Secretary Seward. Herold was at the tobacco barn when Booth was caught. Herold surrendered. He testified at the trial that it was at Lincoln's last speech, on the night of the eleventh, that Booth got the idea to assassinate Lincoln directly. Before that they had plotted to kidnap him. Powell and Herold were both hanged. You should write down as much as you can."

"Why? To build a case for my sanity? I didn't know that Booth was there."

"I know you didn't. And the reason to write it down is that you're an eyewitness, a special one. Because you have another perspective, like an observer who already knows the script. But I know what you mean. It's not like you could mail it off to *Civil War History*."

Joan got to her feet, and Will steadied her. "I don't know whether I'm shaky from all the sitting or the standing." His arms were around her, patting her on the shoulders.

"Now what?" she said.

"I think you're off duty for a while."

She stepped back and looked up at him. "At the last I heard a voice calling my name. Then I was back, though it didn't feel all that sudden, and there you were. But I wasn't sure. The voice sounded a long way off. And when the black man called me 'Sister,' it occurred to me that I was free to move, that I could have walked up to the doorway. Not that they would have let me in, and what would I have said?"

She could see Will fumbling for an answer.

"Well, I didn't do it. I wouldn't have done it." *Do what?* she asked herself. *Go upstairs where he and his wife were? Warn him?* Though he didn't take to warnings and precautions. *Say she'd got the letter? And put her hand on her belly?* Maybe there were limits. To be there at all, did she have to stay here, with Basler? It wouldn't do to write out a note, label it "Urgent," and carry it with her for the next occasion.

"I haven't showed you the letter," she said.

nalism at Northwestern. By now he ought to be back home for the summer. Pointedly, Harry asked no questions of his own, for the little good it did. Luckily, Rita interrupted the inquisition, and the conversation shifted to her visit with her father. Harry wondered if Frank knew the true story of his wife's childhood. Odd what you'll tell a stranger.

Harry glanced outside, then at the clock. It was late enough, but still too light. By ten it should be good and dark. The Triple A map of Evanston showed the campus just a couple of blocks from Matcham's house on Hinman. All he hoped for tonight was to get a sense of the neighborhood: the hotel, Matcham's house, the campus. Broadly, his plan was to get to the core of the impossible letter from Abraham Lincoln to one Joan Matcham of Evanston, Illinois. And no better way than to go to the horse's mouth. Precisely how he would achieve that, he didn't know. Which was all right—he could improvise with the best of them. All those years selling suits and fur coats should be good for something.

He carved another wedge of caramel roll. Almost time. He slipped the map back in his pocket and set his napkin on the table. In the corner booth, finishing off hamburgers, sat two male students in earnest conversation. Something about the one facing him, tall and dark-haired, struck a familiar note. Miriam's son David was still in town? Harry hadn't seen him since he was kindergarten age, but Miriam sent pictures often enough.

Harry paid the damages. In a few minutes he was on campus. Not much to speak of, an architectural hodge-podge, as though the buildings had come from another planet over the last hundred years, and wherever they landed, they took root. Ugly. At the library he reversed his field and headed south. With Midsummer Night less than a week off it was finally getting dark. He crossed Sheridan Road and proceeded down Hinman to the 1600 block, staying on the even side of the street. Obviously an old section of town, with huge trees, maple and elm, lining the sidewalk.

The street wasn't particularly well lit, in part because of the trees—which suited his purposes just fine. *The better for me to see you, my dear.* And to go unseen. The porch light was on at 1607, but the house directly across the street was completely dark, and Harry paused beside an elm whose girth had buckled the sidewalk. Joan Matcham's house was a moderate saltbox structure with a wrap-around porch and a picket fence. Three stories. Lights on downstairs. Front door in the center. After a minute or two Harry continued to the end of the block, lit a cigarette, and turned around. He was just a couple of houses along when Matcham's screen door opened and a skyscraper of a man backed out the door followed by a tall woman. She put her arms around him, probably for a quick kiss, then he headed down the path and through the gate, got in his car, and drove off, the woman waving goodbye. *Hundred to one that's Matcham*, Harry thought.

He walked on past the house, crossed the street, and headed back once more. Two cars were parked in front of her house, a convertible with telltale orange and blue Pennsylvania plates, the other a nondescript sedan with plates from the "Land of Lincoln," a car not unlike Harry's own Plymouth. Her car. And there she was, in plain view, sitting at a desk, with two green-shaded lamps on either side, intent on whatever she was doing and oblivious to the world outside.

Harry prided himself on his farsightedness. He looked closely at her: dark hair, dark eyebrows, no makeup to speak of, not even lipstick, unless it was a rose instead of a red. Hard to judge her looks—kind of like the stereotype of a schoolteacher without the glasses. For now, all he could see was a dark sweater. He drifted on into the next block, crossed Hinman once again, lit another

ing garments. 'Son of my Uncle,' she said, 'word has come that my father is killed in holy war, my mother has died of grief, my brother has suffered the sting of the fatal cobra, and my sister in despair has tumbled from her window, and there is naught I can do but weep.'

"I said only, 'Do as you will; my sorrow goes with you.' For the duration of one year she continued her weeping and wailing, and when the year had returned to its beginning, she asked me if she might build within my palace a tomb with a cupola, and below that a mausoleum. There she might confine her suffering and be less disheartening to me, her Lord and Master. She would name it the House of Lamentations. I said, 'Proceed as you will.' And so she had built a cenotaph with a dome and beneath it a sepulchre worthy of the Prophet himself. What I did not know was that in striking the knave's throat I had not entirely severed the gullet, and with her skill in leechcraft and the aid of her spells, my wife kept his breath alive, though he could neither speak nor perform the deed of darkness. Yet he lived on, for the hour appointed unto his death had not come.

"Each day my wife went to him and gave him wine and rich soup until a second year had completed its circuit, and still I remained patient until the day when I came upon her unawares, weeping, tearing at her hair, and wailing, 'O misery of miseries, grief without end, days without light, stillness and shadow,' the same words over and over until I cried, 'How long is this sorrow to last? Sooner or later every parent must die. Even grief must have its end. What profit in weeping year after year?'

" 'O my cousin,' she said amid her tears, 'Thwart me not, lest I put an end to my misery.'

"I said naught, and for another year she mourned what was not a death but a living death, until I could stand no more. In wrath I entered the cenotaph and cried, 'Enough! What's done is done. The man is as good as dead, and you are not worth the dust the wind blows in your face!' I drew my sword and would have slashed her throat too, but her weeping turned to laughter.

" 'To heel, rude hound,' she said, the scorn in her voice as thick as syrup, and my arm stuck in the air, as though it were fixed in marble. 'Allah has delivered into my palm the very one who did this to me, and my heart is aflame and will not be quenched.' So saying, she pronounced words I understood not, until she concluded, for my benefit, 'Be thou half stone and half man,' and so I became what you see, a being half alive, the other half neither dead nor alive. Moreover, she transformed my city with all its streets and byways and garths and by her gramarye turned each of its four islands into these four mountains. And she bespelled my citizens, Moslem, Nazarene, Jew, and Magian, so now they dwell as fish within the tarn which lies beyond the four mountains, a different color for each faith: red for the Magian, yellow for the Jew, blue for the Christian, and white for the Moslem. Daily I am scourged and whipped with ninety and nine stripes, then dressed again in haircloth, and, over all, these sumptuous robes."

* * *

"Poor devil," said Harry. He glanced at the clock. Before long the alarm would sound, and though no demon would strip him of his sumptuous garb and whip him to a froth, he knew he must sleep. Reluctantly, with the Prince concluding the account of his metamorphosis, Harry turned off the light.

* * *

4:30 in the morning & can't go back to sleep. Dreamed I was locked in a small cell, nothing but a bed and a desk much like this one, really little more than a table. The dream went on day after day, meal after meal, dull food issued through a slot in the door, break-fast, lunch, and dinner. A single light on a cord overhead, on and off in cycles to match the world outside. No windows. No voices.

Two roots to the dream: Burton's tale of the Fisherman and the Jinni and an article from the Chicago Tribune about Rudolf Hess in his prison cell in Berlin. I hadn't made the connection. Hess, the architect of the Nazi "final solution," & Burton's "ensorcelled Prince."

I lay in bed for half an hour after waking, though even awake I couldn't get the dream to let go its hold. Never has a dream seemed so real. Even when my eyes had opened, I saw the shadowy room, the draperies at the window, heard the rumble of a garbage truck, a distant siren, but still I was trapped in the nightmare of the cell. Finally the dream let go and I thanked the gods that it was only a dream. Then I saw a third story, beyond Burton's and Hess's. Mine, which boiled along till I gave up sleep and here I am scrib-bling away, the dream just a stone's throw distant & I am at that desk in my cell trying to make sense of my life. Hess told the inter-viewer that he reads and writes, that's all, a man waiting to die, a man confined not just to a prison, but solely to his own company. What is left but to examine a lifetime of choices?

The shadows are lightening. I've been here at this desk for a good hour. My pen moves in spurts. Burton's story I love, its drive, its twists and turns, the image of the Jinni galloping off to make up for lost time, the Sultan heading off alone by moonlight to find the answer to the transformation of his kingdom. The story of Ru-dolf Hess gives me the chills—an entire prison with but one pris-oner, that's what it will come to, and with that prisoner's death, the razing of the prison. My story is alive and telling itself. It has brought me to this moment. I have mailed the letter. I tell myself I have come here to discover who Joan Matcham is. But that's a lie. Or not entirely a lie, for I do wonder who she is and why she should be privileged to be living a story with Abraham Lincoln as a character and now may be pregnant with his child.

What if I hadn't mailed the letter? I could have held it back— the idea had crossed my mind. Why was it that only after I had mailed it off did I solve its mystery? Would I still have mailed it? To grant her the satisfaction denied me? Can I imagine a letter—or a phone call, a meeting—that would be its match? What miracle could work its way into my life?

I don't play cards, or haven't since I was young, yet it sounds like I am saying I have been dealt a losing hand which only a miracle can save. Here I am then, playing out the game, hoping my opponent will have an even worse hand. And they say the dream at dawn is prophetic. ~~Joan Matcham, to the devil with you~~

XVII SYMPATHY

—Wednesday, June 15, 1955—

The Bistro at Old Orchard Shopping Center, and Joan a bit early for her lunch with Lorraine Riggs. Joan's forty-third birthday. One card, from Liz at the office, no presents. As a childless widow and an only child, Joan had no immediate family; so birthdays didn't amount to much, not since the death of her mother. Of course, there was one living relative, but for the moment it was well hidden and not likely to have sent a card unless she or he could manipulate time and space. And Abraham Lincoln couldn't know the mother's birth date. Not that she was expecting a second piece of mail from the last century.

Just as Joan was wondering if Lorraine had been held up at work, here she was. Joan had almost forgotten how her hair was peppered with gray.

"So," said Lorraine when they had been seated, "tell me, how've you been?"

"If you mean about the baby, the answer's fine. A little queasy sometimes, but no real problems."

"Tell me again how far along you are."

"I can be exact on that one. Nine weeks and four days."

"All right," said the doctor. "So things are fine with the pregnancy, but in some other domain things aren't so fine."

In effect, it was a question. Joan's impulse was to turn it aside. Last week at Zarantanello's had been so easy. Dinner with an old friend, a bond that dated back to the war years, to Robert in uni-

Lorraine was staring at her, no smile, just staring intently. "Abraham Lincoln?" she mouthed. "You did say 'Abraham Lincoln.' President Abraham Lincoln?" She drew the words out one by one.

Joan nodded weakly.

"And you're not kidding. You mean it, don't you? You do. I see that. I think you'd better back up a step or two. At least you weren't abducted by aliens."

"I wasn't abducted by anyone. If anything, it was the other way around. Besides, I'm not sure how an alien species would get me with child."

A hint of a smile from Lorraine. "It's bad enough that one species of alien manages to do that routinely."

The smile helped, humor helped. "I know I sound like a tried and true nut. All I ask is that you hear me out. And promise not to lock me up with a dozen Napoleons."

"I promise," said Lorraine. "Besides, I wouldn't run away from this good a story. Tell on."

Joan waited while the people at the next table gathered up their belongings and departed. "It's really simple enough," she began. "At least it seems simple as I look back. I'll tell just the highlights. Just yesterday I told the same story to my historian."

"I'll bet he has a name."

"William, Will, Studebaker."

"Like the car?"

"Yes, and there the resemblance ends. Back to the story. Easter Sunday, and I was walking the dog by the lake. It was thanks to Rusty that we met him, sitting on a bench by the library. I know I had Emily on my mind—colored eggs and Easter baskets and all that. I don't know what he was thinking about. For him, in 1955, everyone he'd ever known was dead."

"He was just sitting on a bench?"

"Yes, though actually he had arrived the night before, not on the bench—I don't mean to make it comic, but it has those elements. Later he told me that he'd been in his office writing a proposal to Congress about compensating slave owners, though the war was nearly over—he was trying to end the killing. I've looked it up—his Cabinet unanimously rejected it. It was February, 1865. Then without any transition—he didn't whiz through a sparkly time tunnel—he found himself on Howard Street. He said the first thing he noticed were the cars everywhere. And no horses. He poked his head in a few doors, saw television, Jackie Gleason to be specific."

"Jackie Gleason. I can't picture Abraham Lincoln watching Jackie Gleason."

"I can't help you there. It's what he said." Joan caught Lorraine's eye—here came their soup and sandwiches.

"All right," Joan resumed. "We began to talk, about nothing of consequence, and like I said, Emily was on my mind."

Joan stopped. She was botching it. "No, wait. He's sitting on the bench. I noticed him because of Rusty. I didn't recognize him, not a hint of recognition. Just a man. Easter Sunday, thoughts of Emily. Then I was crying, and he was standing, and he put out his hand and said he was Abraham Lincoln and asked if he could walk along with us. But it was the other way around. I said *my* name, and held out *my* hand, and then he said his name. He hadn't meant to give his name—it just spilled out in the heat of the moment. Things happening so fast, his realizing what he'd just done and trying to get around it. He said he had spent the night at the Orrington and had just had breakfast at the Huddle—"

"He spent the night at the Orrington! And breakfast at the Huddle?"

"Yes, pancakes. So much of it is mundane. But I didn't question his story—or only for a moment. It had such a ring of truth, all unrehearsed. It was all so patently real and true. We went back to my house and had lunch. Then we drove downtown, went to the Art Institute, had dinner, saw a movie, had a snack, came home. I forget when he said it, but somehow he knew he'd find himself back in his own time. He asked me if by any chance he had just disappeared from the history books. And what was I supposed to do? Take him back to the Orrington? I wasn't about to let him out of my sight, not if I could help it. I wasn't seduced, and he didn't seduce me. Honest to God, I don't remember how we ended up in the same bed."

"I know another story," Lorraine said. "There was a neighbor of the Lincolns', a man, and Lincoln the husband was away. For whatever reason—maybe it was a fire—the neighbor spent the night in Mary Todd Lincoln's bed, sleeping alongside her. It wasn't improper. I doubt if they had a bundling board in the closet for such occasions. To hear tell, folks wore an array of special clothing at night. Night caps, stockings, night shirts. God forbid the naked body should put in an appearance."

Joan shook her head. "I think we knew what we were doing. In some ways, not all. After—after we made love, and after we talked—it's so hard to come to this moment. After we talked, and talked some more, I just reached for him, and he was gone."

"Oh," said Lorraine, as though it were her story too.

Joan set her soup spoon down, let her breathing slow. She'd told her part. It was Lorraine's turn.

"You said Will Studebaker would vouch for your sanity. Well, I would too, Joan, despite what you're telling me. I've known you for years. I called your mother 'Aunt Anne.' "

"I know," said Joan. "You were so close to her in her later years."

"If anyone asked, I'd say, 'I know Joan Matcham well.' " She was searching for the right words. "No one would accept, would believe your story. It's too fantastic. It's so impossible. But why would you make it up? I know you're pregnant. I know you don't lie. It's like an asteroid crashing into your backyard—it doesn't happen, but it's too solid to deny."

"I know," said Joan.

Lorraine's gaze was elsewhere. "In some ways I know you better than I know myself." She was talking to herself. "You, I can predict. So I'll say I accept what you've said as the truth. But I won't say I believe it. Is this Will Studebaker like a character witness, or is he judging from some hard evidence?"

"Both, I hope," said Joan. "There's a letter. It came last week." Joan paused, and took a bite of her sandwich.

"A letter?"

"Yes. From him."

"From him! How could you get a letter from Abraham Lincoln?"

"It's not all that complicated when you think about it. He wrote it a few days after he got back, addressed it, and left instructions for it to be mailed long after he was dead. His young secretary, John Hay, was charged with the duty, though Hay didn't know what it was all about."

"He must have wondered."

"I know, but the system worked, and Will says everything about the letter looks genuine. And I know that no one but Abraham Lincoln could have known what to write."

"What did he write?"

"It was a comical letter in a lot of ways. He knew how odd it was to write to someone far in the future, and what he was writing about was intimate, so he spoke indirectly, with oblique references. I knew what he meant, but a stranger would read it differently."

"Such as?"

"Well, he said the trip downriver was uneventful, and it's true he had just been on a boat, the *River Queen*, from Hampton Roads at the mouth of the James, then back up the Potomac to the capital, but he meant the River of Time. The letter reads like a bread and butter note: thank you for your hospitality, lunch was delicious, especially the crêpes. And he apologized for his sudden departure. Hoped it hadn't alarmed me."

"I see what you mean when you say only he could've written it."

"Yes," said Joan. "He packed a whole chapter's worth into a few words."

"And here I am at the Lincoln Clinic! Pity I can't write it up for the *Harvard Medical Journal*: 'Presidential sperm remains viable during temporal transit.' Don't choke, dear, it's not good for the fetus. What else did he say?"

"Lorraine," Joan said when she finally managed to swallow, "you're just amazing. Not that I've doubted my sanity, but keeping this all bottled up has been worse than—I don't know what it's been worse than, but I'll think of something."

"How about the Spartan boy who hid the fox under his shirt and didn't cry out when the fox bit him?"

"That's pretty good, but not quite what I had in mind. What else did the letter say? Well, he hinted at the possibility of pregnancy. 'Once is all it takes,' he wrote, and then he apologized for writing lightly of something quite serious. He said that if his visit bore fruit, he would be at a loss for words."

"Almost not a metaphor there."

"I know. The whole letter is like that, with double entendres. And he as much as said what I myself feel: that he wouldn't want to undo what happened. Then he said there was a lot more to say but I'd just have to understand more from less, and that from small acorns great oaks grow. And the last thing was 'Give Rusty my love.' "

"Rusty? Oh, your dog."

"Yes. Rusty provided the introduction, as it were, sniffing at the cuff of his pants."

"Amazing. He must have thought the letter had a fair chance of getting through."

"Yes. John Hay was young at the time. Lincoln sent him on all kinds of confidential missions. Hay kept a diary off and on, which was published not all that long ago. No mention of the letter of course."

"I suspect Lincoln knew his man. You wouldn't be interested in dessert by any chance? They have a rum torte here that I almost forgot about. I want to hear your story, but I don't want to miss out on that cake. We could split it if you like."

"Do we have to split it?"

"Suits me," said Lorraine, and she signaled the waitress over. "Two rum tortes. And I'll have coffee, black."

"And milk for me, please," said Joan.

"I was wondering," Lorraine said when the waitress was out of earshot, "how he knew how to address it."

"He must've seen my address on a letter or a magazine. That must have given John Hay a moment's thought."

"To say the least," Lorraine said. "Okay, I'd call the letter hard evidence. How he did his personal traveling is another matter. You have no idea how the transit was effected? Pardon the phrasing; I read a little science fiction."

"I think that's just it. There is no science, no H. G. Wells, and no time machine. I've thought about it, and the best I can offer—I shouldn't say 'best,' because that makes it sound plausible—is that it's some kind of sympathy. You know how someone has one of those involuntary shudders, and says, 'Somebody must be walking on my grave.' Overlapping times. Though I really haven't a clue."

"Hold on a moment," said Lorraine. "Here comes that dessert." Then, a couple of bites further on, "You used the word 'sympathy.' You know there's a term, 'sympathetic magic,' for talking about things like voodoo—pins in wax figures, and the person grabs their leg like they've been stabbed. The sort of thing that people want your fingernail clippings or hair for. So they can work a spell. It's like the magic provides a link between two disparate entities. A simultaneous union of arbitrarily distant acts. I sound like a textbook."

"That's all right," Joan said. "What else does the textbook say?"

"It tells a story," said Lorraine. "Imagine a rabbi, somewhere in Asia, who deliberately knocks over a glass of wine at his dinner table, and simultaneously the emperor in his palace, about to sign an edict that would call for the extermination of all the Jews in his empire, accidentally tips over the inkwell, and that's it. He's had it with such vindictive folly. He won't go forward with it. It's not that one causes the other. It's that the two are inextricably bound together. Love potions must work the same way. Do something with A, and B resonates. Not that I believe in it. You won't see it treated seriously in a physics text. But as a doctor I know better than to chalk all the moments of our lives up to our well-being, or ill-being for that matter, according to a strict physiological analysis."

"Maybe that's the sort of thing I had in mind," Joan said. "But that would mean that something drew him out of his time and into ours, or corresponded with him in our time. Then when he did what he needed to do, he slipped back? But that's all so contrary to the twentieth century and reason and anything I ever learned in school. And what did he need to do? Besides, there's something else."

Lorraine rolled her eyes. "You're quite a woman, you know. Not just any old stray from the pound. Abraham Lincoln in your net. Then a historian named Studebaker, just like that. And now something else."

"But all my life, nothing like this has ever happened to me. I'm so out-and-out ordinary."

" 'Ordinary' is not the word I associate with Joan Matcham, with or without Abraham Lincoln."

"Yet my daily life is so ordinary. It's just that lately I seem to be caught up in a whirlwind, or maelstrom. I could use an Edgar Allen Poe or a Frank Baum to tell my story. Listen, I have a request. It's already half past two, though I'm not pressed for time."

"Neither am I. Remember, it's Wednesday afternoon. The good doctor is off duty."

"I remember. But even so I want to save the 'something else' till later. Can you come to dinner Friday night? I'd like you to meet my historian. And I'll bake a birthday cake, though today's my birthday."

"Today's your birthday? Will surprises never end?"

Joan knew she had a sheepish expression on her face.

"Friday night's fine," said Lorraine. "And happy birthday. What else do you have cooking in that fertile brain of yours?"

"Well, it's just that Will can bear witness. And you can see the letter. Then—maybe if you're there, plus Will . . ." Her voice trailed off.

"What? What is it you're afraid of?"

"I'm not sure," said Joan. "I was going to say that you and Will, the two of you, could figure out what's going on. But that isn't exactly it."

"What is it?"

"I don't know. You're right, though. I am afraid. I can't get Lincoln out of my mind. Right now he's with Secretary Stanton talk-

XVIII

AVUNCULAR HARRY

—Wednesday, June 15, 1955—

Harry woke for the umpteenth time and glanced at his travel clock. *Jesus!* Past two. Of course it was really two hours earlier. Who'd think the day would come when Harry Stein would complain about voluntarily sleeping in? All his life he'd preferred late night to early morning. He loved the solitude of the wee hours, when it seemed the whole city slept, all but Harry Stein. Then the sense of highway robbery when, out of nowhere, up rode eight a.m., ordering him to step out of night's sweet carriage and prepare for the long day's journey.

Then, to add insult to injury, it had been his job to open Truman Levine's Fur Salon no later than nine o'clock. Not that Truman got there that much later. Or maybe that was the point. Let Miriam's good-for-nothing, crossword-puzzle-working, indolent, non-salesman of a brother be the one whose job it was, come rain or shine, hell or high water, to work his way through the hurly-burly of Truman's rough-and-ready employees to unlock the brass double doors, as though they were the doorway to a temple for the gods of ancient Rome.

Harry's diary was a living reminder of those days, with almost every entry, Monday through Saturday, beginning with eight miserable words: *Downtown early as usual and opened the store.* Or variations on the theme: *Down early and just as I opened, Truman got there too. The bastard. Rode downtown via the Pitt hill and Centre & Webster Aves. It's a little longer, but I keep on going and don't have to creep along in the traffic jam that starts at the Phipps Conservatory and lasts until the Boulevard of the Allies. Opened at 8:50.* Some respite. Or, all too often, chagrin and ensuing guilt: *Overslept and when I got to the store, at 9:05, Truman had already opened.* His nemesis. Nemesis no more.

Downstairs at the Huddle, with a booth all to himself, Harry ordered pancakes and sausages. Across the street, according to the waitress, were the Northwestern Apartments, a brand-new girls' dormitory. The Orrington Hotel, he realized, was the dividing line between the university and downtown Evanston. Very handy, what with Matcham working on campus at the History Department. He'd resolved not to rush it. It didn't matter that he had slept late— he wasn't about to use the term "overslept." Last night's phone call with Miriam had paved the way for easy access to Lincoln's paramour. And there'd be ample time for a stroll along Michigan Avenue, for dinner at the Buttery, even for Cousin Rose if he felt like it.

Harry glanced at the morning *Tribune*—damn little news to speak of: the U.S.S.R. supplying atomic research equipment to Hungary and Bulgaria, as though they were disparate countries, and on the other side of the fence, the International Bank announcing that it was lending money to Austria. Tit for tat. The Cold War. And sometime today, in keeping with the muscle flexing, the U.S. would test its civil defenses against a hydrogen bomb attack. From his secret headquarters, Eisenhower was scheduled to sign a simulated state of national emergency. That should produce a lot of ripples in the pond.

The Bookshop was just around the corner from the hotel, and sure enough, there was David Levine sitting at a rolltop desk, book in hand. He glanced up as Harry walked in, then returned to his book. A couple of customers were browsing. A nice enough looking lad, resembling neither his father nor his older brother. A blood relative—odd to have such a thought after all these years.

Harry looked around. It was a bookstore, plain and simple. Books, books, and more books. No overblown displays guaranteed to catch the eye, no stacks of *Not As a Stranger* or *Gift from the Sea*, or the perennial best-seller, Norman Vincent Peale's *The Power of Positive Thinking*. Harry walked over to the desk, and David looked up expectantly. "Anything I can help you with? Mr. Hohenstein should be back in a bit."

"Who's this Mr. Hohenstein?" Harry asked.

David looked at him strangely, pushed back on his chair, and stood up. He was tall, at least six feet. "Mr. Hohenstein owns this store. He can tell you just about anything you want to know about the books here."

"And what about you?" Years ago it was Harry Stein's avuncular role to test his nephews and nieces on such matters as state capitals, who was the vice president, who was the winning general at the Battle of Waterloo, and where potatoes originated. David's older brother Gene was a smart cookie—together he and Harry used to listen to *Information Please* on the radio.

David's quizzical look intensified. "I can direct you around a little. What were you looking for?"

"Oh, I kind of like the British writers, a generation or two back, Conrad, Hudson, tales of foreign lands, the sea, adventure, but not without depth, character."

"Well," said young Levine, "fiction's downstairs. It's arranged by nation and then alphabetically by author. We have lots of Conrad and some Hudson. For Hudson you might also look in autobiography—that's also downstairs."

"Hudson wrote an autobiography?"

David nodded. "*Long Ago and Far Away*, or maybe it's *Far Away and Long Ago*."

"Any other writers you'd recommend?" Harry knew he was pushing it.

"No hurry, and good to meet you, Mr. Stein," and Emmanuel Hohenstein headed for his desk.

"Here," said David, "I'll jot down my phone number. It's actually Mrs. Matcham's number, my landlady sort of, though she usually doesn't rent out rooms." He wrote the number out for Harry on a slip from alongside the cash register. "The address is there too, an easy walk. Hinman's just a few blocks toward the lake. 'Landlady' is a funny term for her. I think of stern little old ladies who keep an eye on you and make sure you're following the rules, like remembering to put the lid tight on the garbage can."

Harry smiled in spite of himself. "I take it she's a horse of a different color."

"Yes," said David, "she is," leaving Harry to figure out the other color.

Harry thought a moment, then asked, "How does Thursday night sound for dinner?"

David nodded. "Sounds fine to me. I look forward to it after all I've heard from my folks." The last was said with a bland smile. No guessing at what they'd filled his ears with in Pittsburgh.

"Good," said Harry. "In case you need to get hold of me, I'm at the Orrington. See you tomorrow."

Good enough, Harry said to himself outside The Bookshop. Curious boy. On the one hand he seemed ingenuous, but at times he also had a devious air about him. Harry could think of any number of next moves, but for now he wanted to see Evanston in daylight.

* * *

It was seven thirty. It would be best to be certain sure that no one but Matcham would be home. Good, her Dodge was parked in front of the house, and David's Buick had vacated the premises. Earlier in the afternoon Harry had walked over to Hinman to make sure his nephew hadn't driven to work. What Harry wanted was time alone with Matcham.

Harry had spent what remained of the afternoon familiarizing himself with the campus. He had walked past Harris Hall, but there was no reason to go inside. Matcham might well be there, but he wanted to meet her at her home. It was funny how all those horrid Pittsburgh years came in handy—stopping off on the way home from Truman's store as the weather warmed up, to sell a few bucks' worth of moth crystals. He could strike up conversations with people from any walk of life, from the Mallingers in Squirrel Hill to the Schipanis on Epiphany Street. By seven he'd had a snack in downtown Evanston, then headed back to the Orrington to change into his new clothes—seersucker jacket with the wrinkles pressed out, khaki slacks, repp tie—and here he was, back on Hinman.

Harry rang the bell and spotted movement inside. The door opened, and there stood the object of so many years of scrutiny—his own, Alton Sweeney's, Del Hay's, John Hay's, not to mention Abraham Lincoln's. By her side was a panting Labrador retriever. "You must be the Mrs. Matcham David told me about," and then before she could object, "I'm his uncle, Harry Stein."

"Oh yes," she said, "David said his uncle from Oregon had come into The Bookshop this afternoon. Rusty, you sit."

"It was a surprise to find him," Harry said, pleased to hear the dog's name said aloud, a name that Abraham Lincoln knew ninety years ago. "I hadn't expected to find David still at school this late in the year, but I happened to phone his mother, and she told me the good news. His mother speaks so highly of him that I wish I traveled more or didn't live so far away. And Mr. Hohenstein sings his praises to the sky." Harry hated the sound of his voice—pure salesman, ice-cold on the doorstep, the words as false as instant coffee.

time back home. Imagine that getting back to Miriam: tightwad Harry goes berserk.

"Good," she said. "He's a Lincoln scholar, and I'm sure you two would have a lot to talk about."

True enough, thought Harry, if all he was interested in was Civil War talk, especially talk that praised Lincoln to the skies. For now he'd had enough to last a lifetime.

* * *

Outside and free to be himself, Harry was in no hurry to get back to his hotel room. Things had gone better than he could have hoped. Matcham would leave a message at his hotel. Meanwhile he had dinner with David scheduled for tomorrow, as well as the invitation to lunch, though that could be nixed easily enough. It might prove interesting to have this tête-à-tête with Matcham's scholar, knowing full well that Matcham had cards up her sleeve she thought the other two didn't know about.

What Harry would love, if there were a way, was getting Matcham in a tight place, just the two of them, and him in charge, and saying, *I'm the one who mailed the letter.* Just watch her eyes then. *And in case you're pregnant, I know who the father is, the man it was who left a little something behind.* He could do worse, though he didn't think of himself as a violent man. Yet here was the "Great Emancipator," holier than any thou in American history, playing the little game of rut-and-run and thinking he could get away with it.

Harry had a hamburger and a hot fudge sundae at the Huddle. He wasn't about to call Cousin Rose. If she were the rosy-cheeked seventeen-year-old up at Conneaut Lake, wearing the Japanese silk kimono with wide sleeves and nothing on underneath, it would be a different matter; but nearly forty-five years of icy winters and muggy summers would have more than withered the bloom from the cheek of dear old Cousin Rose.

Up in his room he took a cool shower, put on his pajamas and robe, and sat down with a little Scotch on the rocks and the next installment of "The Ensorcelled Prince."

* * *

"O peerless youth," said the Sultan, "where is the mausoleum where lies the wounded slave?"

"The Witch built her House of Lamentations adjoining my castle that she might go freely to the lowly wretch. Every morning after she wakes she comes to me, strips this garb from my shoulders, and with a leather scourge administers her ninety and nine strokes, my cries to no avail, her heart as stony as my lower limbs. Finally she reclothes me, leaving me with yesterday's scraps from the table of her worthless slave."

"I have not come all this distance to hear a woeful tale and do nothing about it," said the Sultan. "Come morning she may scourge you, but it will be the last time."

The Sultan remained by the side of the Prince till nightfall, when he lay down and slept. With the false dawn he woke and removed his outer garments. Taking up his sword, he found the mausoleum where the slave and his paramour lay. He then stood aside and waited. Come the dawn the wife appeared without regard for her disarray and hurried to the palace of the Prince. Immediately, the Sultan entered the mausoleum. The way was lit by lamp after lamp, and he had but to follow the trail of incense to come to the sodden bed of the filthy slave. With a single stroke he slew him and removed the corpse from sight. He then donned the clothing of the slave, and with his sword by his side, he wrapped himself in the covers. When the wife of the Prince returned, heated from the scourging of her husband, woefully she cried, "O husband mine, why will you not speak to me?"

The Sultan then, with a feeble whisper and a gnarled tongue, and in the fashion of speech of the least of all slaves, spoke: "Woe and alack, there is no Might save in Allah, the Glory, the Great!"

When she heard these words, she leaped for joy. "Is it true you have gained the power of speech?"

Whereupon the Sultan said in the same diminished voice, "Why should I bother to talk with the likes of you? Why, every morning when you lay your whip on that husband of yours, he cries till I think my head will burst. Every stroke on him is two upon me. Turn him loose, and I will recover more than speech."

"To hear is to obey," she said. Directly she went to the palace of the Prince, where she took a silver bowl, filled it with water from the fountain nearby, and spoke over it certain words which brought the liquid to a boil as though it were a cauldron and beneath it a great fire. That done, she sprinkled the head of her husband with the water and said, "By virtue of these words, forsake the stone and resume thy true shape."

Lo and behold, the Prince straightened his shoulders and stood upon his feet, crying aloud, "There is no god but *the* God, and in very truth Mohammed is His Apostle, whom Allah bless and keep."

"Go forth and return not," said the daughter of his uncle. "Should I see you ever again, truly I will slay you." The youth departed, but waited close by the pavilion.

His wife then returned to the mausoleum and said unto the slave, "I have done your will, my Lord."

The Sultan then spoke once more: "You have done nothing! The branch is cut, but the root is strong."

"What root is strong?" she asked.

"Do you not hear the voices in the night? They come from the people of the city and the four islands. They lift their heads from the water and cry out against the ill fortune that has turned them from their true shape. Then they weep and wail till the stars themselves shun the skies, and this is why I am kept from my health. Go at once and return them to their true shape. Then I will embrace you, for already I feel strength returning to my limbs."

"I hear and obey, my Lord," and in no time she was standing by the tarn. With its waters in the palm of her hand, she spoke words not even the crows understood, and the fish of four colors rose from the waters and became the citizens of the city, Jew and Magian, Christian and Moslem. The tarn became the crowded mainland, and the four mountains the four islands. This done, the false wife returned to her lover, who was not her lover, and flinging off her gown she spoke. "Take my hand, my Lord, that I may draw you to your feet and we may embrace."

"Nearer, my love," said the Sultan, his voice faint but breathless with a promise of lust. Whereupon she knelt by his side, her head flung back in ecstasy, and the Sultan, swifter than the blink of an eye, thrust his sword between her breasts with such force that its point appeared between the blades of her shoulders, and her false blood, as red as rust, ran swift as the mountain stream down her back. The Sultan rose to his feet, withdrew his sword, and like a stone the witch fell forward upon the soiled bedding. The Sultan smote her a second time, then with a single stroke cut her in twain. He dragged the two halves of her flesh outside, where the foul flesh of her beloved slave lay upon a heap of offal surrounded by a troop of feasting buzzards. "Thus forever an end unto tyranny," he spoke for all to hear. The Sultan then returned to the mausoleum, stripped off the sodden clothing of the rude slave, and kneeling at the fountain, washed away the morning's filth.

* * *

Odd, thought Harry, the story had a familiar ring, as though it were not simply this story but another. He'd worry about that another day. So saying, Harry V. Stein rose to his feet and removed his terry cloth robe. The room had grown warm. The ice was melted from his Scotch, and he tipped the glass to his lips until it was empty. Upon the morrow Harry would reopen his Burton, and the young Prince, ensorcelled no more, would hear the satisfying news of vengeance twice over.

XIX
GHOSTS

—Thursday, June 16, 1955—

Joan looked up from her typewriter. It was Will.

"Liz out to lunch?"

"She just went. Anything I can do?"

He rolled his eyes.

"Men," she said, "all alike."

"Actually," he said, "just the opposite. I was wondering if you'd let me fix you a dinner tonight at my place. Quiche and a salad. Any dietary restrictions I should know about?"

"I think we just skipped a step, but yes, I'd love it. Thanks. And no, I eat most anything."

"Good," he said. "I know that I'm ready for a break. The term ended, but I just keep going."

"All work and no play. So, what *do* you do when you're not teaching and not doing research?"

He scratched his chin. "Let's see. Kind of depends. Research is a catchall term for a historian, but I guess I read, I ride my bicycle, I garden a little, I putter around. And I cook, though I'm more of a baker than an all-around cook."

She raised an eyebrow. "Mind if I ask what kind of a housekeeper you are?"

He laughed. "Talk about skipping a step! You'll find that out tonight, won't you?"

"I guess so, but what if you do a massive cleaning job between now and then, like a wolf in sheep's clothing?"

"Now that's what I call stretching a simile. Besides, I might do just the opposite and messify things, to preserve my singletude."

"Ow," she said, making a face. "It hurts when you do that to the language. Well, far be it from me to interfere with your bachelorhood, though I do have a question, and I'm serious for the moment. About tomorrow: I was going to ask if you could come to dinner. I tried phoning you last night, but there was no answer, and I didn't want to call too late."

"It would've been all right," he said. "I was at the Newberry Library and didn't get home till close to ten."

"Sorry," she said. "I didn't mean to put you on the spot."

"Actually, that's where I want to be. If I wasn't afraid of being too pushy, I'd ask you to go bicycling this afternoon—you're off at one, aren't you?"

She hesitated. "Well, sure. I'll have to check with David to see if he's fixed up my bicycle, though I doubt if he's got around to it. I can call The Bookshop and ask. He may be out to lunch with his uncle. And when do you find time to fix quiche?"

"It's already done," he said. "I woke up at five from a dream and couldn't go back to sleep—something about birds, though all I have now are bits and shreds, a Steller's jay landing on a limb outside my window and staring at me, as though it had a message, or I did. That's when I woke up. The image was so intense; I kept seeing that bird, its eyes on mine. I couldn't tell whether it was male or female—it wasn't a bright blue like the males, but it had such a shine to it. And you know how your mind works when you wake up, it's first light, and you hear nothing but birds—finches and thrushes and crows. So I began to think about all the birds I used to see as a kid. Then I got to thinking about you and Lincoln and the letter and asking you over for dinner and cooking and what I'd need from the grocery store, and finally I gave up the ghost. While water was on for coffee, I started rooting for ingredients. Luckily I had everything, at least for the quiche. So I fixed it then and there."

"Thanks," she said. "What a Steller's jay?"

"Oh, it's a beautiful bird, actually. The only crested jay. You see them mostly at higher altitudes, and only west of the Rockies. And I think they're more iridescent than other jays. Why don't you go ahead and call David. If he hasn't fixed up the bike, we can stop by the Schwinn place—they rent bikes. There's no reason to avoid bicycling, is there?"

"No," she said, lowering her voice. "Pregnant women aren't disabled, not in this day and age."

He shrugged. "I just wanted to be sure. Listen, I'm going to wind things up in my office. I'll check back in a bit," and he was gone.

Joan got David on the phone. Yes, he was having lunch with his uncle, and yes, he had fixed up her bicycle. It was the other bike that needed a tire, and he hadn't picked one up yet. She hung up the phone. Good. She hadn't said anything to Will about David's uncle, and was almost sorry she'd said anything about getting him together with Will. There was something odd about the man that she couldn't put her finger on.

* * *

Scenery drifted by. Will drove his Studebaker intently, checking frequently to make sure the bicycles were safe up on the rack. He'd arrived a bit before two and made her test ride her old Raleigh up and down the street. The day was clear and mild, and she had brought along a sweater just in case. She hadn't been this far north of Evanston in ages.

When she had shown Will the letter from Lincoln, he had read it through silently. He had acknowledged its surface features: the paper, the ink, the kind of pen used, phrasing, diction, handwriting, the signature—everything but the content. That he didn't speak to. Its story was her business, not his. For him it must have represented such an odd paradox. Old business and new. Events which transpired more than ninety years ago by one reckoning; events which were but two months old by another. She had felt her color rising as he read the cryptic message, laden with innuendoes about Abraham Lincoln's short time with her. A time might or might not come for annotation.

Will had said he loved her, or rather that he thought he loved her—there was a difference. She didn't know which to trust more, the blatant declaration or the ambivalence. She couldn't remember a time with Robert when she had declared her love for him, though surely the words were said. Time had washed those memories dim. With Abraham Lincoln words hadn't been instrumental in leading them to her bed. She glanced to her left, and Will smiled back. *Trust*, she thought. *I trust this man.* That was enough for now. She was here; she wanted to be here.

"Have you always been tall?" she asked, and as soon as the words escaped her lips, she heard the folly of the question.

"I think so," he said. "My mother says I was a real string bean from the moment I was born. When I was in fifth grade, I was six feet tall, and for a while it seemed I was done growing. I had another spurt a couple of years later. Then, thank the Lord, it tapered off and quit. So maybe there was an interval back when I was about fourteen when I wasn't the tallest person I knew."

"Did you play basketball?"

"Not on a team, if that's what you mean. The high school coach was my history teacher, and we hit it off pretty good. I played some as a kid, and I was even all right. But when my height came on, no. Maybe it was the undue advantage—it wasn't anything I earned. Besides, I preferred baseball, and there my size was a hindrance. My best friend Warren and I used to play catch for hours on end in the summers. As I look back now, it was the finesse that we loved, fielding the ball and making the throw back to nab the imaginary runner. What about you?"

"Sports, you mean? No, not unless you count bicycling. That I got from my mother. She was born just after the Civil War ended, in '67, and she used to bicycle up to Evanston—she and her friends had a club. They'd have a picnic and then ride back. That must've been around the turn of the century. She was still bicycling the year she died, 1946. After the plane crash, I just quit—it wasn't a deliberate choice. The bicycles just sat."

He nodded and patted her arm. "It's hard," he said.

They hadn't spoken of the plane crash. Odd that it hadn't come up. It always seemed to, if she was around someone long enough. "You knew about the crash, didn't you?"

"Yes, I did. I knew early on. Somebody mentioned it to me, I don't remember who. I knew it had happened a few years before I came to Northwestern. A matchmaker, maybe, or probably just so I'd know. Now I wish I had paid more attention, as if it's time wasted. Though I know it's not like that."

"No," she said. "I don't think you could've reached me."

"What do you think made the difference?"

"A good question," she said. The car was cruising along an all-but-deserted road, a hill or two, a few curves, woods, occasionally a glimpse of the lake. What made the difference? That now was the hour, now was the time for one good gentleman to come to the aid of the party. And Will a specialist in the party system. Her thoughts were rambling away. There was no mention of political parties in the Constitution, and what they were like in Lincoln's time was hard to grasp. Lincoln was a Whig, then a Republican, not a Democrat like Douglas. But was Douglas all that different from Lincoln? Yes, no. How different was the South from the North?

"Time, I guess," she said. "Meeting him when I did." Then she realized she'd answered the wrong question, as though Will had asked *How was it that Lincoln could reach you?* But maybe that's what he meant.

He glanced her way. "I'm sorry. My question came out wrong. Not for a million dollars—"

"It's all right," Joan said. "It doesn't matter which way you meant it. I was answering in my head as though you meant Lincoln, and then I heard it meaning us, now."

The car slowed some. There were tears in his eyes.

"Honestly," she said, "it doesn't matter. The ice isn't that thin. And it *was* a good question. Whatever your words were saying, I heard a question about me and Abe Lincoln. So I said, 'Time.' Healing is part of it. And you on the horizon, you waiting to happen. I don't know. The day with him, it was wonderful. I'll tell you about it sometime, as best I can. It was an all-purpose question, I guess."

"Thanks," he said. "You're a generous woman."

"Maybe, maybe not. I wouldn't dare to label myself one way or the other. Maybe a *daily* woman. No day taken for granted."

"Then you hit the jackpot," said Will.

"Not my choice of metaphors," she said. "I'd say it's more like the surprise box at a church auction: you lift the lid and it says, 'A Day with President Lincoln,' with a little extra thrown in."

He laughed aloud. "I don't think they would auction that off, not at the churches I know about. Hey, we're almost there, just up ahead. Here's as good a place as any," and he pulled off onto the shoulder. "It's a little before three, so if we're back at the car by five, that gets us home easily by six. Then a bit to warm up the quiche, dinner at seven. How's that sound?"

"Like bliss." And what crossed her mind was the analogue of Appomattox. Would she spend the rest of her life comparing everything to the Civil War? Especially when an evening with Will Studebaker was nothing like a victory, where one side has surrendered.

* * *

Mostly Will let her go ahead, then he'd be racing down a hill and waiting for her at the top of the next—she kept hitting the brakes on the downhill. There were no cars on the road. Now he was in front again. Every few minutes, especially when they came round a bend, he'd look over his shoulder to make sure she was there. He'd brought along a few apples, some cheese, and he made sure they both had water. Mostly it was thickly wooded country, though you could never be sure what was beyond the next curve, a meadow, a blackberry thicket, an old farmhouse, a pasture, a pair of buzzards on a fence, their wings spread wide like fans.

Will looked strange on his bike. Its frame was so tall, and the seat was so high up, like a scene from the circus, with the giant on one of those old-fashioned front-wheelers. She'd seen pictures of the rider using a platform to climb aboard. But Will would just swing a leg up and over like the next person. She had kissed him once, but only once. There was no rush. And there was no need not to. He was just what the doctor ordered. But the doctor hadn't ordered anyone. No one had ordered either one of them, neither Abraham Lincoln nor William Clemens Studebaker. Like magic they had materialized in her path.

The road narrowed, twisted; Will would be waiting for her at the crest. She was in first gear and working hard at the ped-als. Ahead was an odd sound, like a horse trotting. She lifted her head. A tall man on an easy-going gray horse. He was wearing a black suit and a tall black hat. He looked over his shoulder, looked hard, and pulled back on the reins. She rode up cautiously behind him.

"Hello," she said, and he tilted his head and looked at her strangely, as though he hadn't quite seen or heard her. It was him of course. Lincoln.

He looked left and right. A ways ahead was a small troop of men on horseback idling along, his bodyguard.

"I can just stop for a moment," he said. "It feels like I'm talking to a ghost."

"I'm right here," she said.

"I know," he said. "I won't ask what you're doing on this road, but what *are* you doing?"

"Nothing much," she said. "I was just riding a bicycle, one of those two-wheeler contraptions. Remember, we saw a couple on the campus, at Northwestern." He was smiling. "What are you doing?" she asked.

"I'm heading to the Soldiers' Home," he said. "Then I'll turn back. It isn't much, but it lets me get away from the press of folk seeking this, seeking that. You'd think after Lee's surrender things would calm down." He patted his horse. "Old Abe, all he wants is exercise and fresh air. Which of us is Old Abe?"

"I got your letter," she said. "It came last week. Very much a surprise, but thank you."

"Oh," he said. "My letter."

She could almost touch him, but she didn't want to reach out for fear her hand would come on nothing but thin air. Like the last time.

"I *am* pregnant," she said, stressing the "am." "Two months along. Our child."

"Oh," he said, and he bowed his head slightly. "At my age." And he sighed. "I wish," he began to say, but his voice faltered.

The tip of her right foot was keeping the bicycle balanced. It was a dusty road, unpaved. "There's a man who loves me," she said, "at least he thinks he loves me. He's up the road a bit, waiting for me at the crest, a kind man, like you. Tall, even taller than you. Tonight he'll be fixing dinner for me and I love you, I'll love you forever."

Old Abe nodded and Abraham Lincoln nodded too, and the big gray horse took a step forward, then another and another. Before long he caught up to the others, and her toe was still planted in dust. Then he was out of sight, and the dusty road wasn't dusty anymore. It was paved.

"Goodbye," she called softly. "Goodbye."

* * *

She was still rooted to the spot when she saw Will, tall on his tall bicycle coasting back down the hill. "You all right?" he asked.

She nodded. She looked at the road, thinking maybe there would be hoofprints. "He was here just now, on horseback. Said he was heading to the Soldiers' Home. To get away from the press of callers. A small troop of soldiers was guarding him, but they were up ahead, and we talked for a few minutes, him on his horse, Old Abe, me on my bicycle. I told him I got his letter. I told him I was pregnant, two months. I told him about you, not much, that you would fix dinner tonight, that you, that you were even taller than he is."

"Oh boy," said Will, and she saw he was breathing heavily, holding back tears.

"Lee has surrendered. It's that week. He said, 'You'd think things would calm down after the surrender.' "

"I don't know what to say."

"You don't have to say anything. Then at the end he just went ahead." Joan waved her left hand, a sweeping gesture. "And they rode out of sight."

Will dismounted from his bike and leaned it up against an old rail fence, then leaned hers against his. He rummaged in his pack.

"Whatever you've got, I'd like some," she said. He got out a small cloth, two apples, and a hunk of cheddar cheese, and from his pocket his jackknife. They sat on a downed tree. She took a bite of the red apple.

"Unexpected," she said.

He nodded.

"You didn't notice anything?"

He shook his head. "You seemed to be taking longer than usual, so I circled back, and there you were in the middle of the road. I kind of wish I had come sooner, but maybe that's against the rules."

"It's complicated," she said. "Before, it was my time and light-hearted, like a holiday. But this was nothing like a holiday. I was back in his time. We were on a dusty road and I could see his bodyguard. It was more as if there were a weight hanging over us. He said it was like seeing a ghost."

"It sure is an adventure being with you," Will said. "I don't mean that in a trite way."

"I know," she said. She wiped away a few tears. "I can't help but think of Ford's Theater and Good Friday, but that wasn't what I was thinking. I guess I don't know what I was thinking besides what we said, and both the surprise and the inevitability of his being there, and then being fearful of trying to do more than talk, of touching him or his horse. What's the word? Evanescent? Before it was as though he had stepped outside of history and could afford to be ordinary. But this time he was back in it."

They finished their apples and cheese and satisfied their thirst. It was time to head back. "It's funny," Will said as they rode side by side, "but I wonder what if I had kept you within my sight? I wonder what I would have seen, or if it could've happened at all?"

"I don't know," Joan said. "I can't remember exactly what I was thinking before he appeared. It was something to do with you and how you came along, and how he came along, except you happened upon me and I happened upon him, but both were accidents."

Will nodded. Lost in thought, she guessed, lost in wonder.

"The other thing," she said, "is that I think there's a pattern. Accident is part of it, but not all of it is chance. It's as though threads are weaving in and out, holding the universe together, which sounds like puppets and a master puppeteer. That's like the metaphor of the clock and God's hand winding it to begin with and there's your universe. But something's meddling."

Will was about a bike length behind, and mostly she was talking on faith. If he couldn't hear, he'd say something. *Meddlers*, she wondered. *Us, me, who?* But it was leading up to tomorrow. She hadn't expected anything today. Twice now she could have warned him, and twice she had said nothing.

* * *

They stopped by her place to drop off her bike and to feed Rusty. David was there with his uncle, the two of them just on their way out to dinner. Joan introduced the uncle to Will, who was undoing her bike from the rack. She'd forgotten all about Harry Stein and his fascination with the Civil War and her promise to bring the two men together. David and his uncle were an unlikely duo, she thought as they drove off, the top down on David's Buick, the uncle in his sporty clothes waving a hearty goodbye, more like a character in a movie than a real person. As though the whole scene were arranged for her benefit, with Rusty the tail-wagging dog nothing but a prop, and the car having no place really to go to, just clearing the set.

Will's house was on Sherman and was smaller than small. It was composed of an entryway with pegs for hats and coats, then a living room that served as library and study, then an archway to the kitchen which was just short of a decent size. It had open shelves for dishes, sugar and creamer, a Brown Betty teapot, and odds and ends, and in the middle a small dining table.

"Bathroom?" she inquired. Will pointed to a narrow flight of stairs off the living room. Joan poked her head into the one bedroom: a four-poster bed made up with a quilt, a couple of bookshelves, an end table, a tall, dark chest of drawers. Neat as a pin. She couldn't remember being in a man's house, ever. Robert had lived with his family when they were going out. And since then she'd led such a narrow life.

Will was at the kitchen sink when she returned. "Anything I can do?" she asked.

"Sure. You could slice some red onion and chop those almonds, not too fine. There's no rush—it'll take a few more minutes for the quiche to warm up. By the time I've washed these spinach greens, we'll be ready to eat."

As she chopped and sliced, she thought of her grandmother, though granddaughter and grandmother had never met—Sarah Morrow dying before the turn of the century at about the age of eighty. Her marriage to Grandfather Morrow had been her second marriage, just after the Civil War. She too had lost a husband and a daughter, to a flood. She too had known Abraham Lincoln, and she too was party to the crime, if meddling with time was criminal. Joan hadn't said anything about the penny to Will—the poor man's credulity was stretched to the breaking point as it was.

"A penny for your thoughts."

She looked at him sharply.

"What's that for?" he asked.

"Nothing," she said. "I guess I'm on edge. I was just thinking about a penny. It's a long story, and I was going to save it for another day. It concerns my grandmother, whose life stretched almost from one end of the nineteenth century to the other."

"That's up to you," he said. "I'm almost done here. Then we can eat. There's dressing in the fridge in a clear jar. Have you ever seen this trick?" He was shoveling the washed spinach leaves into a pillowcase; then he headed out the back door to the garden, where he swung the pillowcase round and round, water spraying like a Catherine wheel on the Fourth of July. Back inside they put the salad together, took the golden quiche from the oven, got out the plates and silverware.

"Are you allowed to have wine, a little?"

"A little."

"Good," and he produced a bottle of Chianti from the cupboard. They sat down and he lifted his glass. "Mazel tov."

"Mazel tov," said Joan, clinking their glasses. Dinner proceeded, tentative bites of salad and quiche, then bravos for the cook, and for the almond chopper too.

"I have a question," she said. "Where'd you come by all this old furniture? It looks so mid-nineteenth century."

"That's what it is. Oh, some of it's from my family. Then in graduate school I had a friend who had inherited all his father's woodworking tools, and we used to go off on weekends into the countryside, barn sales and that sort of thing—we'd watch the ads. I bought a few books on old furniture and refinishing. When I got the teaching job in North Dakota it was as if I had found King Solomon's mine. It satisfies the historian in me."

After they went back for seconds, Joan told the story of the penny, her finding it among her grandmother's pen points, and then the diary that told the story of how Sarah Morrow got the penny from Abraham Lincoln in Richmond. "It's like there's a loop, and it's so complete that you can't find its beginning."

"I'm beginning to wonder how many of these stories you have tucked up your sleeve."

"I think that's the last one."

"Not that I want it to be. I heard of a man who had two holes in one in a single round of golf, and I'll bet he was hoping for the third. You know, I wish I had just seen, say, his shadow, today. But I saw something even better."

"What's that?" asked Joan.

"You."

Silence fell. As though he had said more than he meant to, or she had caught the echoes from what he was thinking three layers down.

"Tomorrow," she said, "I've also invited Lorraine Riggs, my doctor—we're old friends. She knows the story too, of the letter, everything. And tomorrow is the fourteenth of April—"

"I know," he said, "Ford's Theater."

"And you saw what happened today, kind of. I didn't have Basler open. I don't need a book. I don't even know for sure when it was, other than the week."

"It was—or it is—Thursday, April the thirteenth."

"How do you know?"

"I did some checking yesterday. He met with Grant and Stanton, and Gideon Welles, and Maunsell Field. And he rode out to the Soldiers' Home. It must've been in the afternoon, late afternoon."

"Oh."

"What time is dinner tomorrow?" Will asked.

"How about six, to be on the safe side?"

"Sure," he said. "Maybe I could come a little earlier. I could help with dinner. I worry about you being alone."

"It's later that worries me. I do wonder about today. If you had come back while he was there, what would you have seen on the road? It's so strange. It's like a seance, but I don't believe in any of that. I'm so straightforward. Thanks, I'd love it if you'd come over earlier tomorrow. I have no idea what we'll have for dinner."

"We'll figure something out."

"Thank you," she said. "It's like you dropped from out of the blue. I know you've been here all along. Then—was it just last Friday?"

"Last Friday," he said, "by the lake, and you and your brother-in-law."

"You're part of it," she said, and she smiled. "Not a footnote, not a postscript, or relegated to the appendices. You're not somebody incidental, like the newsboy who delivers the newspaper with the story that has the last clue, the last piece to the puzzle."

DELIVERANCE

The Buttery, Chicago's finest restaurant. Harry leaned forward slightly, his elbows planted on the arms of the plush dining chair, his hands folded as though in devout prayer. He'd polished off his Caesar salad. David was working on his French onion soup. Rarely had Harry felt so expansive. Dinner was well worth the small fortune it was costing, if for no better reason than how far the tale of this meal would carry him forward in Miriam's esteem. David had taken the invitation at face value. *Anything you like. Oysters, soup, salad, steak, lobster, anything but oatmeal—I'll bet they have that too for folks with troubled stomachs, same as they have peanut butter and jelly sandwiches for the finicky kids. Though it won't show its ugly face on the menu. You have no idea how long I've dreamed of an occasion like this, Harry and his long-lost nephew.* Pure blarney, but in character, the well of words was well stocked tonight.

And didn't he and David cut quite a figure, the two of them dressed to the nines and cruising in David's handsome Buick convertible, creamy white with green leather upholstery? Granted, the car was already a good seven years old, but those first postwar cars, loaded to the gills with extras, already were classics. David's car had been Miriam's the first six years of its life, so if it went beyond Murray Avenue and the Giant Eagle grocery store, it was an adventure. Would you believe it had under twenty thousand miles?

"Harry," David said, looking up from his soup, "I've been wondering. Not just since yesterday when I kind of met you for the first time, really. A five-year-old's memory doesn't count for much."

"No, kiddo, I guess not. You were saying?" Harry, master of the grand gesture, was reminded of the Sultan and the Prince from Burton. Without the Sultan, the Prince was doomed to be a no-body, worse off than the meanest slave.

"Well," David went on, "I know, unlike Dad who studied business administration at the University of Pennsylvania, you chose Yale and you majored in the arts."

"Righto," said Harry. "Classics, *magna cum laude.*"

"Well, there are a couple of things I've always wondered," David continued. "Maybe not always, but ever since I learned how to wipe my own nose."

"Yes," said Harry encouragingly.

"So, with that kind of background, what kept you from, say, teaching, or writing, or diplomacy?" Before Harry could defend himself, David pushed ahead. "I know the story of Grandpa and Lou Gehrig's Disease, though he had it before Lou Gehrig, and how you had to look after things. But how come—" There his sentence ran out of steam, and his eyes looked to Harry's for help.

Harry wasn't sure whether it was impertinence or innocence speaking. *Why haven't you made more of yourself?* Backhanded praise. Almost like the old joke about your taste in neckties being not half as bad as they say. He could invoke the tale of Cincinnatus, but Harry hadn't quite saved the Republic, nor was he a simple farmer. "Kiddo," he said finally, "there are stories, and then there are stories. When I graduated from Yale in 1915, the world was my oyster. With two exceptions. Any guesses?"

"A war, World War I."

"Yes," said Harry. "What was called the Great War, the war to end all wars. We weren't in it yet; it was just a matter of time. I could launch myself on the academic highway, but how far would

I get before Uncle Sam made his claim? Alton Sweeney—he was my mentor at Yale—was all for my pushing ahead. We were almost like father and son." *A sweeping generalization there*, Harry thought. *There's always the case of Oedipus.*

"They didn't have deferments then, I guess."

"Not really, and not for scholars. That's one exception. The other has to do with the little matter of religion."

Harry glanced up. A busboy, a smile frozen on his face, cleared the table, refilled their water glasses, brought more French bread. David waited for Harry to continue.

"All right, how many Jewish diplomats can you name? The ambassador to the Court of St. James, a Jew! Can you imagine? An Israelite? Besides, there are just two ways to get ahead in diplomacy: either you underwrite a presidential campaign to the tune of a million bucks, or you deliver a constituency at the polls. And that's if you're a Gentile. I suppose I could've started at the bottom of the ladder as a career diplomat. It's not a bad life, kowtowing to the political appointee of the hour, the trivia of lost passports, rubbing shoulders with the local gentry." Harry was thinking of Del Hay in Pretoria, having a real job to do and rising to the occasion, the poor son of a bitch. "It would've helped if your grandfather were the Secretary of State or happened to be named Andrew Mellon."

The waiter brought the main course, steak and mushrooms for David, halibut with almondine sauce for Harry. Conversation drifted. Just as well. Harry didn't care for the direction it was heading, a damper to the evening. Talk of how doors gradually slammed shut one by one on his future. The damned army and its waste of good time—two years' worth—supervising clerks, a glorified bookkeeper. Truman meanwhile getting to play baseball at Fort Benning. Fun and games. Then with the war ending, the first signs of his father's illness. If the disease had taken him swiftly the way it was supposed to, some money would have been left over, but by 1931 it had all but run down the drain. Plus the crash of '29, and Harry and his mother moving into that hellhole of a one-bedroom apartment. How could he have done it? And the whole time—from 1925 on—waiting for Alton Sweeney to keel over and set Harry Stein free. To un-ensorcell him. As a Sultan, Sweeney left a little to be desired. And what if his mother hadn't been scared to death in 1940? She could easily have gone on, with nitroglycerine tablets under her tongue, another twenty years.

Harry looked at his fish, half eaten, a corpse. The thought of his mother still alive was enough to kill any appetite. David was working earnestly with knife and fork on his steak. An innocent, Harry decided. And he willed himself to take a bite of fish and then another. He did love the buttery almonds.

He thought back over the last couple of weeks. It would be two weeks tomorrow, after waiting thirty long years, that he had licked a purple three-cent stamp bearing a bust of Thomas Jefferson, stuck it on Abraham Lincoln's envelope, and slipped it through the slot at the main post office. The fewer hands on it the better. Then the unfolding of events that brought him to this very moment, with Joan Matcham like a fly in amber a few miles to the north. *But,* he asked himself, *to what end? The long-lost nephew asks why his uncle hadn't made more of his life. A question the uncle is doing his best to keep at bay. Let the moment tell its own story, so that Uncle Harry need not ask his wherefore.*

"What is it, Uncle Harry?"

Startled, Harry blinked, saw in the silvery distance a mirrored figure who bore a passing resemblance to a one-time Pittsburgh lad, sitting at table with its double, a youth named David whose visage was unsettled, like a troubled pond.

"Woolgathering," said Harry; *Woolgathering,* the image repeated. Alongside the man and the youth sat a sturdy dog, a Labrador retriever, shaking its head. *No*, it was saying, *no*. "What is what?" said Harry, looking once more at his nephew across the table.

"I dunno exactly," said David. "It's just you seemed a million miles away, staring off into space, like a spell had been cast. Everything so still. I could hear the ticking of a clock somewhere, maybe someone's pocket watch. I worry about Mrs. Matcham, about Joan."

"Mrs. Matcham?" It was as though an electric current were surging through Harry. "Joan Matcham?"

David set his knife and fork on his plate. "Probably nothing," he said. "I see her sitting at her desk. It's like her mind is somewhere else. Not always, of course. That would be craziness. Like schizophrenia. Did you know that her daughter and her husband were killed in a plane crash?" Said with such a pained expression.

"I didn't," said Harry. "A long time ago?"

"Depends, I guess," said David. "You know how time is. She said it was in 1947. I think that's partly why I'm living there—to make the house less lonely for her. Anyhow, you had that same look, like Joan's."

Distracted, thought Harry, *forever being drawn away from the moment*.

"I read too much," said David, as though giving himself a scolding. "I don't mean books—you can't read too many books."

"No," said Harry. "No such thing."

"I mean, like reading into what the other person is thinking, that kind of reading. Especially girls. Always thinking what they must be thinking, which leaves me with nothing to say. It's stupid, I know. That's why I like having this job at The Bookshop. It's so—" he looked for the right word "—concrete. I always know what to say next."

Harry's knife and fork were also crisscrossed on his plate. This boy was so like himself, the self he once was. He hadn't caught the telltale ticking of David's imaginary timepiece. What he did catch was the lad's genuine concern for Joan Matcham, the haunting of her house by an airplane plummeting to earth, and David's own inwardness, which, like the sharp note of a tuning fork, resonated, not with the youthful Harry so much as this Harry, costumed as a bon vivant, yet a man whose days had been reduced to the narrowness of self.

"I was thinking," said Harry, "about youth, yours and mine, of blasted hopes, and wishing better for you." Which was not at all what he had been thinking, but was thinking now. "Of the Great War, 'the war to end all wars,' sowing the seed for another world war, not a war to end all wars, for in no time at all, there's a war with China. Imagine! A war with China, halfway round the world. Yes, I mean China, not Korea. A world at war. And more wars brewing, wars ever brewing."

David was looking at his uncle sideways, doing his best to grasp his words, as though it were the Delphic Oracle herself speaking.

"And worst of all," said Harry, "this fish—" here Harry rotated his plate a hundred and eighty degrees, so that the glazed eye was now focused on David "—were it not for this buttery almondine sauce, to my jaundiced eye, this fish would resemble a corpse." Whereupon Harry took a nibble and smacked his lips.

"Uncle Harry—"

"Please. 'Harry.' Any 'Harry' but 'Uncle.' "

"Harry," said David, "Harry evermore, you were on your way to ruining a very good dinner." And he fell to eating.

Two tables over was an attractive girl who had just gained David's surreptitious attention, a blonde and blue-eyed beauty with a peaches-and-cream complexion, a pert Gentile nose, and beneath her black cashmere sweater a delectable build that reminded Harry of young Cousin Rose. It was quite a family: the father, boisterous and bald, the mother demure and washed-out, an impoverished version of the daughter. From the tidbits of conversation Harry could pick up, they were celebrating the sacred rites of college graduation, the father waxing on as though he were God's gift to Chicago, clinking his water glass with his knife for the necessary sound effects. Something to do with the law—obviously he was a lawyer. When the daughter put her napkin beside her plate and excused herself, David followed suit, and the story died down.

Good luck, David. In his day, Harry thought wistfully, he would have aimed at an exchange of telephone numbers, and the next thing you know, what lies behind the cashmere wouldn't be a guess. Not that he would have been free to take the next step. Such fruit was forbidden to the likes of Harry, thanks to the prevailing sentiments of a so-called "all men are free and equal" society that considered Jews as less than human. And thanks also to the iron fist of his half-turned-to-stone father, threatening to cut him off without a penny if he ever so much as looked at another shiksa. By 1925 and Alton Sweeney's rash promise, Harry was thirty-two years old, and just about every limb in every orchard, Jew and Gentile, had been stripped clean. Fifteen years later, when the rigid tyrant had finally died, Harry himself was turning to stone, lying awake at nights on his half of a twin set of beds, his mother snoring away on the other. Your mother, your twin. Matricide, now there would have been a solution. Why didn't he think of the gambit of the prankster at the door?

David returned, nature satisfied, so to speak. You don't need to travel in time to bed a woman. Harry glanced at his watch, a little after eight. If all went well, he and David would return to Matcham's around nine, paths would cross, and like the resourceful Sultan, Harry would see what was to be seen.

"Have you ever thought of writing?" David asked out of the

blue. Seeing the startled look on Harry's face, David backed up a step. "I mean, you read everything under the sun—you're a match for Mr. Hohenstein. And from what you say you have the time. Not that you have to be a writer just because you read. The world would be flooded with books if it was like that. Though that's what I'd do if I had the freedom not to worry about a job." David had neatly unasked his question.

"You want to write?" Harry had to bite his tongue. *The twit. Wants to match wits with Chekhov and Tolstoy, Poe and Hawthorne? Steady, Harry.*

"I would. I do. Not that there's much opportunity what with the grind of school. But yes."

"Well, good for you," said Harry. "A noble calling to be one with the Muse. And to answer your question, I did think of being a writer once upon a time—you see right there that I've got the tail before the nose. As though my story might end with 'And that's what happened once upon a time.' But my efforts came to naught."

"You just gave up? Did you show what you wrote to anyone? Though that can be risky enough."

"No, I didn't. I didn't need another's eyes to recognize my limitations. And so I burnt it, every last page."

"You did!" cried David.

"It's all right, kiddo," and Harry exchanged conspiratorial looks with David's blonde chippy. He should invite her to the table to hear the story of the lost literary treasure of Harry V. Stein. "Take my word on this one," Harry said. Then he added, seemingly off-the-cuff, "Say, how would it be if we took dessert home with us? I'm stuffed. Maybe you could make me a cup of coffee. And we could even take something back for your landlady. You pick it out."

* * *

David let them in the house, then flicked on the porch light. Matcham was still out with her tall history professor. Good. "Might as well put her cake in the refrigerator," Harry said. "No knowing when she'll get home." Though Harry guessed it wouldn't be all that late for a middle-aged woman with child. "We might as well go ahead and polish off our cake." Back at the restaurant it had been hard for Harry not to crown the dinner there and then. God knows what David would serve up under the name of coffee.

David put water on to boil, and sure enough, got out a tall jar of Nestle's instant best. Harry poked around in a cupboard or two—a well-enough-organized kitchen—the house a worthy nest for little Lincoln. Obviously David had no inkling that the mistress of the house might be with child. And speak of the devil, they both turned at the sound of the door opening and the rush of Rusty to the hallway.

"It's just me," said Matcham. "How you doing, old girl?" Rusty's reply was inaudible.

"Hello," David called from the kitchen. "My Uncle Harry's here."

"I hope I'm not intruding," Harry said loud and clear. "We brought dessert back, from the Buttery. There's Black Forest chocolate cake—not the whole cake. Oh yes, some rice pudding. David said you like rice pudding."

"Hi, Joan," David said as she walked into the kitchen. "There's also this weird marbled sourdough cake."

"A Bundt cake," Matcham said. They were all arrayed on the counter. "I'm afraid I've just had more than enough dinner at Will's, so maybe I'll just have a nibble of the rice pudding and then head up to bed. Thanks for thinking of me. How was your dinner?"

"Delicious," said David. "It's like a show there, with the service, everything about as good as it can be. How's this for the rice pudding?"

Her mind's elsewhere, thought Harry, as David handed him his Nescafé, then sat at the table with a slice of the Black Forest cake.

"I forgot about you, Harry."

"I'll try some of that Bundt cake, kiddo. Thanks."

Matcham was leaning against the counter eating her pudding in tiny bites.

"I take it," Harry said, hoping to break the spell, "that you and your friend from History, a mighty tall man, were bicycling today. Would you believe that I once rode in a race from Boston to New York?"

"Really, Uncle Harry, on a bicycle?"

"A bicycle, and not all that different from the bikes I saw today. The Sturmey-Archer gear is basically unchanged since the turn of the century. You can repair old ones with new parts—they're still interchangeable. Hard to believe in this day and age when folks buy a new car every year."

"How'd you make out in the race, Harry?" Matcham asked.

"I completed it. Which put me in the top ten. I did finish about a day behind the winner. But mind you, he had placed second in the Tour de France a year or so before. The war pretty much put an end to bicycle racing, except for the seniors."

"You don't still ride, do you?" asked David.

"Actually, I do," which of course wasn't the truth, but it sounded good to his ears. "Like they say, *Mens sana in corpore sano*—'Sound mind in a sound body.' No races anymore, just utilitarian cycling: to the library, to the store, and once in a while around Mt. Hood."

"All the way around Mt. Hood?" Poor David was being stretched beyond his limits, and for sure this would get back to Pittsburgh.

"No," said Harry, "I mean in the vicinity of Mount Hood. Remember, I'm closer to being Methuselah than I am to Superman." A line which provoked a smile from Matcham. Good, that's what he was looking for. Icebreakers.

"Have you heard anything about how your client's doing?" Matcham again.

"Not bad, more shaken up than he realized. He's in his mid-eighties, though his health is surprisingly good, aside from the usual arthritis." There was no end to what Harry could make up about this mythical cousin of the Sweeneys'. "He's going to lie low for a couple of days, being battered and bruised, as they say. Take two aspirin and get a good night's rest. I'll probably putter around on the campus tomorrow. David said he'd take me to the Art Institute sometime over the weekend."

"Sounds like you're in good hands," she said. "And thanks for the pudding. I'm going to turn in now. I have to be at work by eight. David, you and your uncle make yourselves at home."

Harry listened to her soft tread on the stairs, then to her walking about upstairs, readying herself for bed. He and David finished their cake and coffee. "Leave the dishes to me," David said, and Harry acquiesced graciously. He didn't mind washing dishes in his own kitchen, but he hated anyone else's routine. They agreed to check about plans sometime during the day—Harry knew where to reach David. And Harry departed.

Finally, he thought, time to himself. An afternoon on stage, then the evening's performance was enough to drive him crazy. But it was worth it to get a taste of Joan Matcham in her element, to see what was on her bookshelves, in her refrigerator, on her desk. With a little luck he'd soon get to poke about upstairs. With David living in her house, no door was barred. If she were a book, he'd soon be in the thick of it. Tonight she definitely was off the mark, as though she had gotten bad news and once up-

242 | Good Friday

stairs could ease aside her mask. Who doesn't wear a mask?

The evening was mild, mid-June in the Midwest. Two months from now they'd be sweltering like suckling pigs. Harry whistled his way back to the hotel, spun through the revolving door, rode up the elevator, achieved his inner sanctum, and washed away the day's filth (somewhat less bloody than the Sultan's). He donned his pajamas, then slipped under the covers and settled his shoulders against the rack of plump Orrington pillows.

"We're home," he said softly. All the cards were on the table, and he was the dealer. Burton lay to his right. Yet Harry was reluctant to pick it up, to listen to Shahrazad spin out the obligatory last word. All too neat, too pretty: the Sultan thinking himself but a two-day walk from his Sultanate, whereas in truth a year's journey separates him from all he has ever known—daunting news, solved with the flick of a page. Were it Harry, a being of flesh and blood, what would he say upon such news? Harry half-whispered the word, "Fuck!" But not the Caliph. Harry found the passage:

> "A year!" exclaimed the Caliph. "May the wonders of Allah never cease. Let us rejoice and begin preparation to visit my kingdom. From this day forth I proclaim you my son, for I have never been blessed with issue."

"Such pap," said Harry. Within a paragraph the Sultan and the Prince had crossed the vast desert and were married to the Fisherman's two daughters, each a beauty with eyes like jet and a face as round as the moon. Good thing they don't smell like Limburger cheese.

Harry set the book aside, *A Thousand and One-Too-Many Nights*. He had no stomach for such fairy-tale endings.

Now what? The Gideon's Bible from the nightstand drawer? Sooner the phonebook. He could turn on the TV. With his luck it'd be Jimmy Stewart's drawling kisser. What about his diary? He could map out his grand plan. Save that he had no grand plan. At the Buttery, with David across the table gobbling up his steak like a turkey, it had seemed too good to be true, the gleaming yellow-brick-road leading straight to Matcham's doorstep. How many years had he been waiting for this moment?

He lay there puzzled. What had happened to the sure-footed Harry who could rattle off every state capital and knew the roots of "assassin" and "dungaree"? David Levine, the upstart nephew, asked, *So why didn't you do something with your life?* And Rita Griffin capped Harry's woes with the bitter story of her father, then reduced Harry to utter silence with her frigid *Do you mind if I read for a while?*

Harry's lips were dry as dust. He'd come all this way, to what end? So that he could live happily ever after? So many years he'd been feeding on the enigma of Lincoln in one century and Matcham in the next. What did he expect to find? A story, but not this story.

When he got home he'd get himself a goddamn dog, man's best friend. And a bicycle for Mount Hood? Or what about hiking in Forest Park, just Harry and his faithful companion? Harry laughed aloud at the thought of this latest transformation. And how in God's name could any son of Truman Levine turn into this book-loving David!

"I give up," Harry muttered. Five minutes later he was dressed and, hands in pockets, was out for a midnight stroll, like a will-o'-the-wisp, bound for nowhere.

NOW AND THEN

—Friday, June 17, 1955—

Joan was sitting on the porch, her rocker tilting back and forth, when Will's Studebaker drove up, a blue as pale as the sky. Rusty sat at her side, her ears alert to the newcomer—Rusty, a link between Emily and now. And to Lincoln.

Joan had been sitting for more than an hour, the unread book upon her lap, her eyes seeing and not seeing, her thoughts unremarkable and unremembered. She had to will herself to rise as Will opened the gate. It was beginning. Friday evening, the fourteenth of April.

"Hello there," said Will. He had a couple of grocery bags in his arms. "I took the liberty of going shopping. If you don't like what I got, or don't like my ideas for the menu—"

"It's okay," she said. "I was going to go shopping. I just couldn't do it. It's like my legs were made of lead. So I finally came out here with a book, maybe an hour ago. I don't even know the title."

He glanced at the spine. "*Moby Dick*."

"*Moby Dick*! I don't even own *Moby Dick*."

"My attempt at a joke. Sorry. It's *The Collected Stories of Katherine Mansfield*."

"More like it. Well, come on in, and we'll see what I'm cooking for dinner," and she held the screen door open for him.

He unloaded the sacks onto the kitchen counter: cans and boxes and this and that, plus salad makings and a loaf of French bread.

"Lasagna?" she asked doubtfully.

"How'd you ever guess, aside from the box of lasagna noodles?"

"Just clever, I guess. You really fix lasagna? I figured only grand-mothers born in Milan cooked lasagna."

"Maybe so," he said. "Me, mostly I follow the directions on the noodle package. With a few afterthoughts. Besides, my grand-mother was from Milan."

"No," she said. "You're kidding, aren't you?"

"Yes. What time did you tell the doctor to be here?"

"She said she'd be here around six, if she doesn't get held up."

"Good. And did David say anything about his plans for the evening?"

"He said he's doing something with his uncle, like dinner and a movie."

"So with Dr. Riggs getting here sometime after six, we've got plenty of time. Let's see," said Will. "It's half past four. What if I put this together now? Then we can have it in the oven around, say, six o'clock? Ready to eat by seven, and we finish eating by eight at the latest. I won't try to fit the dirty dishes into the equa-tion. How's that sound?"

"Like any girl's dream. What can I do?"

"Well, put a pot of water on to boil for the noodles, and I'll take care of the rest. If you don't have enough pans and baking dishes, I have some in the car. You can keep me company or go back to not reading your book."

"I'll watch," she said. "I like to watch others work. It's hearten-ing. How'd you say you learned to cook?"

"Working alongside my mother. She knows her way around a kitchen, and for my twenty-first birthday she gave me Rombauer and Becker, mother and daughter, *The Joy of Cooking*—it was a pretty new book in those days."

Joan sat at the table and watched. Will worked intently, some-times whistling, sometimes humming. He'd make funny gestures with his hands, which she was sure he was unaware of. She was reminded of her own mother in the kitchen. When the time came to build the lasagna, it was like seeing the last pieces of a jigsaw puzzle come together. "There," he said. "Six. Right on the button." Five minutes later and the kitchen looked pristine once more. "Any objections to my drinking a bottle of beer out on the porch in the heart of WCTU-land?"

"Nope. A woman's home is her castle."

Rusty led the way, then sat in front of Will. "All right. Just one," and from his pocket he removed a large milk-bone biscuit.

"You think of everything." Halfway to a question.

He smiled. "It's what comes of having run off to the circus at the age of twelve—everything's a performance. Actually," he said, "I get wound up once I get going, and then it takes me a while to come back down. I'll be all right. The beer will help."

"I hope I don't ever take you for granted," she said.

"I hope not. And that's one I'll drink to. Cheers."

* * *

It was six thirty when Lorraine Riggs drove up. Joan performed her ritual with the introductions. Dinner was in the oven. Will got himself and Lorraine each a glass of wine, and all three sat for a while. Joan let the two of them handle their own conversation. They talked about their jobs, where they lived, where they were raised, and how they both happened to be single, the last topic in response to a direct question from Lorraine, which Will turned back on the questioner.

"I have no general objections to the race of man," Lorraine said. "It's just that by the time I was done with all the hurdles on the way to becoming a doctor, the particulars were already snapped up, and the remainder represented one sorrowful deficiency or another."

"Such as?" said Will, his jaw extended, as though he might be precisely such a case.

"Oh," she said, "too small a brain, too much wealth, too set in their ways, too scornful of women, too full of themselves—a whole host of reasons. Right now I'm running through the mental catalog of Men I Have Known." Joan could hear the capital letters. "Not that there weren't a couple of possibilities. But, you know, there are reasons why a good man might shy away from a woman like me—not that I plan to go into detail as to what those reasons might be, not tonight, not with tomorrow being my birthday. Half a century, in case you're wondering."

Joan's chair abruptly ceased its rocking. "Tomorrow's your fiftieth birthday?"

Lorraine nodded matter-of-factly. "You think you're the only one allowed to hide a birthday?"

"Now what's all that about?" asked Will.

"Just that Wednesday, two days ago, was this one's birthday—" Lorraine directing her thumb back at Joan "—a fact that leaked out at lunch. It was the lure of her baking herself a birthday cake that clinched my decision to come tonight."

"Did you?" he asked Joan.

Joan shook her head guiltily.

"Well, Dr. Riggs, will you settle for spumoni and a raincheck— let's see—in eight days? One week plus one night from tonight?"

Joan looked at him doubtfully. "Just what does that arithmetic add up to?"

"I too get to have a birthday—the twenty-fifth of June."

Lorraine laughed. "Looks like we know what six people a generation ago were doing come harvest season. Which is all right by me. Without babies, I'd be out of a job."

Will glanced at his watch. "Almost seven. I need to get the lasagna out of the oven, let it cool for a few minutes, and fix the salad.

You two stay here. I'll call when I'm ready." And in he went.

"I like that man," said Lorraine. "Like him a lot. I'm sure he has his faults—because no man comes free of the blot of Adam. But I'd say, in a pinch, he'll do."

Joan nodded. "I like him a lot too. He's a good man. I may even love him. I have a hard time putting the two together, loving and men."

Lorraine raised an eyebrow. "So you say; so we all say. Granted it can be well-nigh impossible, yet the human race goes on."

"Maybe so," said Joan. "At times I wondered at the word 'love'—at least between a man and a woman. How we feel with a child, or even with a dog like Rusty—that's so much easier, more absolute."

"In my case," said Lorraine, "it's that ounce of hesitation that's held me back over the years, like a diver perched on the high board who can't get his knees to flex and let loose. Listen, I'm going to see if Will could use a hand."

"Remember," said Joan, "he's mine."

Joan wasn't sure Lorraine had heard the last bit. She had said it softly, as Lorraine was heading round the bend, and was surprised when she realized what she'd said.

Rusty was looking so earnestly Joan's way. Heart to heart. As though she should be in on the conversation. "Come here, old girl." Joan reached down and scratched Rusty's cheek. Rusty leaned into it—sheer sensual delight. "All this talk," said Joan, "and not a word said about Abe Lincoln, not directly." Rusty pressed against Joan's hand. *Wake up, get with it!* And Joan's hand did.

Little things matter, Joan thought. Gestures, petting a dog a moment longer, one extra step, or one less, a moment's delay, a slip of the tongue—little things. She'd seen the illustration from *Harper's Weekly* of John Wilkes Booth on stage just after the assassination, Booth with his right arm upraised, knife in hand; he's just said the Latin words from the seal of the state of Virginia, *Sic semper tyrannis—Thus always to tyrants*. The audience is in an uproar. There's screaming from the President's box, though in the picture all you see is how it's draped with flags. The actor Harry Hawk is in shadow, far from the footlights, alone on stage. Or he had been alone, till Booth fired his shot and leaped the twelve feet from the balustrade. About to climb on stage is a man named J. B. Stewart, a lawyer, taller than any other man in the city of Washington, and ready to give chase.

* * *

They'd eaten the lasagna, the salad, the garlic bread, then had spumoni and coffee and sung "Happy Birthday." To look at Will, you'd have expected him to eat that much more than everybody else, but he didn't appear to. Now he and Lorraine were doing a fast washup of the dishes, and it was a little past eight. Joan excused herself and went upstairs to the bathroom.

Time was passing. The room was smaller than she remembered. She ran water in the sink and watched it swirl away. She kept her eyes from the silvery reflection in the medicine-cabinet mirror. Mirrors had made her uneasy for as long as she could remember. She'd learned not to talk about it because of the way people took it. They'd display a queer smile, and maybe there'd be an awkward laugh—as though in the next moment they'd turn tail and scamper away, then scrub their hands at the nearest opportunity. She could will herself to be reasonable. If she smiled and was enthusiastic, the person in the mirror would forego her stern judgment and join in the celebration. Joan glanced up.

It held her gaze, the mirror, the other Joan. It was almost a stranger, scrutinizing her, worrying about her, worried about that other Joan who mimicked her. Joan squeezed her eyes closed, turned her head, and her body. She twisted the doorknob to open the door, but it didn't budge, and she felt sudden chills. She tried pulling back on the door and this time it opened normally. Like a mirror, she'd gotten the door reversed. But mirrors only reverse left and right, not in and out or up and down, and why that was she didn't know. Alice had trouble with looking-glasses. So many things have their opposites, but mirrors don't reflect every opposite, do they? Life, death. Joy, sorrow. Now, then. Good, ill. In its own fashion, the mirror is relentless. Joan could walk away, but would the mirror cease its reflecting? Joan closed the door. The mirror was looking for her, would come after her.

Downstairs, both Will and Lorraine looked strangely at her, held her in their gaze, saying nothing. Then Will ran toward her and caught her as she fell.

* * *

She was in her easy chair by the fireplace, and Lorraine was kneeling beside her. Will was across the room, his back against the wall. Lorraine had asked Will to explain, to the best of his ability, what was going on. "Joan said you understood."

"Yes," he said. "You already know the basic story. It's okay for me to go on, isn't it, Joan?"

Joan nodded. "Yes."

"We've been avoiding it—I certainly have—ever since we got here, though it's always been right there on the tip of my mind. Joan's notion—and it's real enough, for her at least—that this evening, June 17, 1955, matches up precisely with April 14, 1865—Good Friday—the night Abraham Lincoln went to Ford's Theater and was assassinated. I hate to put words to it. Some parts of Joan's story are factual, or material, verifiable. Like the letter, her pregnancy, probably more—the register at the Orrington Hotel. People she and Lincoln saw that Saturday, if they'd remember. And there's Joan's grandmother's diary that talks about a penny from the middle of the twentieth century."

"I'm trying not to ask questions," Lorraine said with a wry smile. "Go on."

"For the last week or so Joan has been having—I don't know the right term—"

"Visions," said Joan.

"Okay, visions. I keep backing away from the words that best tell the story. It so goes against the grain of how we're brought up, to be reasonable. Leastways that's what we tell ourselves. Everything has its label. We know what's a fact, what's just a myth, what's true or false, what's a dream, what isn't."

"Don't worry about any of that," said Lorraine, who was now sitting opposite Joan. "I've known Joan a long time. Just tell the story."

"So Joan's been having visions this past week. It's as though she has two clocks, one keeping time in 1865, the other in 1955. Mostly she lives according to the 1955 clock, but all of a sudden she finds herself living by the other. Unexpectedly, but always in relation to events in Lincoln's life. I could call it a psychic clock. It's very accurate. Do you follow me at all?"

"Oddly enough, I do. Go on."

"Monday morning, then Tuesday night, Joan was there at the White House, in the midst of a huge crowd outside by the portico, during the Serenades, listening to speeches from the President. Appomattox was two days before, on Sunday. So the city was rejoicing, illuminations every night. Remember, it wasn't just a Sunday in April of 1865. It was also our Sunday, five days ago. How am I doing?"

"You're doing all right," said Joan. "Go on."

"Okay," he said. "At the second Serenade Joan heard a small knot of men talking angrily, swearing that this was it, the last straw. One of them said something like, 'I'll run him through.' It was John Wilkes Booth. And from her description, I recognize the other men. Booth's co-conspirators. I was here the whole time, in this room, with Joan in this room, and she didn't know who they were. I did. Then yesterday, when we were bicycling, she crossed over again. Not that she disappears from my sight, and not that I have the privilege of seeing into the past. Though I wondered about yesterday. I wish I had been by your side."

"I know," said Joan, though the conversation would have been different. But she couldn't picture it, with introductions and Will trying to be matter-of-fact about his leap into the past.

"I was at one of her crossings, at lunch on Wednesday," said Lorraine. "Lincoln and Stanton were talking about reconvening the Virginia Legislature."

"Really?" he said. "So much was going on after Appomattox. I know a lot about the Civil War, and I've been reading up on the last few days this week, but I don't have perfect knowledge, far from it. Reports come from so many places: newspapers, diaries, interviews, memoirs, letters, telegraph records, receipts, and not just from Basler—Roy Basler, the editor of *The Collected Works*. There's a project afoot to chronicle Lincoln's life day by day. That'll probably be its title, *Lincoln Day by Day*."

"No wonder Joan said you could bear witness."

He nodded. "I guess I'm the next best thing to an *amicus curiae*, a friend of the court. I should be enough to silence any devil's advocate. If you'll accept me."

"Which I do," said Lorraine. "Knowing you're a historian, that you've seen the letter, just knowing you and knowing that you accept the story—" She paused, shook her head as though to clear it. "What I'm trying to say is that right now I'm with you. I believe. It sounds like a testimonial, and maybe it is. Twenty-four hours from now, I don't know."

"That's true for me too," said Joan. "As though I could wake up and realize that none of this had ever happened."

"So," said Will, "today, in the afternoon, around five, the President and Mrs. Lincoln went for a carriage ride to the Navy Yard to see three monitors—steel-clad ships—and the President talked about going home to Springfield and living a quiet life. Back at the White House he talked with old friends from Illinois, and he read aloud some chapters out of Petroleum V. Nasby, who was really David Locke—comic stories that Lincoln loved dearly. Then around half past eight the Lincolns picked up Major Rathbone and Clara Harris, the daughter of one of the Iowa senators—she and the Major were engaged, and their life was a tragedy all its own—around half past eight, to see *Our American Cousin*. It's a British play, with Laura Keene, who by then was in her forties. She was famous for the role, the way O'Neill's father was famous for *The Count of Monte Cristo*, or Edwin Booth was for *Hamlet*. Here, in Evanston, it's almost nine o'clock, and with the hour difference between Washington and Illinois, that makes it ten there. In about fifteen minutes—"

"No!"

They both looked at Joan. Her hands were clenched, and she was leaning forward.

"I'm sorry," said Will. "I'm thoughtless to have gone on like that."

"It's all right," Joan said. "I think someone's on the porch."

It was David and his uncle. David opened the door—it wasn't locked. The two men entered, stopping to look at the silent tableau in the living room. "Joan," said David's uncle, "I want to—"

"Not now, Harry," she said urgently, "not now." And Joan found herself sitting in a theater. On stage an actor was delivering lines about lighting a cigar. Then he took a sheet of paper from his breast pocket and set it afire, and held it with his fingertips till it was ashes.

The audience was enjoying itself. Every single woman wore a hat; nearly every man had a mustache, and many had beards. It was Ford's Theater. The President's box, above and to her right, was draped with banners and flags, red, white, and blue. In the middle hung a framed portrait of George Washington. It was too shadowy within the box to make anything out. A hand pushed the banner aside, the better to see; then the person leaned forward. The audience was intent upon the action onstage. It was Lincoln, the President, wearing his black suit and black tie. He was looking for someone in particular, his eyes methodically working their way along the rows. Joan raised her right hand, a slight gesture, as though she were at a silent auction, and their eyes met. He started back, then turned to his right, maybe said something, then leaned forward again.

The audience was laughing now. Joan could read the question on his face: *What are you doing here?* As though she could stand up and deliver her answer from the middle of her row. She wouldn't know what to say. She had seen a production of *Othello* in college, and it took a deliberate act of will not to stand up during the last scene and shout out, *Don't believe a thing he says. Don't get on that bed. He thinks you've been unfaithful. He's going to kill you.* But she had stayed silent. She had sat in her seat and watched the murder happen.

He was out of sight again, but his hand was on the balustrade holding the banner aside. She was only a few rows from the musicians. "Excuse me," she said to the woman to her left, and laboriously she worked her way along the row and out to the aisle, then up to the lobby. A couple of men in dark suits were lounging at the end of the aisle, indifferent to the play, to each other, even to her. The lobby was small—they didn't waste space on anything that wasn't for sitting or acting. She crossed the lobby, nodded to a small man at what had to be the cashier's office, and headed up the long, curving flight of stairs on the same side of the theater as Lincoln's box.

What if, when their eyes made contact, she had pointed her finger at her head, pantomiming a gun? What would he have understood? At the top she realized she couldn't get to the President's box from there. She went back down, recrossed the lobby, and went up the other flight of stairs. Now she had to cross the width of the theater. She made her way behind the last row of seats, to a narrow aisle with a doorway at the end that must lead to the boxes.

A man dressed in some kind of gray uniform, but not a soldier, looked her way, almost a challenge. Joan knew that whoever had the duty of guarding the President's box had deserted his station that night, either to watch the play or to leave the theater altogether and get himself a drink in a nearby tavern. She smiled at him, and he nodded slightly, then he looked beyond her to another man, small, with a black mustache and fierce-looking eyes, wearing dark clothes and a dark felt hat. He nodded familiarly at the man in the gray uniform, then passed by her. She was nobody. But she recognized him: the stylish man who was so agitated at the notion of the Louisiana Negroes achieving the franchise. The man as angry as Rumplestiltskin. John Wilkes Booth. He was opening the door leading to the boxes, and she just managed to slip through behind him.

She was in a small passageway with two more doors, one slightly ajar and leading to the farther box, and the other to her left and closed. Beyond the closed door were the Lincolns with

Major Rathbone and Clara Harris. Booth stood with his back to the wall, waiting for her to cross in front of him and go through the open door to the next box. When she was just beyond him, she turned abruptly, facing forward, and raised her fist to knock at the President's door. Suddenly she was hit from behind, and instead of striking the door, she stumbled to her knees. There was blood on her arm, and the image of Harry Stein flooded her mind, Harry's voice and the passage from the Second Inaugural, all the years of blood drawn from the lash and blood drawn from the sword. She cried aloud one word. "Booth!" The door to the box opened, and there stood Lincoln. His eyes met hers. "Joan," he said, and a gunshot rang out. Lincoln staggered and fell back, and Booth was leaping from the edge of the box onto the stage.

* * *

Joan was sitting on the floor by the fireplace. "What happened?"

"Hold still," said Lorraine, examining Joan's arm.

"We don't know," said Will.

"It's not a serious injury," Lorraine said, "but I think we should get you over to the emergency room. You should have stitches."

"Can you do it?"

"Yes, but I'd rather you had proper care."

"You can't do it?"

"Yes, I can do it. It's a clean cut. David, get my keys from my purse. My black bag's in the trunk of my car. But I want you to hold off on questions for a while, and we'll do the same."

They led Joan to the kitchen, and Lorraine organized a small surgery, with Will as her assistant. Occasionally Joan could hear the muted voices of David and his uncle from the other room. Joan kept playing the scene at the theater over and over. *All that, and still Booth shoots the President.*

"That should do. Tomorrow evening I can check on it. It will be my birthday present from you, a healthy wound."

Will led Joan back to the living room. He looked at Lorraine for permission to speak, and she nodded. "Are you feeling well enough to tell us what happened?"

"Yes."

David looked at Will. A lot was being said without anyone speaking. "Is it okay for my uncle and me to stay?"

"Joan?" asked Will.

"They were here the whole time, weren't they?"

Will nodded.

"Then it's all right with me." Things seemed so matter-of-fact. She'd never been in shock before. Was this what it was like, a preternatural calm? "Can I ask one question: would you tell me what happened at Ford's Theater?"

Will looked at her out of the corner of his eye. "That's just what we were going to ask you."

"Oh," she said. "I guess that makes sense. Let me ask it another way. I know it will sound strange. What happened to President Lincoln the night of April fourteenth?"

They looked at each other dumbly, and then all eyes settled on Will. "He was at Ford's Theater, and he was shot by John Wilkes Booth, who then leaped from the Presidential box onto the stage, said a few words, and escaped, though he broke his leg in the fall. He was killed about two weeks later after they set fire to the barn where he was hiding. The man who shot him was a crazy soldier named Boston Corbett."

It was Joan's turn to nod. "The man who had castrated himself to avoid temptation and wore his hair long to look like Jesus."

"Yes. He'd been a hatter, a mad hatter."

"And the President?" she asked. She was still trying to see, to remember what she had seen, but all she could picture was Lincoln's figure filling the doorway, then the shot and him falling away, and Booth leaping out of sight.

There was no way around the next question. "Tell me where the bullet struck him."

"The bullet hit Lincoln in the right shoulder."

She could feel the rise and fall of her chest, tried to keep her voice calm. "Then?"

"Well, mayhem, of course. Booth onstage, theatrically proclaiming the words from the great seal of Virginia, *Sic semper tyrannis*, though there's conflicting evidence as to exactly when he said it."

"Did Major Rathbone try to stop him?"

"Yes, but Booth in his frenzy slashed the Major's arm, and then leaped to the stage. Rathbone wasn't a big man."

"So Booth ran across the stage and escaped, and Stewart couldn't catch him. What about the President?"

"There was an army surgeon in the house, Charles Taft, and people handed him up to the box. It wasn't very high, and it was quicker than going all the way up and around. He gave immediate attention."

"So he survived." It wasn't quite a question. If the wound had been mortal, surely by now someone would have said so. But still she was afraid to ask the question directly.

No one said anything. They looked stunned.

"He did survive, didn't he?" Joan wanted the answer to be crystal clear. She wanted to hear the words.

"Yes," said Will, "he survived. It turned out to be a minor wound. Though the danger in those days was more from infection. In less than two weeks he was back at his desk."

David Levine looked like he was ready to jump out of his skin. "The whole time you said just one word: 'Booth.' "

"David's right," said Will. "You said only the one word, though I'll swear I saw your lips move once or twice, saying something. But I can't read lips."

260 | Good Friday

"I said 'Excuse me.' That was about all I said the whole time. Except when I yelled his name. 'Booth.' What happened to my arm?"

Lorraine's turn to answer. "You were sitting in the chair—I'd say in a trance, but not rigid. It's as if your muscles were flexing in a miniature version of something else. Tiny movements. We were afraid to intervene, to break the spell. We just watched. None of us has training for this."

"How long was I in this trance?"

"Ten or fifteen minutes. It seemed like forever. I did look at my watch once or twice. Then suddenly you pitched forward and hit the coffee table."

"Does my arm look like it hit a table? Wouldn't that just bruise me? I've fallen before, but never drawn blood, not like this."

"I know," said Lorraine, "but what can I tell you other than what I saw? What's your story about what happened?"

Joan hesitated.

"There's something I need to say." Now it was Harry Stein speaking. He swallowed once. "I'm the one who mailed the letter." He spoke deliberately, carefully.

David looked at his uncle. "Letter? What letter?"

"David," said Harry, "there's a lot of explaining to do, and I can catch you up on some of it. But for now, just listen."

"So it was you who mailed the letter," said Joan. "Someone had to mail it. And you know what it said, don't you?"

Harry nodded. "I'm sorry. For thirty years I had the letter. I think at first I was like the others. You couldn't help but wonder about it. But the level of trust was so powerful that I shunted my curiosity aside. Then came a time when it didn't matter so much. I'd say the temptation wore me down. Or circumstances. But it wasn't that. It was me. I had changed. And so I violated his trust, Lincoln's. I broke the chain. Only me. Everyone else did the right thing."

"You're not really here on business, are you?"

"No. I came to see you. To find out for sure what happened. Then what, I don't know. That David was living with you was an impossible coincidence. It gave me an in, but it changed things. It made a difference. I can't ask for your forgiveness."

"Well," said Joan, "I forgive you. At the last moment, it was you I saw in my mind's eye, or heard, or saw and heard—your voice, your words, his words, the words from the Second Inaugural: 'If God so wills it, the years of blood drawn from the lash shall be paid by blood drawn from the sword.' That's what it might take to even the long equation. And that's the moment when I cried his name aloud, to warn him. Cried, 'Booth!' It was crazy. As though Abraham Lincoln already knew what we all know, and the sound of John Wilkes Booth's name would serve as a warning." She was telling herself the story as much as anybody else.

"So you were there," said Will. "I knew that, but I wanted to hear it from your own lips. Without asking."

"Yes," she said. "David and Harry came in, and suddenly I found myself sitting in the theater, close to the stage. I saw him in his box, and he saw me, and I wanted to warn him. It was like swimming through molasses to get to his box. Finally, when I was almost there, Booth, with a nod from the guard, got ahead of me. But I was right on his heels. Then I was with Booth in the little hallway leading to the two boxes."

"The vestibule."

"I guess, the vestibule. I squeezed in right after Booth. He thought I was heading for the farther box. I really didn't know what I was going to do. Anything to stop him. I could pound on the door to the Lincoln box, and I was just about to. Maybe I did. I think I did. Then he struck me from behind. He had a knife in one hand and a gun in the other. Like Hamlet with the dagger and the rapier. I remember seeing the knife in his hand, with blood on it. I was on my knees, and that's when Lincoln opened the door, saw me on the ground. Then Booth shot him."

"Can I ask one question?"

"Go ahead, Harry."

"Professor Studebaker, how do they explain why John Wilkes Booth didn't just sneak up on Lincoln and shoot him while he was watching the play, like a sitting duck? No one's ever mentioned a woman in the vestibule, have they?"

"No," said Will, and it was hard to read his expression, whether he was solemn, or smiling inwardly. Something in his eyes said the latter. "No mention of a woman. All the theories end up pretty much in thin air. No one really knows why Booth botched it. A failure of nerves? Lincoln said he heard a commotion just beyond the door. Surely he knew the guard wasn't much of a guard, though that kind of thing never concerned him all that much. Nor did the guard say anything about a woman.

"Anyway, Lincoln did a stupid thing—he admitted it was stupid. He opened the door. He should've sat tight. But I can see where you wouldn't do that, especially an active man like Abraham Lincoln. Reason says, *Send Major Rathbone to investigate.* Lincoln himself had suggested that Major Eckert accompany the Presidential party to protect them—Eckert was a powerful man. But he had work to do, and Stanton said he couldn't spare him—Stanton was probably still hoping to dissuade Lincoln altogether from going to the theater that night. There really are only two explanations. Either Booth deliberately made the commotion, knowing that Lincoln was sitting closest to the door, figuring that he'd be the one to open it. Which he did! Or Booth's plan fell apart. Whatever it was, hindsight tells you how to commit a crime in a way that would have worked. I think Booth thought he'd succeeded, that he'd killed the President. That's what he was thinking when he leaped to the stage and raised the knife and cried, *Sic semper tyrannis.* 'Down with tyrants.' To me that sounds like the cry of a victorious man. Lincoln wasn't much help with the whole affair. He was always somewhat muddled about what had happened. Which is allowable when you've been shot."

"I suppose," said Joan.

"You know the rest, don't you? The attack on Seward, the failure of the plan to kill the vice president?"

Joan nodded and then spoke, again more to herself than to the others. Not a lot needed to be said. "And so Lincoln served out his second term. That's not a question," she added. It was beginning to filter through. Andrew Johnson never was the president. Abraham Lincoln lived on till his mid-seventies. How he and Mary toured Europe. His retirement in Springfield. The new reality. Her new world. Wasn't Will Studebaker in for a history lesson?

EPILOGUE

Harry watched the edge of Lake Michigan drift by in serene silence—the dirigible's engines were said to be set farther to the rear than ever. Oh, modernity! Harry loved the paradox that the slower the form of transportation, the more it cost. Slowest of all were the ships of the Cunard Fleet, the two *Queens*, and the most recent edition of the *Titanic*. If you were in a hurry, expect to spend your time as cramped as a sardine.

Harry Stein and David Levine had caught the noon flight from Meigs Field, thanks to a ride from Will Studebaker and Joan Matcham, Harry's first ride in a Studebaker and the first ride for both Harry and David on a Goodyear R-101, *The City of Pittsburgh*. Harry had asked David's boss to spare the lad for a week's leave, and Emmanuel Hohenstein, who seemed to have a wider perspective than most, declared he could use a week off and had David hang a "Closed" sign in the window of The Bookshop.

This was Harry's treat, no strings attached, wherein it differed considerably from the dinner at the Buttery. How long had it been since Harry was free from the web of the past?

David swiveled his chair to get a better view. He was doing his best to take the trip in stride, as though he traveled in such gross luxury any old day of the year. Joan Matcham had given Harry permission to share the story of the letter with David, since without him, who knows how the tale would have played out? David's presence at the house on Hinman had made a difference to Harry, and Harry's conversation over pie and coffee had made a difference for Joan at Ford's Theater.

Harry took a deep breath. By the skin of his teeth he had averted disaster. He thought of his last travel companion, Rita Griffin, and how he'd terrorized her, or did his best to, with tales of disaster. Hard to imagine being under such a spell.

They had reservations for one o'clock in the dining room of the R-101. It was as though he had been wearing blinders all these years, like the sorriest plow horse, except the one direction he couldn't see was straight forward. Only the crooked path, convoluted and gnarled. It seemed so sudden, this clarity, this depth of perspective.

"Harry," David said, "I think I've finally got the story straight—maybe."

"Still there, are you, kiddo? Well, it's one hell of a story with all its loops and twists and turning in on itself, like the snake with its tail in its own mouth. What's holding you up?"

"Well, there's Lincoln's visit two or so months ago. And Joan's visions during Appomattox week. And the way the two times overlapped for her."

"All right," said Harry. "If you've got that, you've got a lot. Most people would just freeze up and do their best to explain it away, no matter what, for the sake of their sanity." Harry was reminded of Burton's Fisherman, who lived in a world where Jinnis, as uncommon as they were, were still not unheard of. Of course you know how stupid they are and can use that to your advantage. So when your net gives you the copper urn, you just deal with it. As though you are at a party and it turns out the concert pianist is a vampire, and instead of getting the hell out of there, you start looking for wooden stakes.

"What I don't get," said David, "is what Joan was doing at the theater, or what she was trying to accomplish. She said she wanted to warn Lincoln, and I'm sure it's no fun to be shot. She even admits that what she did was senseless, crying out Booth's name."

"I know," said Harry, "time travel must be confusing as all hell." Which had to be the most remarkable utterance of his entire life.

"So, according to Professor Studebaker, we know something no one else knows: we know what caused the commotion in the vestibule. It was Joan, who was there, and then she wasn't."

Harry smiled. *There was a little man who wasn't there*—and damned if he could remember how the rest of the nonsense rhyme went.

"Could it be," David asked, "that there was something like a hole in reality? An event had happened, but its cause had gotten short-circuited. History has Lincoln getting up and going to the door—no one else ever said they heard anything. They say nature abhors a vacuum, and so it finds this really weird solution. It wants its fabric complete, so it comes up with the remedy."

"It could be something like that," Harry said. "I do like the elegance of the hypothesis. Nature doesn't like a loose end."

"On the other hand," said David, "it all seems so pointless. Things are no different from what they ever were."

"Maybe, maybe not," said Harry. "He did see her one more time. He must've understood what she was doing, was trying to do. That would make a difference to me. It was almost as though we were there, wasn't it?"

The lake was far to the rear now, and ahead lay patches of farm country. *Then there's me*, thought Harry, *heading east, toward a family in Pittsburgh that I haven't seen in fifteen years. Ripples in a pond. The joy of paradox. And a baby. The child of Abraham Lincoln.*

AUTHOR'S NOTE

To quote John Crowley, "this is a book made out of other books." The "Tale of the Fisherman and the Jinni," as Harry Stein notes, appears in the first volume of Richard F. Burton's "plain and literal translation" of *The Book of the Thousand Nights and a Night* (privately printed by the Burton Club, 1885, 17 volumes.). The version that Harry recalls and later reads derives from Burton's text, but it is my own much-truncated variation. I have taken to heart the example of Italo Calvino in his *Italian Folktales*, where the story-teller is expected to render the story faithfully but at the same time has the freedom to dress the tale in fresh attire.

I have tried my best to be true to Lincoln scholarship as was current in 1955. Roy P. Basler's then recent edition of *The Collected Works of Abraham Lincoln* was indispensable for Joan Matcham and for me as well. J. G. Randall's four volumes on the presidency of Abraham Lincoln sustained me for many a night. The character of the Civil War historian William C. Studebaker is my invention, and any professional inadequacies he may reflect are to be laid at my doorstep.

My representation of John Hay and his son Adelbert derives in part from Tyler Dennett's *John Hay: From Poetry to Politics* (Dodd, Mead & Company, 1933). John Hay's letter to Theodore Roosevelt appears in that volume. Del Hay, alas, did perish in a fall from a window in 1901 while at his second reunion at Yale. Alton Sweeney is my fabrication entirely, as are Joan Matcham's contemporaries (in the twentieth century). I have, however, drawn on the diaries willed to me by my late uncle, Samuel V. Sanger, for inspiration in imagining Harry Stein. (Sammy, wherever you are, I hope you're smiling at my portrait of Harry.) I also owe a debt to

Oscar Lewis, whose *The Lost Years: A Biographical Fantasy* (Alfred A. Knopf, 1951) showed me one way to another ending.

Lastly, on Christmas Eve, 1985, Robert Todd Lincoln Beckwith died at the age of eighty-one. He was Abraham Lincoln's last descendent outside this novel (Mark E. Neely, Jr., and R. Gerald McMurtry, *The Insanity File*).

AUTHOR'S ACKNOWLEDGMENT

For the first of these Lincoln stories, *Abraham Lincoln, a Novel Life*, I expressed my gratitude to a host of teachers and friends who have made this writing life what it is, one of the centers of my life. Today, once again, I want to thank Dennis Stovall, Karen Kirtley, Susan Applegate, Lake Bogan, and the rest of the team at Ooligan Press (in particular Chris Huff for his careful design). And thanks again to dear Libby Solomon, who lived to hold in her hand the novel which her generosity had launched into daylight.

I also want to take time to thank Ursula Le Guin, who in 1975, when I was delegated to approach her about teaching a science fiction writing class for the Division of Continuing Education at Portland State, said, "Let's do it together." At the time I was a lit teacher, pure and simple. My obsession with writing, dating back to my early teen years, had quietly expired when I began graduate studies in English in 1959. I said Yes to Ursula's suggestion, not knowing what I was in for. (We split the DCE wage of $600, that's how long ago it was.) Within a couple of weeks I realized that like everyone else in the class, including Ursula, I was expected to produce some science fiction. I was an SF teacher but not an SF writer. I began a short story about a man named Charley who is building a miniature house, as I was doing at the time. He soon is obsessed with its authenticity, that it should be a duplicate of his own house. At some point in my fledgling story Charley came alive, and I found myself weeping into my old Remington typewriter. I was writing. Now, thirty-two years later, I want to say *Thank you* one more time to Ursula. You have changed my life. Thank you.

About the Author:

Tony Wolk has taught at Portland State University since 1965, specializing in Dante Alighieri, William Shakespeare, Jorge Luis Borges, Italo Calvino, and Philip K. Dick, as well as writing classes.

He is the author of *Abraham Lincoln, a Novel Life*, published in 2004 by Ooligan Press.

About the Artist:

Jessica Wolk-Stanley began life in Oregon as an infant, nearly devoid of drawing skills. In the intervening years, she perfected her craft and now lives in Seattle, Washington, with a husband and two children. Her work often appears in teen magazines, and other children's publications, always in a vastly different style from what is in this book. More can be viewed at:

www.olk-stanley.com.

Photo by Lindy Delf.

Acquisitions:
Vinnie Kinsella – Manager
Katrina Hill – Manager

Editing:
Joanna Schmidt – Manager
Haili Graff – Manager
Karen Brattain – Copyediting
Susan Landis-Steward
                    – Copyedting
Pamela Ivey – Proofreading
Kari Smit – Proofreading

Design:
Abbey Gaterud – Manager
Peggy Lindquist – Manager
Chris Huff – Interior Design
Cliff Hansen – Cover Design

Marketing:
Jenn Lawrence – Manager
Terri Davis – Manager
Jake Keszler – Book Lead

Ooligan would like to also thank: Emilee Newman Bowles, Karen Brattain, Liz Buelow, Karli Clift, Allison Collins, Audrey Coulthurst, Brie Delvin, Monica Garcia, Laura Howe, Ryan Hume, Pamela Ivey, Rob Jackson, Susan Landix, Cameron Marshall, Jessica Pricer, Cassie Richoux, Rachel Tobie, Janie Webster, and Erin Woodcock.

Colophon

This text was typeset in Palatino LT Standard, designed by Hermann Zapf.